Thornes Classic Novels

The Strange Case of
DR JEKYLL and MR HYDE
and
THE BEACH OF FALESÁ

by

ROBERT LOUIS STEVENSON

EDITED BY JOHN SEELY

SERIES EDITOR: JOHN SEELY

Stanley Thornes (Publishers) Ltd

The Strange Case of Dr Jekyll and Mr Hyde first published 1886.
The Beach of Falesá first published under the title *Urma* in the Illustrated London News, 1892.

This edition first published in 1995 by:
Stanley Thornes (Publishers) Ltd
Ellenborough House
Wellington Street
CHELTENHAM GL50 1YD
England

A catalogue record for this book is available from the British Library.

ISBN 0–7487–1829–X

Acknowledgements

The author and publishers are grateful to the following for permission to reproduce illustrations and photographs:
Pictures on p.2, Mansell Collection.
Pictures on p.3, Mary Evans Picture Library.

Illustrated by Trevor Parkin
Typeset by Melanie Gray and Maggie Jones
Printed and bound in Great Britain at T J Press (Padstow) Ltd, Cornwall

Contents

How to use this book

This edition of *The Strange Case of Dr Jekyll and Mr Hyde* and *The Beach of Falesá* is designed to help you get the most out of these exciting stories. The book begins with some information about the writer of the stories. Each story is then presented in three parts:
- an introduction to the characters and the setting of the story;
- the story itself;
- the study guide – questions to help you understand what you have read.

INTRODUCTIONS

These contain an illustrated introduction to the characters and setting of each story. You can read this material before starting the stories, or you can leave it until later. If you get confused about people or places while reading the stories, the introductions will make things clearer for you.

THE STORIES

As well as the complete stories themselves, there are a number of other things to help you enjoy and understand them:
- at the beginning of each chapter, advice on what to look out for;
- on each page, a commentary that explains what is happening;
- on each page, notes that explain difficult words or expressions;
- 'fast forward' and 'rewind' sections (see below);
- illustrations of key moments;
- illustrations to help explain difficult words or expressions.

Fast forward/rewind sections

Some people like to read a story quickly to find out 'what happens next' missing out the less important sections. If you like to do this, the sections you can jump are marked. A 'fast forward' box (▶▶) tells you which page to jump to, a sign in the margin tells you where to start reading again, and a 'rewind' box (◀◀) tells you what was on the pages you have skipped.

STUDY GUIDES

These contain advice and activities to use while you are reading the stories and after you have finished them. There is a more detailed explanation of how to use the study guides at the beginning of each one.

About the writer

ROBERT LOUIS STEVENSON

Stevenson was born in Edinburgh in 1850. He spent his youth in Scotland, mainly in Edinburgh, and studied at university there. He was never strong and was often ill.

His father was an engineer, responsible for designing, maintaining and inspecting harbour works and lighthouses. For some time he hoped that his son would follow in his footsteps, and, later, that he would follow another 'respectable' profession, but he was disappointed.

Although Stevenson qualified as a lawyer, his one ambition was to become a writer. With support from his father he was able to do so. Some of his most popular works are historical novels set in

Photograph of Edinburgh in 1866, in Stevenson's youth

Scotland: *Kidnapped* (1886), *The Master of Ballantrae* (1898) and *Catriona* (1893). Probably his most famous book is a story for children, *Treasure Island*, published in 1883.

Stevenson had many friends in London, and often visited the city, which forms the setting for his second great success, *The Strange Case of Dr Jekyll and Mr Hyde*, published in 1886.

Stevenson travelled widely and spent a lot of time in France. It was here that he met a married American woman, Fanny Osbourne, with whom he became very friendly.

One of his earliest books was a description of a journey he made in southern France, *Travels with a Donkey* (1879).

An illustration from an early edition of Treasure Island

For most of his life, Stevenson suffered from chronic chest disease, so that he was forced to spend a lot of time ill in bed. He searched constantly for new places, not only to stimulate him as a writer, but also for the sake of his health.

In 1879 he travelled to America to be with Fanny and in the following year, after her divorce, they were married.

The couple spent some time living at a deserted gold mine, high in the mountains of California.

Frontispiece from
Travels with a Donkey

After various travels, in 1888 Stevenson and Fanny sailed from San Francisco bound for the South Pacific islands. They decided to settle in Samoa and built a house, which they called Vailima.

A photograph of Stevenson at the age of 40

Stevenson lived there for the rest of his life and wrote, among other books, *The Beach of Falesá*. He loved Samoa and its people and was loved by them. They called him 'Tusitala', the storyteller.

He died suddenly in 1894 and was buried in Samoa.

Vailima – Stevenson's house in Samoa

The Strange Case of
DR JEKYLL and MR HYDE

by
ROBERT LOUIS STEVENSON

Introduction

THE CHARACTERS

Mr Edward Hyde

Sir Danvers Carew

Mr Richard Enfield   Mr Gabriel Utterson

Poole

Dr Henry Jekyll

Dr Hastie Lanyon

THE SETTING

① The door

② Dr Jekyll's door

Courtyard

Dr Henry Jekyll's House

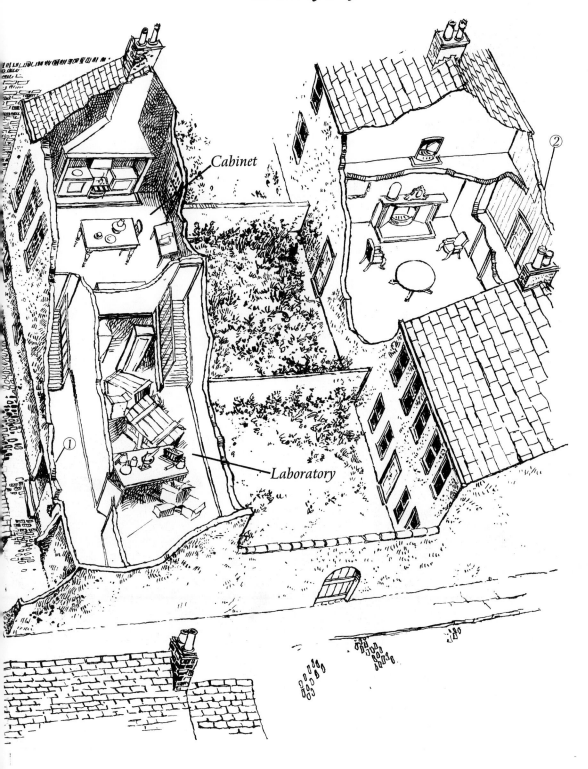

Cabinet

Laboratory

1 Story of the Door

Look out for...
- the personality of Utterson, the storyteller – what are your first impressions of him?
- the setting of the story. Try to form a picture in your mind of the London streets where the story takes place.

FAST FORWARD: to page 12

Mr Utterson the lawyer was a man of a rugged countenance, that was never lighted by a smile; cold, scanty and embarrassed in discourse; backward in sentiment; lean, long, dusty, dreary, and yet somehow lovable. At friendly meetings, and when the wine was to his taste, something eminently human beaconed from his eye; something indeed which never found its way into his talk, but which spoke not only in these silent symbols of the after-dinner face, but more often and loudly in the acts of his life. He was austere with himself; drank gin when he was alone, to mortify a taste for vintages; and though he enjoyed the theatre, had not crossed the doors of one for twenty years. But he had an approved tolerance for others; sometimes wondering, almost with envy, at the high pressure of spirits involved in their misdeeds; and in any extremity inclined to help rather than to reprove. 'I incline to Cain's heresy,' he used to say quaintly: 'I let my brother go to the devil his own way.' In this character it was frequently his fortune to be the last reputable acquaintance and the last

COMMENTARY
We meet the severe and apparently dull lawyer, Mr Utterson. Despite his appearance, he is a likeable person.

countenance: face
discourse: conversation
backward in sentiment: slow to show emotion
austere: strict
mortify a taste for vintages: get rid of his love for good wine
Cain's heresy: in the bible story, Cain (who had murdered his brother) asked, 'Am I my brother's keeper?'

good influence in the lives of down-going men. And to such as these, so long as they came about his chambers, he never marked a shade of change in his demeanour.

No doubt the feat was easy to Mr Utterson; for he was undemonstrative at the best, and even his friendships seemed to be founded in a similar catholicity of good-nature. It is the mark of a modest man to accept his friendly circle ready made from the hands of opportunity; and that was the lawyer's way. His friends were those of his own blood, or those whom he had known the longest; his affections, like ivy, were the growth of time, they implied no aptness in the object. Hence, no doubt, the bond that united him to Mr Richard Enfield, his distant kinsman, the well-known man about town. It was a nut to crack for many, what these two could see in each other, or what subject they could find in common. It was reported by those who encountered them in their Sunday walks, that they said nothing, looked singularly dull, and would hail with obvious relief the appearance of a friend. For all that, the two men put the greatest store by these excursions, counted them the chief jewel of each week, and not only set aside occasions of pleasure, but even resisted the calls of business, that they might enjoy them uninterrupted.

It chanced on one of these rambles that their way led them down a by street in a busy quarter of London. The street was small and what is called quiet, but it drove a thriving trade on the week-days. The inhabitants were all doing well, it seemed, and all emulously hoping to do better still, and laying out the surplus of their gains in coquetry; so that the shop fronts stood along that thoroughfare with an air of invitation, like rows of smiling saleswomen. Even on Sunday, when it veiled its more florid charms and lay comparatively

---

REWIND: …enjoy them uninterrupted.

Mr Utterson is a reserved and apparently dull lawyer, who seems to have no pleasures. He is friendly with Richard Enfield, a 'man about town'. Every Sunday they go out for a walk together.

COMMENTARY

All his friends are either relatives or people who have known him a long time. Mr Richard Enfield, 'a well-known man about town', is a distant relative and the two of them get on well, although they seem to have nothing in common.

down-going men: men whose careers are on a downward path

And to such…his demeanour: he always treated them exactly the same as he did everyone else

was undemonstrative: did not show his thoughts or feelings

even his friendships…good-nature: he was easy-going with all his friends

emulously hoping…coquetry: competing to do better by spending money to make their shops more attractive

empty of passage, the street shone out in contrast to its dingy neighbourhood, like a fire in a forest; and with its freshly painted shutters, well-polished brasses, and general cleanliness and gaiety of note, instantly caught and pleased the eye of the passenger.

Two doors from one corner, on the left hand going east, the line was broken by the entry of a court; and just at that point, a certain sinister block of building thrust forward its gable on the street. It was two storeys high; showed no window, nothing but a door on the lower storey and a blind forehead of discoloured wall on the upper; and bore in every feature the marks of prolonged and sordid negligence. The door, which was equipped with neither bell nor knocker, was blistered and distained. Tramps slouched into the recess and struck matches on the panels; children kept shop upon the steps; the schoolboy had tried his knife on the mouldings; and for close on a generation no one had appeared to drive away these random visitors or to repair their ravages.

negligence: lack of care and maintenance
The door: see illustration above
distained: stained

Mr Enfield and the lawyer were on the other side of the by street; but when they came abreast of the entry, the former lifted up his cane and pointed.

'Did you ever remark that door?' he asked; and when his companion had replied in the affirmative, 'It is connected in my mind,' added he, 'with a very odd story.'

'Indeed!' said Mr Utterson, with a slight change of voice, 'and what was that?'

'Well, it was this way,' returned Mr Enfield: 'I was coming home from some place at the end of the world, about three o'clock of a black winter morning, and my way lay through a part of town where there was literally nothing to be seen but lamps. Street after street, and all the folks asleep – street after street, all lighted up as if for a procession, and all as empty as a church – till at last I got into that state of mind when a man listens and listens and begins to long for the sight of a policeman. All at once, I saw two figures: one a little man who was stumping along eastward at a good walk, and the other a girl of maybe eight or ten who was running as hard as she was able down a cross-street. Well, sir, the two ran into one another naturally enough at the corner; and then came the horrible part of the thing; for the man trampled calmly over the child's body and left her screaming on the ground. It sounds nothing to hear, but it was hellish to see. It wasn't like a man; it was like some damned Juggernaut. I gave a view halloa, took to my heels, collared my gentleman, and brought him back to where there was already quite a group about the screaming child. He was perfectly cool and made no resistance, but gave me one look, so ugly that it brought out the sweat on me like running. The people who had turned out were the girl's own family; and pretty soon the doctor, for whom she had been sent, put in his appearance. Well, the child was not much the worse, more frightened, according to the Sawbones; and there you might have supposed would be an end to it. But there was one curious circumstance. I had taken a loathing to my gentleman at first sight. So had the child's family, which was only natural. But the doctor's case was what struck me. He was the usual cut-and-dry apothecary, of no particular age and colour, with a strong

remark: notice
replied in the affirmative: said 'yes'
Juggernaut: a huge creature or machine
   that crushes all before it
view halloa: the huntsman's shout when
   the fox is sighted
Sawbones: slang word for doctor
apothecary: literally a person who
   prepares and sells medicines – so here
   another word for doctor

COMMENTARY
Mr Enfield tells a strange story connected with the door. Very early one morning, he passed the place. He saw a strange man collide with a young girl and knock her over. Instead of stopping, he trampled on her and kept going. Mr Enfield stopped him and the child's parents arrived with a doctor.

Edinburgh accent, and about as
emotional as a bagpipe. Well, sir, he
was like the rest of us: every time he
looked at my prisoner, I saw that
Sawbones turned sick and white with
the desire to kill him. I knew what
was in his mind, just as he knew
what was in mine; and killing being
out of the question, we did the next
best. We told the man we could and
would make such a scandal out of
this, as should make his name stink
from one end of London to the
other. If he had any friends or any
credit, we undertook that he should
lose them. And all the time, as we
were pitching it in red hot, we were
keeping the women off him as best
we could, for they were as wild as
harpies. I never saw a circle of such
hateful faces; and there was the man
in the middle, with a kind of black

sneering coolness – frightened too, I could see that – but carrying it off, sir,
really like Satan. "If you choose to make capital out of this accident," said he,
"I am naturally helpless. No gentleman but wishes to avoid a scene," says he.
"Name your figure." Well, we screwed him up to a hundred pounds for the
child's family; he would have clearly liked to stick out; but there was something
about the lot of us that meant mischief, and at last he struck. The next thing
was to get the money; and where do you think he carried us but to that place
with the door? – whipped out a key, went in, and presently came back with the
matter of ten pounds in gold and a cheque for the balance on Coutts's, drawn

COMMENTARY
The people present decided to force
the man to pay compensation to the
child's parents. He agreed and went
through the door into the building. He
returned with cash and a cheque.

credit: reputation, good name
pitching it in red hot: 'giving it to him good
    and strong'
harpies: creatures from Greek mythology
    – they were half-woman and half-bird
    and attacked human beings
struck: agreed

payable to bearer, and signed with a name that I can't mention, though it's one of the points of my story, but it was a name at least very well known and often printed. The figure was stiff; but the signature was good for more than that, if it was only genuine. I took the liberty of pointing out to my gentleman that the whole business looked apocryphal; and that a man does not, in real life, walk into a cellar door at four in the morning and come out with another man's cheque for close upon a hundred pounds. But he was quite easy and sneering. "Set your mind at rest," says he; "I will stay with you till the banks open, and cash the cheque myself." So we all set off, the doctor, and the child's father, and our friend and myself, and passed the rest of the night in my chambers; and next day, when we had breakfasted, went in a body to the bank. I gave in the cheque myself, and said I had every reason to believe it was a forgery. Not a bit of it. The cheque was genuine.'

'Tut-tut!' said Mr Utterson.

'I see you feel as I do,' said Mr Enfield. 'Yes, it's a bad story. For my man was a fellow that nobody could have to do with, a really damnable man; and the person that drew the cheque is the very pink of the properties, celebrated too, and (what makes it worse) one of your fellows who do what they call good. Blackmail, I suppose; an honest man paying through the nose for some of the capers of his youth. Blackmail House is what I call that place with the door, in consequence. Though even that, you know, is far from explaining all,' he added; and with the words fell into a vein of musing.

From this he was recalled by Mr Utterson asking rather suddenly: 'And you don't know if the drawer of the cheque lives there?'

'A likely place, isn't it?' returned Mr Enfield. 'But I happen to have noticed his address; he lives in some square or other.'

'And you never asked about – the place with the door?' said Mr Utterson.

'No, sir: I had a delicacy,' was the reply. 'I feel very strongly about putting questions; it partakes too much of the style of the day of judgment. You start a question, and it's like starting a stone. You sit quietly on the top of a hill; and away the stone goes, starting others; and presently some bland old bird

COMMENTARY

The cheque had been signed by another person. They made him cash it in their presence because they did not trust him. Mr Enfield tells Utterson that the name on the cheque was that of an honest and good man, so he concluded that this evil-looking character must be blackmailing him.

bearer: whoever took it to the bank
looked apocryphal: seemed suspicious
the very pink of the properties, celebrated: a very respectable and well-known person
the drawer: the person who signed it
had a delicacy: was sensitive (about it)

it partakes too much of the style of the day of judgment: it is too much like Judgment Day (when Christians believe we shall all be questioned about our lives)

(the last you would have though of) is knocked on the head in his own back garden, and the family have to change their name. No, sir, I make it a rule of mine: the more it looks like Queer Street, the less I ask.'

'A very good rule, too,' said the lawyer.

'But I have studied the place for myself,' continued Mr Enfield. 'It seems scarcely a house. There is no other door, and nobody goes in or out of that one, but, once in a great while, the gentleman of my adventure. There are three windows looking on the court on the first floor; none below; the windows are always shut, but they're clean. And then there is a chimney, which is generally smoking; so somebody must live there. And yet it's not so sure; for the buildings are so packed together about that court, that it's hard to say where one ends and another begins.'

The pair walked on again for a while in silence; and then – 'Enfield,' said Mr Utterson, 'that's a good rule of yours.'

'Yes, I think it is,' returned Enfield.

'But for all that,' continued the lawyer, 'there's one point I want to ask: I want to ask the name of that man who walked over the child.'

'Well,' said Mr Enfield, 'I can't see what harm it would do. It was a man of the name of Hyde.'

'Hm,' said Mr Utterson. 'What sort of a man is he to see?'

'He is not easy to describe. There is something wrong with his appearance; something displeasing, something downright detestable. I never saw a man I so disliked, and yet I scarce know why. He must be deformed somewhere; he gives a strong feeling of deformity, although I couldn't specify the point. He's an extraordinary-looking man, and yet I really can name nothing out of the way. No, sir; I can make no hand of it; I can't describe him. And it's not want of memory; for I declare I can see him this moment.'

Mr Utterson again walked some way in silence, and obviously under a weight of consideration. 'You are sure he used a key?' he inquired at last.

'My dear sir...' began Enfield, surprised out of himself.

'Yes, I know,' said Utterson; 'I know it must seem strange. The fact is, if I

COMMENTARY

They discuss the strange door and the house into which it leads. Enfield reveals that the name of the brutal man was Hyde and is surprised when Utterson asks him if Hyde used a key to open the door.

Queer Street: a slang expression meaning 'getting into trouble' or 'getting into debt'

do not ask you the name of the other party, it is because I know it already. You see, Richard, your tale has gone home. If you have been inexact in any point, you had better correct it.'

'I think you might have warned me,' returned the other, with a touch of sullenness. 'But I have been pedantically exact, as you call it. The fellow had a key; and, what's more, he has it still. I saw him use it, not a week ago.'

Mr Utterson sighed deeply, but said never a word; and the young man presently resumed. 'Here is another lesson to say nothing,' said he. 'I am ashamed of my long tongue. Let us make a bargain never to refer to this again.'

'With all my heart,' said the lawyer. 'I shake hands on that, Richard.'

gone home: got through to me
pedantically exact: extra careful about the
    details

COMMENTARY
He tells Enfield that he already knows the name of the man who signed the cheque. Enfield confirms that Hyde did use a key to open the door. The two men agree never to speak of the matter again.

2 Search for Mr Hyde

Look out for...
- Jekyll's will: why is it so important?
- Dr Lanyon's opinion of his old friend Jekyll.
- Utterson's suspicions about Hyde's relationship with Jekyll: what is he so worried about?

That evening Mr Utterson came home to his bachelor house in sombre spirits, and sat down to dinner without relish. It was his custom of a Sunday, when this meal was over, to sit close by the fire, a volume of some dry divinity on his reading-desk, until the clock of the neighbouring church rang out the hour of twelve, when he would go soberly and gratefully to bed. On this night, however, as soon as the cloth was taken away, he took up a candle and went into his business room. There he opened his safe, took from the most private part of it a document endorsed on the envelope as Dr Jekyll's Will, and sat down with a clouded brow to study its contents. The will was holograph; for Mr Utterson, though he took charge of it now that it was made, had refused to lend the least assistance in the making of it; it provided not only that, in case of the decease of Henry Jekyll, M.D., D.C.L., LL.D., F.R.S., & C., all his possessions were to pass into the hands of his 'friend and benefactor Edward Hyde'; but that in the case of Dr Jekyll's 'disappearance or unexplained absence for any period exceeding three calendar months,' the said Edward Hyde should step into the said Henry Jekyll's shoes without further delay, and

COMMENTARY

When Utterson goes home that evening, he looks again at the strange will made by Dr Jekyll. In it he has left all his possessions and money to Mr Hyde in the event of his death or disappearance for more than three months.

volume of some dry divinity: boring book about religion
endorsed: marked
holograph: written in Jekyll's handwriting
decease: death
M.D., D.C.L., LL.D., F.R.S.: Doctor of Medicine, Doctor of Civil Law, Doctor of Laws, Fellow of the Royal Society – Jekyll is clearly a very highly qualified and respected scientist
benefactor: a person who has done good or kindness to another

free from any burthen or obligation, beyond the payment of a few small sums to the members of the doctor's household. This document had long been the lawyer's eyesore. It offended him both as a lawyer and as a lover of the sane and customary sides of life, to whom the fanciful was the immodest. And hitherto it was his ignorance of Mr Hyde that had swelled his indignation; now, by a sudden turn, it was his knowledge. It was already bad enough when the name was but a name of which he could learn no more. It was worse when it began to be clothed upon with detestable attributes; and out of the shifting, insubstantial mists that had so long baffled his eye, there leaped up the sudden, definite presentment of a fiend.

'I thought it was madness,' he said, as he replaced the obnoxious paper in the safe; 'and now I begin to fear it is disgrace.'

FAST FORWARD: to page 22

With that he blew out his candle, put on a great coat, and set forth in the direction of Cavendish Square, that citadel of medicine, where his friend the great Dr Lanyon, had his house and received his crowding patients. 'If any one knows, it will be Lanyon,' he had thought.

The solemn butler knew and welcomed him; he was subjected to no stage of delay, but ushered direct from the door to the dining room, where Dr Lanyon sat alone over his wine. This was a hearty, healthy, dapper, red-faced gentleman, with a shock of hair prematurely white, and a boisterous and decided manner. At sight of Mr Utterson, he sprang up from his chair and welcomed him with both hands. The geniality, as was the way of the man, was somewhat theatrical to the eye; but it reposed on genuine feeling. For these two were old friends, old mates both at school and college, both thorough respecters of themselves and of each other, and, what does not always follow, men who thoroughly enjoyed each other's company.

COMMENTARY

Utterson dislikes the will because it is irregular. Now he dislikes it even more because he fears Hyde may have some power over Dr Jekyll. He decides to go and talk to an old friend of his and Jekyll's, Dr Lanyon.

burthen: burden
sane and customary: healthy and normal
the fanciful was the immodest: anything unusual or imaginative was incorrect
citadel: centre of excellence

After a little rambling talk, the lawyer led up to the subject which so disagreeably preoccupied his mind.

'I suppose, Lanyon,' he said, 'you and I must be the two oldest friends that Henry Jekyll has?'

'I wish the friends were younger,' chuckled Dr Lanyon. 'But I suppose we are. And what of that? I see little of him now.'

'Indeed!' said Mr Utterson. 'I thought you had a bond of common interest.'

'We had,' was his reply. 'But it is more than ten years since Henry Jekyll became too fanciful for me. He began to go wrong, wrong in mind; and though, of course, I continue to take an interest in him for old sake's sake as they say, I see and I have seen devilish little of the man. Such unscientific balderdash,' added the doctor, flushing suddenly purple, 'would have estranged Damon and Pythias.'

This little spirt of temper was somewhat of a relief to Mr Utterson. 'They have only differed on some point of science,' he thought; and being a man of no scientific passions (except in the matter of conveyancing), he even added: 'It is nothing worse than that!' He gave his friend a few seconds to recover his composure, and then approached the question he had come to put.

'Did you ever come across a *protégé* of his – one Hyde?' he asked.

'Hyde?' repeated Lanyon. 'No. Never heard of him. Since my time.'

That was the amount of information that the lawyer carried back with him to the great, dark bed on which he tossed to and fro until the small hours of the morning began to grow large. It was a night of little ease to his toiling mind, toiling in mere darkness and besieged by questions.

Six o'clock struck on the bells of the church that was so conveniently near to Mr Utterson's dwelling, and still he was digging at the problem. Hitherto it had touched him on the intellectual side alone; but now his imagination also was engaged, or rather enslaved; and as he lay and tossed in the gross darkness of the night and the curtained room, Mr Enfield's tale went by before his mind in a scroll of lighted pictures. He would be aware of the great field of lamps in a nocturnal city; then of the figure of a man walking swiftly; then of a child

---

COMMENTARY

Utterson asks Lanyon if he has heard of Hyde, but is disappointed when he is told that he has not. Lanyon also criticises Jekyll's scientific ideas, of which Utterson knows nothing. Utterson returns home and goes to bed. He cannot sleep for thinking about this monster Hyde.

Damon and Pythias: two Greek friends (correctly named Damon and Phintias) who were absolutely devoted to each other. When one was condemned to death, his friend wanted to take his place but was refused. Neither of them wanted to live at the expense of the other.

conveyancing: transferring a house or other property to a new owner

protégé: person he has helped or protected

running from the doctor's; and then these met, and that human Juggernaut trod the child down and passed on regardless of her screams. Or else he would see a room in a rich house, where his friend lay asleep, dreaming and smiling at his dreams; and then the door of that room would be opened, the curtains of the bed plucked apart, the sleeper recalled, and, lo! there would stand by his side a figure to whom power was given, and even at that dead hour he must rise and do its bidding. The figure in these two phases haunted the lawyer all night; and if at any time he dozed over, it was but to see it glide more stealthily through sleeping houses, or move the more swiftly, and still the more swiftly, even to dizziness, through wider labyrinths of lamp-lighted city, and at every street corner crush a child and leave her screaming. And still the figure had no face by which he might know it; even in his dreams it had no face, or one that baffled him and melted before his eyes; and thus it was that there sprang up and grew apace in the lawyer's mind a singularly strong, almost an inordinate, curiosity to behold the features of the real Mr Hyde. If he could but once set eyes on him, he thought the mystery would lighten and perhaps roll altogether away, as was the habit of mysterious things when well examined. He might see a reason for his friend's strange preference or bondage (call it which you please), and even for the startling clauses of the will. And at least it would be a face worth seeing: the face of a man who was without bowels of mercy: a face which had but to show itself to raise up, in the mind of the unimpressionable
▶▶ Enfield, a spirit of enduring hatred.

REWIND: …of enduring hatred.
Utterson has been to visit a friend of his and Jekyll's, Dr Lanyon. He has asked him about Jekyll's friends, only to discover that Jekyll and Lanyon have fallen out over Jekyll's 'science'. Lanyon says he has never heard of anyone called Hyde. Utterson begins to be obsessed with the figure of Hyde: he is determined to see him.

---

labyrinths: twisting, complicated paths
  or tunnels
inordinate: out of all proportion
bondage: imprisonment
bowels of mercy: any sense of mercy
unimpressionable: not easily moved to
  strong emotion

COMMENTARY
Utterson dreams of Hyde crushing the little girl and his dreams develop into terrible nightmares. He decides that the only way to get rid of this obsession is to see Hyde for himself.

From that time forward, Mr Utterson began to haunt the door in the by street of shops. In the morning before office hours, at noon when business was plenty and time scarce, at night under the face of the fogged city moon, by all lights and at all hours of solitude or concourse, the lawyer was to be found on his chosen post.

'If he be Mr Hyde,' he had thought, 'I shall be Mr Seek.'

And at last his patience was rewarded. It was a fine dry night; frost in the air; the streets as clean as a ball-room floor; the lamps, unshaken by any wind, drawing a regular pattern of light and shadow. By ten o'clock, when the shops were closed, the by street was very solitary, and, in spite of the low growl of London from all around, very silent. Small sounds carried far; domestic sounds out of the houses were clearly audible on either side of the roadway; and the rumour of the approach of any passenger preceded him by a long time. Mr Utterson had been some minutes at his post when he was aware of an odd light footstep drawing near. In the course of his nightly patrols he had long grown accustomed to the quaint effect with which the footfalls of a single person, while he is still a great way off, suddenly spring out distinct from the vast hum and clatter of the city. Yet his attention had never before been so sharply and decisively arrested; and it was with a strong, superstitious prevision of success that he withdrew into the entry of the court.

The steps drew swiftly nearer, and swelled out suddenly louder as they turned the end of the street. The lawyer, looking forth from the entry, could soon see what manner of man he had to deal with. He was small, and very plainly dressed; and the look of him, even at that distance, went somehow strongly against the watcher's inclination. But he made straight for the door, crossing the roadway to save time; and as he came, he drew a key from his pocket, like one approaching home.

Mr Utterson stepped out and touched him on the shoulder as he passed. 'Mr Hyde, I think?'

Mr Hyde shrank back with a hissing intake of the breath. But his fear was only momentary; and though he did not look the lawyer in the face, he

COMMENTARY

Utterson begins to spend his spare time watching the door that Enfield showed him. At last he manages to catch Hyde just as he is about to open the door. Hyde does not show his face.

the rumour…long time: you could hear people coming a long way off

a strong, superstitious prevision: a premonition

answered coolly enough: 'That is my name. What do you want?'

'I see you are going in,' returned the lawyer. 'I am an old friend of Dr Jekyll's – Mr Utterson, of Caunt Street – you must have heard my name; and meeting you so conveniently, I thought you might admit me.'

'You will not find Dr Jekyll; he is from home,' replied Mr Hyde, blowing in the key. And then suddenly, but still without looking up, 'How did you know me?' he asked.

'On your side,' said Mr Utterson, 'will you do me a favour?'

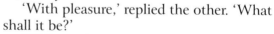

'With pleasure,' replied the other. 'What shall it be?'

'Will you let me see your face?' asked the lawyer.

Mr Hyde appeared to hesitate; and then, as if upon some sudden reflection, fronted about with an air of defiance; and the pair stared at each other pretty fixedly for a few seconds. 'Now I shall know you again,' said Mr Utterson. 'It may be useful.'

'Yes,' returned Mr Hyde, 'it is as well we have met; and *à propos*, you should have my address.' And he gave a number of a street in Soho.

'Good God!' thought Mr Utterson, 'can he too have been thinking of the will?' But he kept his feelings to himself, and only grunted in acknowledgment of the address.

'And now,' said the other, 'how did you know me?'

'By description,' was the reply.

'Whose description?'

'We have common friends,' said Mr Utterson.

'Common friends!' echoed Mr Hyde, a little hoarsely. 'Who are they?'

'Jekyll, for instance,' said the lawyer.

from home: out
fronted about: turned around
à propos: while we are on the
    subject
common friends: friends we
    share

COMMENTARY
Utterson speaks to Hyde and persuades him to show him his face. Hyde also tells him his address – it is in Soho, another part of London. Utterson reveals that he knows Dr Jekyll is a friend of them both.

'He never told you,' cried Mr Hyde, with a flush of anger. 'I did not think you would have lied.'

'Come,' said Mr Utterson, 'that is not fitting language.'

The other snarled aloud into a savage laugh; and the next moment, with extraordinary quickness, he had unlocked the door and disappeared into the house.

The lawyer stood awhile when Mr Hyde had left him, the picture of disquietude. Then he began slowly to mount the street, pausing every step or two, and putting his hand to his brow like a man in mental perplexity. The problem he was thus debating as he walked was one of a class that is rarely solved. Mr Hyde was pale and dwarfish; he gave an impression of deformity without any namable malformation, he had a displeasing smile, he had borne himself to the lawyer with a sort of murderous mixture of timidity and boldness, and he spoke with a husky, whispering and somewhat broken voice, – all these were points against him; but not all of these together could explain the hitherto unknown disgust, loathing and fear with which Mr Utterson regarded him. 'There must be something else,' said the perplexed gentleman. 'There *is* something more, if I could find a name for it. God bless me, the man seems hardly human! Something troglodytic, shall we say? or can it be the old story of Dr Fell? or is it the mere radiance of a foul soul that thus transpires through, and transfigures, its clay continent? The last, I think; for, O my poor old Harry Jekyll, if ever I read Satan's signature upon a face, it is on that of your new friend!'

Round the corner from the by street there was a square of ancient, handsome houses, now for the most part decayed from their high estate, and let in flats and chambers to all sorts and conditions of men: map-engravers, architects, shady lawyers, and the agents of obscure enterprises. One house, however, second from the corner, was still occupied entire; and at the door of this, which wore a great air of wealth and comfort, though it was now plunged in darkness except for the fan-light, Mr Utterson stopped and knocked. A well-dressed, elderly servant opened the door.

fitting: suitable for the occasion

disquietude: anxiety

he gave…malformation: he seemed to be deformed but there was nothing physically wrong with him

troglodytic: like a cave-dweller

Dr Fell: 'I do not like thee, Dr Fell, the reason why I cannot tell. But this alone I know full well: I do not like thee, Dr Fell.'

the mere…clay continent: his idea is that Hyde is so evil that this makes him look ugly and deformed

'Is Dr Jekyll at home, Poole?' asked the lawyer.

'I will see, Mr Utterson,' said Poole, admitting the visitor, as he spoke, into a large, low-roofed, comfortable hall, paved with flags, warmed (after the fashion of a country house) by a bright, open fire, and furnished with costly cabinets of oak.

'Will you wait here by the fire, sir? or shall I give you a light in the dining-room?'

'Here, thank you,' said the lawyer; and he drew near and leaned on the tall fender. This hall, in which he was now left alone, was a pet fancy of his friend the doctor's; and Utterson himself was wont to speak of it as the pleasantest room in London. But to-night there was a shudder in his blood; the face of Hyde sat heavy on his memory; he felt (what was rare in him) a nausea and distaste of life; and in the gloom of his spirits, he seemed to read a menace in the flickering of the firelight on the polished cabinets and the uneasy starting of the shadow on the roof. He was ashamed of his relief when Poole presently returned to announce that Dr Jekyll was gone out.

'I saw Mr Hyde go by the old dissecting-room door, Poole,' he said. 'Is that right, when Dr Jekyll is from home?'

'Quite right, Mr Utterson, sir,' replied the servant. 'Mr Hyde has a key.'

'Your master seems to repose a great deal of trust in that young man, Poole,' resumed the other, musingly.

'Yes, sir, he do indeed,' said Poole. 'We have all orders to obey him.'

'I do not think I ever met Mr Hyde?' asked Utterson.

'O dear no, sir. He never *dines* here,' replied the butler. 'Indeed, we see very little of him on this side of the house; he mostly comes and goes by the laboratory.'

'Well, good-night, Poole.'

'Good-night, Mr Utterson.'

And the lawyer set out homeward with a very heavy heart. 'Poor Harry Jekyll,' he thought, 'my mind misgives me he is in deep waters! He was wild when he was young; a long while ago, to be sure; but in the law of God there is

---

pet fancy: favourite place
dissecting-room: a laboratory used for experiments on dead bodies
repose: place
musingly: thoughtfully

COMMENTARY

It is the house of Dr Jekyll. Utterson asks if he is at home, but Poole, the butler, tells him that he is not. He then asks Poole about Mr Hyde and is told that he usually enters the house by the laboratory door, to which he has a key. (So we learn that the door in the alley leading to the courtyard lets Hyde into the laboratory and from there into Jekyll's house.)

no statute of limitations. Ah, it must be that; the ghost of some old sin, the cancer of some concealed disgrace; punishment coming, *pede claudo*, years after memory has forgotten and self-love condoned the fault.' And the lawyer, scared by the thought, brooded awhile on his own past, groping in all the corners of memory, lest by chance some Jack-in-the-Box of an old iniquity should leap to light there. His past was fairly blameless; few men could read the rolls of their life with less apprehension; yet he was humbled to the dust by the many ill things he had done, and raised up again into a sober and fearful gratitude by the many that he had come so near to doing, yet avoided. And then by a return on his former subject, he conceived a spark of hope. 'This Master Hyde, if he were studied,' thought he, 'must have secrets of his own: black secrets, by the look of him; secrets compared to which poor Jekyll's worst would be like sunshine. Things cannot continue as they are. It turns me quite cold to think of this creature stealing like a thief to Harry's bedside; poor Harry, what a wakening! And the danger of it! for if this Hyde suspects the existence of the will, he may grow impatient to inherit. Ay, I must put my shoulder to the wheel – if Jekyll will but let me,' he added, 'if Jekyll will only let me.' For once more he saw before his mind's eye, as clear as a transparency, the strange clauses of the will.

COMMENTARY

Utterson decides that Hyde must have some hold over Jekyll because of something he did in his youth. That is why Jekyll has made his strange will. He decides he must help Jekyll – if he will let him.

---

statute of limitations: a law that says that you cannot be prosecuted for a crime after a certain period of time

pede claudo: with slow feet

condoned: overlooked

iniquity: injustice

rolls: the scrolls or manuscripts recording a person's history

3 Dr Jekyll was Quite at Ease

Look out for...
- **your first impressions of Dr Jekyll: what does he look like? What is his personality? What kind of life does he lead?**
- **Dr Jekyll's 'painful situation': what do you think he means by this?**

A fortnight later, by excellent good fortune, the doctor gave one of his pleasant dinners to some five or six old cronies, all intelligent reputable men, and all judges of good wine; and Mr Utterson so contrived that he remained behind after the others had departed. This was no new arrangement, but a thing that had befallen many scores of times. Where Utterson was liked, he was liked well. Hosts loved to detain the dry lawyer, when the light-hearted and the loose-tongued had already their foot on the threshold; they liked to sit awhile in his unobtrusive company, practising for solitude, sobering their minds in the man's rich silence, after the expense and strain of gaiety. To this rule Dr Jekyll was no exception; and as he now sat on the opposite side of the fire – a large, well-made, smooth-faced man of fifty, with something of a slyish cast perhaps, but every mark of capacity and kindness – you could see by his looks that he cherished for Mr Utterson a sincere and warm affection.

'I have been wanting to speak to you, Jekyll,' began the latter. 'You know that will of yours?'

had already their foot on the threshold: were already setting off for home
unobtrusive: not showy or demanding
something of a slyish cast: his face sometimes looked just a little bit cunning

COMMENTARY
Two weeks later Utterson attends a dinner party at Dr Jekyll's house. When the two of them are alone together he raises the subject of the will.

A close observer might have gathered that the topic was distasteful; but the doctor carried it off gaily. 'My poor Utterson,' said he, 'you are unfortunate in such a client. I never saw a man so distressed as you were by my will; unless it were that hide-bound pedant, Lanyon, at what he called my scientific heresies. O, I know he's a good fellow – you needn't frown – an excellent fellow, and I always mean to see more of him; but a hide-bound pedant for all that; an ignorant, blatant pedant. I was never more disappointed in any man than Lanyon.'

'You know I never approved of it,' pursued Utterson, ruthlessly disregarding the fresh topic.

'My will? Yes, certainly, I know that,' said the doctor, a trifle sharply. 'You have told me so.'

'Well, I tell you so again,' continued the lawyer. 'I have been learning something of young Hyde.'

The large handsome face of Dr Jekyll grew pale to the very lips, and there came a blackness about his eyes. 'I do not care to hear more,' said he. 'This is a matter I thought we had agreed to drop.'

'What I heard was abominable,' said Utterson.

hide-bound pedant: narrow-minded and old-fashioned thinker
scientific heresies: beliefs that go against established scientific ideas
blatant: proud of it
abominable: terrible, awful

'It can make no change. You do not understand my position,' returned the doctor, with a certain incoherency of manner. 'I am painfully situated, Utterson; my position is a very strange – a very strange one. It is one of those affairs that cannot be mended by talking.'

'Jekyll,' said Utterson, 'You know me: I am a man to be trusted. Make a clean breast of this in confidence; and I make no doubt I can get you out of it.'

'My good Utterson,' said the doctor, 'this is very good of you, this is downright good of you, and I cannot find words to thank you in. I believe you fully; I would trust you before any man alive, ay, before myself, if I could make the choice; but indeed it isn't what you fancy; it is not so bad as that; and just to put your good heart at rest, I will tell you one thing: the moment I choose, I can be rid of Mr Hyde. I give you my hand upon that; and I thank you again and again; and I will just add one little word, Utterson, that I'm sure you'll take in good part: this is a private matter, and I beg of you to let it sleep.'

Utterson reflected a little, looking in the fire.

'I have no doubt you are perfectly right,' he said at last, getting to his feet.

'Well, but since we have touched upon this business, and for the last time, I hope,' continued the doctor, 'there is one point I should like you to understand. I have really a very great interest in poor Hyde. I know you have seen him; he told me so; and I fear he was rude. But I do sincerely take a great, a very great interest in that young man; and if I am taken away, Utterson, I wish you to promise me that you will bear with him and get his rights for him. I think you would, if you knew all; and it would be a weight off my mind if you would promise.'

'I can't pretend that I shall ever like him,' said the lawyer.

'I don't ask that,' pleaded Jekyll, laying his hand upon the other's arm; 'I only ask for justice; I only ask you to help him for my sake, when I am no longer here.'

Utterson heaved an irrepressible sigh. 'Well,' said he, 'I promise.'

COMMENTARY

Jekyll admits that he is in a very difficult situation. Utterson asks him to let him help him, but Jekyll says that it is his business alone. In any case, he can get rid of Hyde whenever he likes. But whatever happens Utterson must respect the terms of the will. He need not like Hyde, but he must give him justice. Utterson promises that he will.

with a certain incoherency of manner: not
   very clearly
painfully situated: in a difficult situation
an irrepressible sigh: a sigh that he could
   not keep in

The Carew Murder Case

Look out for...
- **the attack on Carew: what effect does this description have on you?**
- **your impressions of London as it is described in this chapter.**
- **further information about the character and personality of Hyde.**

Nearly a year later, in the month of October, 18—, London was startled by a crime of singular ferocity, and rendered all the more notable by the high position of the victim. The details were few and startling. A maid-servant living alone in a house not far from the river had gone upstairs to bed about eleven. Although a fog rolled over the city in the small hours, the early part of the night was cloudless, and the lane, which the maid's window overlooked, was brilliantly lit by the full moon. It seems she was romantically given; for she sat down upon her box, which stood immediately under the window, and fell into a dream of musing. Never (she used to say, with streaming tears, when she narrated that experience), never had she felt more at peace with all men or thought more kindly of the world. And as she so sat she became aware of an aged and beautiful gentleman with white hair drawing near along the lane; and advancing to meet him, another and very small gentleman, to whom at first she paid less attention. When they had come within speech (which was just under the maid's eyes) the older man bowed and accosted the other with a very pretty manner of politeness. It did not seem as if the subject of his

COMMENTARY
A year has passed and London is shaken by a terrible crime. It is witnessed by a servant girl looking out of her bedroom window near the Thames. She sees an elegant old man meet a smaller, younger man. The older man speaks to the younger man.

singular: remarkable
romantically given: had a romantic view of life
fell into a dream of musing: started day-dreaming
accosted: spoke to

address were of great importance; indeed, from his pointing, it sometimes appeared as if he were only inquiring his way; but the moon shone on his face as he spoke, and the girl was pleased to watch it, it seemed to breathe such an innocent and old-world kindness of disposition, yet with something high too, as of a well-founded self-content. Presently her eye wandered to the other, and she was surprised to recognise in him a certain Mr Hyde, who had once visited her master and for whom she had conceived a dislike. He had in his hand a heavy cane, with which he was trifling; but he answered never a word, and seemed to listen with an ill-contained impatience. And then all of a sudden he broke out in a great flame of anger, stamping with his foot, brandishing the cane, and carrying on (as the maid described it) like a madman. The old gentleman took a step back, with the air of one very much surprised and a trifle hurt; and at that Mr Hyde broke out of all bounds, and clubbed him to the earth. And next moment, with ape-like fury, he was tramping his victim under foot, and hailing down a storm of blows, under which the bones were audibly shattered and the body jumped upon the roadway. At the horror of these sights and sounds, the maid fainted.

It was two o'clock when she came to herself and called for the police. The murderer was gone long ago; but there lay his victim in the middle of the lane, incredibly mangled. The stick with which the deed had been done, although it was of some rare and very tough and heavy wood, had broken in the middle under the stress of this insensate cruelty; and one splintered half had rolled in

the neighbouring gutter – the other, without doubt, had been carried away by the murderer. A purse and a gold watch were found upon the victim; but, no cards or papers, except a sealed and stamped envelope, which he had been probably carrying to the post, and which bore the name and address of Mr Utterson.

COMMENTARY

She recognises the younger man as Mr Hyde. Suddenly he becomes angry and attacks and kills the old man. The girl faints and when she recovers she calls the police.

old-world kindness of disposition: old-fashioned kindness of personality
high: noble
well-founded self-content: a well-deserved good opinion of himself
insensate: without feeling

This was brought to the lawyer the next morning, before he was out of bed; and he had no sooner seen it, and been told the circumstances, than he shot out a solemn lip. 'I shall say nothing till I have seen the body,' said he; 'this may be very serious. Have the kindness to wait while I dress.' And with the same grave countenance, he hurried through his breakfast and drove to the police station, whither the body had been carried. As soon as he came into the cell, he nodded.

'Yes,' said he, 'I recognise him. I am sorry to say that this is Sir Danvers Carew.'

'Good God, sir!' exclaimed the officer, 'is it possible?' And the next moment his eye lighted up with professional ambition. 'This will make a deal of noise,' he said. 'And perhaps you can help us to the man.' And he briefly narrated what the maid had seen, and showed the broken stick.

Mr Utterson had already quailed at the name of Hyde; but when the stick was laid before him, he could doubt no longer: broken and battered as it was, he recognised it for one that he had himself presented many years before to Henry Jekyll.

'Is this Mr Hyde a person of small stature?' he inquired.

'Particularly small and particularly wicked-looking, is what the maid calls him,' said the officer.

Mr Utterson reflected; and then, raising his head, 'If you will come with me in my cab,' he said, 'I think I can take you to his house.'

FAST FORWARD: to page 34

It was by this time about nine in the morning, and the first fog of the season. A great chocolate-coloured pall lowered over heaven, but the wind was continually charging and routing these embattled vapours; so that as the cab crawled from street to street, Mr Utterson beheld a marvellous number of degrees and hues of twilight; for here it would be dark like the back-end of

COMMENTARY
The old man had been holding a letter addressed to Mr Utterson. The next morning it is delivered to him. He goes to the police station and identifies the body as that of Sir Danvers Carew. He offers to take the police to the home of Mr Hyde and they set off into the fog.

he shot out a solemn lip: his face became serious
grave countenance: serious face
This will make a deal of noise: this will be talked about by everyone
quailed: lost courage
pall: gloom
charging and routing these embattled vapours: driving the fog back

evening; and there would be a glow of a rich, lurid brown, like the light of some strange conflagration; and here, for a moment, the fog would be quite broken up, and a haggard shaft of daylight would glance in between the swirling wreaths. The dismal quarter of Soho seen under these changing glimpses, with its muddy ways, and slatternly passengers, and its lamps, which had never been extinguished or had been kindled afresh to combat this mournful reinvasion of darkness, seemed, in the lawyer's eyes, like a district of some city in a nightmare. The thoughts of his mind, besides, were the gloomiest dye; and when he glanced at the companion of his drive, he was conscious of some touch of that terror of the law and the law's officers which may at times assail the most honest.

As the cab drew up before the address indicated, the fog lifted a little and showed him a dingy street, a gin palace, a low French eating-house, a shop for the retail of penny numbers and two-penny salads, many ragged children huddled in the doorways, and many women of many different nationalities passing out, key in hand, to have a morning glass; and the next moment the fog settled down again upon that part, as brown as umber, and cut him off from his blackguardly surroundings. This was the home of Henry Jekyll's favourite; of a man who was heir to a quarter of a million sterling.

An ivory-faced and silvery-haired old woman opened the door. She had an evil face, smoothed by hypocrisy; but her manners were excellent. Yes, she said, this was Mr Hyde's, but he was not at home; he had been in that night very late, but had gone away again in less than an hour: there was nothing strange in that; his habits were very irregular, and he was often absent; for instance, it was nearly two months since she had seen him till yesterday.

'Very well then, we wish to see his rooms,' said the lawyer; and when the

---

REWIND: …quarter of a million sterling.
They have travelled through the fog to Hyde's house.

COMMENTARY
They arrive at Hyde's house and the door is opened by an unpleasant-looking housekeeper. She tells them that Mr Hyde had come in late that night but had gone out again.

conflagration: fire
slatternly: wretched
dye: colour
gin palace: a gaudy public house
penny numbers: items that could be
    bought for a penny
blackguardly: evil-looking

woman began to declare it was impossible, 'I had better tell you who this person is,' he added. 'This is Inspector Newcomen of Scotland Yard.'

A flash of odious joy appeared upon the woman's face. 'Ah!' said she, 'he is in trouble! What has he done?'

Mr Utterson and the inspector exchanged glances. 'He don't seem a very popular character,' observed the latter. 'And now, my good woman, just let me and this gentleman have a look about us.'

In the whole extent of the house, which but for the old woman remained otherwise empty, Mr Hyde had only used a couple of rooms; but these were furnished with luxury and good taste. A closet was filled with wine; the plate was of silver, the napery elegant; a good picture hung upon the walls, a gift (as Utterson supposed) from Henry Jekyll, who was much of a connoisseur; and the carpets were of many plies and agreeable in colour. At this moment, however, the rooms bore every mark of having been recently and hurriedly ransacked; clothes lay about the floor, with their pockets inside out; lockfast drawers stood open; and on the hearth there lay a pile of grey ashes, as though many papers had been burned. From these embers the inspector disinterred the butt end of a green cheque book, which had resisted the action of the fire; the other half of the stick was found behind the door; and as this clinched his suspicions, the officer declared himself delighted. A visit to the bank, where several thousand pounds were found to be lying to the murderer's credit, completed his gratification.

'You may depend upon it, sir,' he told Mr Utterson. 'I have him in my hand. He must have lost his head, or he never would have left the stick or, above all, burned the cheque book. Why, money's life to the man. We have nothing to do but wait for him at the bank, and get out the handbills.'

This last, however, was not so easy of accomplishment; for Mr Hyde had numbered few familiars – even the master of the servant-maid had only seen him twice; his family could nowhere be traced; he had never been photo-graphed; and the few who could describe him differed widely, as common observers will. Only on one point were they agreed; and that was the haunting sense of unexpressed deformity with which the fugitive impressed his beholders.

COMMENTARY

They go into the house and search Hyde's rooms. He has obviously left in a hurry. They find half the stick which he had broken when attacking Carew and the ashes of various papers he had burned, including the remains of a cheque book. They go to the bank and discover that he has several thousand pounds in his account. The police decide they must search for him, but the problem is that people cannot agree exactly what he looks like.

odious: hateful
napery: table linen
of many plies: thick and expensive

gratification: satisfaction at what he has discovered
familiars: friends

5 Incident of the Letter

Look out for...
- the change that has taken place in Dr Jekyll.
- what Jekyll tells Utterson about the letter.
- what Utterson learns later about the letter.

It was late in the afternoon when Mr Utterson found his way to Dr Jekyll's door, where he was at once admitted by Poole, and carried down by the kitchen offices and across a yard which had once been a garden, to the building which was indifferently known as the laboratory or the dissecting-rooms. The doctor had bought the house from the heirs of a celebrated surgeon; and his own tastes being rather chemical than anatomical, had changed the destination of the block at the bottom of the garden. It was the first time that the lawyer had been received in that part of his friend's quarters; and he eyed the dingy windowless structure with curiosity, and gazed round with a distasteful sense of strangeness as he crossed the theatre, once crowded with eager students and now lying gaunt and silent, the tables laden with chemical apparatus, the floor strewn with crates and littered with packing straw, and the light falling dimly through the foggy cupola. At the further end, a flight of stairs mounted to a door covered with red baize; and through this Mr Utterson was at last received into the doctor's cabinet. It was a large room, fitted round with glass presses, furnished, among other things, with a cheval-glass and a

COMMENTARY

That afternoon Utterson goes to Dr Jekyll's house. For the first time he sees Jekyll's laboratory, which had once been a dissecting theatre. From there he is taken to the doctor's study.

carried: taken
destination: use to which it was put
cupola: a small domed roof (in this case, with windows in it)
cabinet: private study
glass presses: glass-fronted cupboards
cheval-glass: a long mirror which pivots in a frame

business table, and looking out upon the court by three dusty windows barred with iron. The fire burned in the grate; a lamp was set lighted on the chimney-shelf, for even in the houses the fog began to lie thickly; and there, close up to the warmth, sat Dr Jekyll, looking deadly sick. He did not rise to meet his visitor, but held out a cold hand and bade him welcome in a changed voice.

'And now,' said Mr Utterson, as soon as Poole had left them, 'you have heard the news?'

The doctor shuddered. 'They were crying it in the square,' he said. 'I heard them in my dining room.'

'One word,' said the lawyer. 'Carew was my client, but so are you; and I want to know what I am doing. You have not been mad enough to hide this fellow?'

'Utterson, I swear to God,' cried the doctor, 'I swear to God I will never set eyes on him again. I bind my honour to you that I am done with him in this world. It is all at an end. And indeed he does not want my help; you do not know him as I do; he is safe, he is quite safe; mark my words, he will never more be heard of.'

bind my honour to you: give you my word

COMMENTARY
Utterson sees Jekyll sitting in his study by the fire. He looks very ill. Jekyll swears that he has not helped Hyde to escape. He says that no one will ever hear of Hyde again.

The lawyer listened gloomily; he did not like his friend's feverish manner. 'You seem pretty sure of him,' said he; 'and for your sake, I hope you may be right. It if came to a trial, your name might appear.'

'I am quite sure of him,' replied Jekyll; 'I have grounds for certainty that I cannot share with any one. But there is one thing on which you may advise me. I have – I have received a letter; and I am at a loss whether I should show it to the police. I should like to leave it in your hands, Utterson; you would judge wisely, I am sure; I have so great a trust in you.'

'You fear, I suppose, that it might lead to his detection?' asked the lawyer.

'No,' said the other. 'I cannot say that I care what becomes of Hyde; I am quite done with him. I was thinking of my own character, which this hateful business has rather exposed.'

Utterson ruminated awhile; he was surprised at his friend's selfishness, and yet relieved by it. 'Well,' said he, at last, 'let me see the letter.'

The letter was written in an odd, upright hand, and signed 'Edward Hyde': and it signified, briefly enough, that the writer's benefactor, Dr Jekyll, whom he had long so unworthily repaid for a thousand generosities, need labour under no alarm for his safety as he had means of escape on which he placed a sure dependence. The lawyer liked this letter well enough; it put a better colour on the intimacy than he had looked for, and he blamed himself for some of his past suspicions.

'Have you the envelope?' he asked.

'I burned it,' replied Jekyll, 'before I thought what I was about. But it bore no postmark. The note was handed in.'

'Shall I keep this and sleep upon it?' asked Utterson.

'I wish you to judge for me entirely,' was the reply. 'I have lost confidence in myself.'

'Well, I shall consider,' returned the lawyer. 'And now one word more: it was Hyde who dictated the terms in your will about that disappearance?'

signified: said
put a better colour on the intimacy: made
   the friendship look more acceptable
judge for me entirely: do whatever you
   think is right on my behalf

COMMENTARY

Jekyll swears that this is true and tells Utterson he is glad to be rid of Hyde. He shows him a letter from Hyde which he says was handed in at the house. It says that Hyde promises that he will no longer trouble Jekyll. Utterson keeps the letter and asks Jekyll if it was Hyde who suggested the terms of his will.

The doctor seemed seized with a qualm of faintness; he shut his mouth tight and nodded.

'I knew it,' said Utterson. 'He meant to murder you. You have had a fine escape.'

'I have had what is far more to the purpose,' returned the doctor solemnly: 'I have had a lesson – O God, Utterson, what a lesson I have had!' And he covered his face for a moment with his hands.

On his way out, the lawyer stopped and had a word or two with Poole. 'By the by,' said he, 'there was a letter handed in today: what was the messenger like?' But Poole was positive nothing had come except by post; 'and only circulars by that,' he added.

This news sent off the visitor with his fears renewed. Plainly the letter had come by the laboratory door; possibly, indeed, it had been written in the cabinet; and, if that were so, it must be differently judged, and handled with the more caution. The news boys, as he went, were crying themselves hoarse along the footways; 'Special edition. Shocking murder of an M.P.' That was the funeral oration of one friend and client; and he could not help a certain apprehension lest the good name of another should be sucked down in the eddy of the scandal. It was, at least, a ticklish decision that he had to make; and, self-reliant as he was by habit, he began to cherish a longing for advice. It was not to be had directly; but perhaps, he thought, it might be fished for.

FAST FORWARD: to page 41

FAST FORWARD: to page 41

Presently after, he sat on one side of his own hearth, with Mr Guest, his head clerk, upon the other, and midway between, at a nicely calculated distance from the fire, a bottle of a particular old wine that had long dwelt unsunned in the foundations of his house. The fog still slept on the wing above the drowned city, where the lamps glimmered like carbuncles; and through the

COMMENTARY

Jekyll admits that the will was Hyde's idea and Utterson tells him that Hyde had intended to murder him for his money. As Utterson is leaving he asks the butler if he saw the letter handed in and is surprised to learn that no one has handed a letter in that day – so it must have been written inside the house. Very worried, Utterson returns home. He decides to talk to his head clerk, Mr Guest.

seemed seized with a qualm of faintness: looked as if he was going to faint

circulars: junk mail

oration: speech

eddy: whirlpool

unsunned: in the dark

carbuncles: red gemstones

muffle and smother of these fallen clouds, the procession of the town's life was still rolling in through the great arteries with a sound as of a mighty wind. But the room was gay with firelight. In the bottle the acids were long ago resolved; the imperial dye had softened with time, as the colour grows richer in stained windows; and the glow of hot autumn afternoons on hillside vineyards was ready to be set free and to disperse the fogs of London. Insensibly the lawyer melted. There was no man from whom he kept fewer secrets than Mr Guest; and he was not always sure that he kept as many as he meant. Guest had often been on business to the doctor's; he knew Poole; he could scarce have failed to hear of Mr Hyde's familiarity about the house; he might draw conclusions: was it not as well, then, that he should see a letter which put that mystery to rights? and above all, since Guest, being a great student and critic of handwriting, would consider the step natural and obliging? The clerk, besides, was a man of counsel; he would scarce read so strange a document without dropping a remark; and by that remark Mr Utterson might shape his future course.

'This is a sad business about Sir Danvers,' he said.

'Yes, sir, indeed. It has elicited a great deal of public feeling,' returned Guest. 'The man, of course, was mad.'

'I should like to hear your views on that,' replied Utterson. 'I have a document here in his handwriting; it is between ourselves, for I scarce know what to do about it; it is an ugly business at the best. But there it is; quite in your way: a murderer's autograph.'

Guest's eyes brightened, and he sat down at once and studied it with passion. 'No, sir,' he said; 'not mad; but it is an odd hand.'

'And by all accounts a very odd writer,' added the lawyer.

Just then the servant entered with a note.

'Is that from Dr Jekyll, sir?' inquired the clerk. 'I thought I knew the writing. Anything private, Mr Utterson?'

'Only an invitation to dinner. Why? Do you want to see it?'

'One moment. I thank you, sir'; and the clerk laid the two sheets of paper

---

COMMENTARY

Over a glass of fine wine, Utterson tells Guest his worries and shows him the letter. Guest is a handwriting expert and agrees with Utterson that the writing is strange. At that moment, a letter arrives from Jekyll and Guest asks to see it.

In the bottle...stained windows: the wine has matured in the bottle so that its taste has mellowed and its colour has deepened

elicited: led to

autograph: document written in his own handwriting

alongside and sedulously compared their contents. 'Thank you, sir,' he said at last, returning both; 'it's a very interesting autograph.' ◄◄

There was a pause, during which Mr Utterson struggled with himself. 'Why did you compare them, Guest?' he inquired suddenly.

'Well, sir,' returned the clerk. 'there's a rather singular resemblance; the two hands are in many points identical; only differently sloped.'

'Rather quaint,' said Utterson.

'It is, as you say, rather quaint,' returned Guest.

'I wouldn't speak of this note, you know,' said the master.

'No, sir,' said the clerk. 'I understand.'

But no sooner was Mr Utterson alone that night than he locked the note into his safe, where it reposed from that time forward. 'What!' he thought. 'Henry Jekyll forge for a murderer!' And his blood ran cold in his veins.

REWIND: ...a very interesting autograph.'
Utterson has invited Guest, his head clerk, to have a drink with him. They have talked about the death of Sir Danvers and Utterson has shown Guest the letter from Hyde. Guest has compared the handwriting with a note that has been delivered from Dr Jekyll.

◄◄

COMMENTARY
Guest points out to Utterson the similarity between Hyde's writing and Jekyll's. Utterson tells him to keep this to himself. He believes that Jekyll must have forged Hyde's note.

sedulously: very carefully
quaint: strange

6 Remarkable Incident of Dr Lanyon

Look out for...
- **sudden changes in Dr Jekyll: what do you think may be the cause of these?**
- **the rapid decline in Dr Lanyon's health and the possible causes of it.**
- **how all this affects Utterson.**

Time ran on; thousands of pounds were offered in reward, for the death of Sir Danvers was resented as a public injury; but Mr Hyde had disappeared out of the ken of the police as though he had never existed. Much of his past was unearthed, indeed, and all disreputable: tales came out of the man's cruelty, at once so callous and violent, of his vile life, of his strange associates, of the hatred that seemed to have surrounded his career; but of his present whereabouts, not a whisper. From the time he had left the house in Soho on the morning of the murder, he was simply blotted out; and gradually, as time drew on, Mr Utterson began to recover from the hotness of his alarm, and to grow more at quiet with himself. The death of Sir Danvers was, to his way of thinking, more than paid for by the disappearance of Mr Hyde. Now that the evil influence had been withdrawn, a new life began for Dr Jekyll. He came out of his seclusion, renewed relations with his friends, became once more their familiar guest and entertainer; and whilst he had always been known for charities, he was no less distinguished for religion. He was busy, he was much in the open air, he did good; his face seemed to open and brighten, as if with

injury: loss, disaster
ken: knowledge

COMMENTARY
Time has passed, but although the stories about Hyde have multiplied, he has never been sighted. Dr Jekyll begins to live a happier and more sociable life.

an inward consciousness of service; and for more than two months the doctor was at peace.

On the 8th of January Utterson had dined at the doctor's with a small party; Lanyon had been there; and the face of the host had looked from one to the other as in the old days when the trio were inseparable friends. On the 12th, and again on the 14th, the door was shut against the lawyer. 'The doctor was confined to the house,' Poole said, 'and saw no one.' On the 15th he tried again, and was again refused; and having now been used for the last two months to see his friend almost daily, he found this return of solitude to weigh upon his spirits. The fifth night he had in Guest to dine with him; and the sixth he betook himself to Dr Lanyon's.

There at least he was not denied admittance; but when he came in, he was shocked at the change which had taken place in the doctor's appearance. He had his death-warrant written legibly upon his face. The rosy man had grown pale; his flesh had fallen away; he was visibly balder and older; and yet it was not so much these tokens of a swift physical decay that arrested the lawyer's notice, as a look in the eye and quality of manner that seemed to testify to some deep-seated terror of the mind. It was unlikely that the doctor should fear death; and yet that was what Utterson was tempted to suspect. 'Yes,' he thought; 'he is a doctor, he must know his own state and that his days are counted; and the knowledge is more than he can bear.' And yet when Utterson remarked on his ill looks, it was with an air of great firmness that Lanyon declared himself a doomed man.

'I have had a shock,' he said, 'and I shall never recover. It is a question of weeks. Well, life has been pleasant; I liked it; yes, sir, I

He had his death warrant written legibly upon his face: it was clear from his face that he was dying

COMMENTARY

This happy state of affairs continues for two months. Early in the New Year, however, Jekyll again shuts his door to visitors and will not even let Utterson in. Utterson visits Dr Lanyon and finds him a sick man. He tells Utterson that he has had a bad shock.

used to like it. I sometimes think if we knew all, we should be more glad to get away.'

'Jekyll is ill, too,' observed Utterson. 'Have you seen him?'

But Lanyon's face changed, and he held up a trembling hand. 'I wish to see or hear no more of Dr Jekyll,' he said, in a loud, unsteady voice. 'I am quite done with that person; and I beg that you will spare me any allusion to one whom I regard as dead.'

'Tut, tut,' said Mr Utterson; and then, after a considerable pause, 'Can't I do anything?' he inquired. 'We are three very old friends, Lanyon; we shall not live to make others.'

'Nothing can be done,' returned Lanyon; 'ask himself.'

'He will not see me,' said the lawyer.

'I am not surprised at that,' was the reply. 'Some day, Utterson, after I am dead, you may perhaps come to learn the right and wrong of this. I cannot tell you. And in the meantime, if you can sit and talk with me of other things, for God's sake, stay and do so; but if you cannot keep clear of this accursed topic, then, in God's name, go, for I cannot bear it.'

As soon as he got home, Utterson sat down and wrote to Jekyll, complaining of his exclusion from the house, and asking the cause of his unhappy break with Lanyon; and the next day brought him a long answer, often very pathetically worded, and sometimes darkly mysterious in drift. The quarrel with Lanyon was incurable. 'I do not blame our old friend,' Jekyll wrote, 'but I share his view that we must never meet. I mean from henceforth to lead a life of extreme seclusion; you must not be surprised, nor must you doubt my friendship, if my door is often shut even to you. You must suffer me to go my own dark way. I have brought on myself a punishment and a danger that I cannot name. If I am the chief of sinners, I am the chief of sufferers also. I could not think that this earth contained a place for sufferings and terrors so unmanning; and you can do but one thing, Utterson, to lighten this destiny, and that is to respect my silence.' Utterson was amazed; the dark influence of Hyde had been withdrawn, the doctor had returned to his old tasks and amities; a week ago,

---

allusion to: mention of

darkly mysterious in drift: its overall meaning was a complete mystery

I mean…seclusion: from now on I intend to live entirely alone

to lighten this destiny: to make my fate easier to bear

amities: friendships

COMMENTARY

Utterson tells him that Jekyll, too, is ill. Lanyon asks him never to mention Jekyll again. Perhaps one day he will discover why. Utterson writes to Jekyll asking why he will not see him and receives a reply telling him that Jekyll wants to live entirely alone from now on. He has sinned and suffered, but it is his business and no one else's.

the prospect had smiled with every promise of a cheerful and honoured age; and now in a moment, friendship and peace of mind and the whole tenor of his life were wrecked. So great and unprepared a change pointed to madness; but in view of Lanyon's manner and words, there must lie for it some deeper ground.

A week afterwards Dr Lanyon took to his bed, and in something less than a fortnight he was dead. The night after the funeral, at which he had been sadly affected, Utterson locked the door of his business room, and sitting there by the light of a melancholy candle, drew out and set before him an envelope addressed by the hand and sealed with the seal of his dead friend. 'PRIVATE: for the hands of J. G. Utterson ALONE, and in case of his predecease *to be destroyed unread*,' so it was emphatically superscribed; and the lawyer dreaded to behold the contents. 'I have buried one friend to-day,' he thought: 'what if this should cost me another?' And then he condemned the fear as a disloyalty, and broke the seal. Within there was another enclosure, likewise sealed, and marked upon the cover as 'not to be opened until the death or disappearance of Dr Henry Jekyll.' Utterson could not trust his eyes. Yes, it was disappearance, here again, as in the mad will, which he had long ago restored to its author, here again were the idea of a disappearance and the name of Henry Jekyll bracketed. But in the will, that idea had sprung from the sinister suggestion of the man Hyde; it was set there with a purpose all too plain and horrible. Written by the hand of Lanyon, what should it mean? A great curiosity came to the trustee, to disregard the prohibition and dive at once to the bottom of these mysteries; but professional honour and faith to his dead friend were stringent obligations; and the packet slept in the inmost corner of his private safe.

It is one thing to mortify curiosity, another to conquer it; and it may be doubted if, from that day forth, Utterson desired the society of his surviving friend with the same eagerness. He thought of him kindly; but his thoughts were disquieted and fearful. He went to call indeed; but he was perhaps relieved to be denied admittance; perhaps, in his heart, he preferred to speak

COMMENTARY

Not long afterwards Dr Lanyon dies. Utterson receives a letter from him. He opens the envelope and discovers that it contains another sealed envelope which he is not to open until the death or disappearance of Dr Jekyll. He puts it in his safe.

tenor: course
melancholy: sad
in case of his predecease: if he dies before (i.e. before Dr Lanyon)
it was emphatically superscribed: it had written boldly on the outside
A great curiosity…prohibition: he was dying to disobey the instruction
stringent obligations: strict duties
mortify: subdue
disquieted: anxious

with Poole upon the doorstep, and surrounded by the air and sounds of the open city, rather than to be admitted into that house of voluntary bondage, and to sit and speak with its inscrutable recluse. Poole had, indeed, no very pleasant news to communicate. The doctor, it appeared, now more than ever confined himself to the cabinet over the laboratory, where he would sometimes even sleep; he was out of spirits, he had grown very silent, he did not read; it seemed as if he had something on his mind. Utterson became so used to the unvarying character of these reports, that he fell off little by little in the frequency of his visits.

bondage: imprisonment

COMMENTARY
Utterson continues to visit Jekyll's house but is never allowed to see him.

7 Incident at the Window

Look out for...
● the strange and sudden change in Jekyll in the middle of the conversation: what do you think causes it?

It chanced on Sunday, when Mr Utterson was on his usual walk with Mr Enfield, that their way lay once again through the by street; and that when they came in front of the door, both stopped to gaze on it.

'Well,' said Enfield, 'that story's at an end, at least. We shall never see more of Mr Hyde.'

'I hope not,' said Utterson. 'Did I ever tell you that I once saw him, and shared your feeling of repulsion?'

'It was impossible to do the one without the other,' returned Enfield. 'And, by the way, what an ass you must have thought me, not to know that this was a back way to Dr Jekyll's! It was partly your own fault that I found it out, even when I did.'

'So you found it out, did you?' said Utterson. 'But if that be so, we may step into the court and take a look at the windows. To tell you the truth, I am uneasy about poor Jekyll; and even outside, I feel as if the presence of a friend might do him good.'

The court was very cool and a little damp, and *full of premature twilight,*

COMMENTARY
One Sunday, Utterson is taking his usual walk with Enfield. They come to 'that door'. They go into the courtyard to view the back of Jekyll's house.

full of premature twilight: already getting dark, although it was early

although the sky, high up overhead, was still bright with sunset. The middle one of the three windows was half way open; and sitting close beside it, taking the air with an infinite sadness of mien, like some disconsolate prisoner, Utterson saw Dr Jekyll.

'What! Jekyll!' he cried. 'I trust you are better.'

'I am very low, Utterson,' replied the doctor drearily; 'very low. It will not last long, thank God.'

'You stay too much indoors,' said the lawyer. 'You should be out, whipping up the circulation like Mr Enfield and me. (This is my cousin – Mr Enfield – Dr Jekyll.) Come, now; get your hat and take a quick turn with us.'

'You are very good,' sighed the other. 'I should like to very much; but no, no, no, it is quite impossible; I dare not. But indeed, Utterson, I am very glad to see you; this is really a great pleasure. I would ask you and Mr Enfield up, but the place is really not fit.'

'Why then,' said the lawyer, good-naturedly, 'the best thing we can do is to stay down here, and speak with you from where we are.'

'That is just what I was about to venture to propose,' returned the doctor, with a smile. But the words were hardly uttered, before the smile was struck out of his face and succeeded by an expression of such abject terror and despair, as froze the very blood of the two gentlemen below. They saw it but for a glimpse, for the window was instantly thrust down; but that glimpse had

---

COMMENTARY

They see Jekyll at an open window and speak to him. The conversation is interrupted when Jekyll suddenly looks horrified and slams the window shut.

---

disconsolate: sad
whipping up the circulation: getting the
  blood moving round the body (by
  vigorous exercise)
abject: wretched

been sufficient, and they turned and left the court without a word. In silence, too, they traversed the by street; and it was not until they had come into a neighbouring thoroughfare, where even upon a Sunday there were still some stirrings of life, that Mr Utterson at last turned and looked at his companion. They were both pale; and there was an answering horror in their eyes.

'God forgive us! God forgive us!' said Mr Utterson.

But Mr Enfield only nodded his head very seriously, and walked on once more in silence.

traversed: walked the length of

COMMENTARY
Horrified, Utterson and Enfield go on their way in silence.

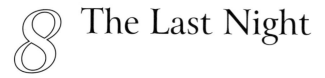# The Last Night

Look out for...
- **the way in which the tension mounts in this chapter: how does the writer achieve this?**
- **the atmosphere in Jekyll's house and the terror of his servants.**
- **Utterson's growing realisation of what has happened.**

FAST FORWARD: to page 53

Mr Utterson was sitting by his fireside one evening after dinner, when he was surprised to receive a visit from Poole.

'Bless me, Poole, what brings you here?' he cried; and then, taking a second look at him, 'What ails you?' he added; 'is the doctor ill?'

'Mr Utterson,' said the man, 'there is something wrong.'

'Take a seat, and here is a glass of wine for you,' said the lawyer. 'Now, take your time, and tell me plainly what you want.'

'You know the doctor's ways, sir,' replied Poole, 'and how he shuts himself up. Well, he's shut up again in the cabinet; and I don't like it, sir – I wish I may die if I like it. Mr Utterson, sir, I'm afraid.'

'Now, my good man,' said the lawyer, 'be explicit. What are you afraid of?'

'I've been afraid for about a week,' returned Poole, doggedly disregarding the question, 'and I can bear it no more.'

The man's appearance amply bore out his words; his manner was altered for

be explicit: explain precisely and clearly what you mean
doggedly disregarding the question: ploughing on and taking no notice of the question

COMMENTARY
One evening Utterson receives a visit from Poole, Jekyll's butler. Poole is very worried about Jekyll, who has shut himself up in his room for a week.

the worse; and except for the moment when he had first announced his terror, he had not once looked the lawyer in the face. Even now, he sat with the glass of wine untasted on his knee, and his eyes directed to a corner of the floor. 'I can bear it no more,' he repeated.

'Come,' said the lawyer, 'I see you have some good reason, Poole; I see there is something seriously amiss. Try to tell me what it is.'

'I think there's been foul play,' said Poole, hoarsely.

'Foul play!' cried the lawyer, a good deal frightened, and rather inclined to be irritated in consequence. 'What foul play? What does the man mean?'

'I daren't say, sir,' was the answer; 'but will you come along with me and see for yourself?'

Mr Utterson's only answer was to rise and get his hat and great coat; but he observed with wonder the greatness of the relief that appeared upon the butler's face, and perhaps with no less, that the wine was still untasted when he set it down to follow.

It was a wild, cold, seasonable night of March, with a pale moon, lying on her back as though the wind had tilted her, and a flying wrack of the most diaphanous and lawny texture. The wind made talking difficult, and flecked the blood into the face. It seemed to have swept the streets unusually bare of passengers, besides; for Mr Utterson thought he had never seen that part of London so deserted. He could have wished it otherwise; never in his life had he been conscious of so sharp a wish to see and touch his fellow-creatures; for, struggle as he might, there was borne in upon his mind a crushing anticipation of calamity. The square, when they got there, was all full of wind and dust, and the thin trees in the garden were lashing themselves along the railing. Poole, who had kept all the way a pace or two ahead, now pulled up in the middle of the pavement, and in spite of the biting weather, took off his hat and mopped his brow with a red pocket-handkerchief. But for all the hurry of his coming, these were not the dews of exertion that he wiped away, but the moisture of some strangling anguish; for his face was white, and his voice, when he spoke, harsh and broken.

COMMENTARY
Poole tells Utterson that he is afraid that violence has been done at Jekyll's house. He leads Utterson through the windy night to the house.

amiss: wrong
perhaps with no less: he was probably just as surprised
a flying wrack...texture: thin high clouds were blowing across the moon
there was borne...calamity: his mind filled with dread at what they would find

not the dews...anguish: the sweat on his face was caused not by effort but by his mental agony

'Well, sir,' he said, 'here we are, and God grant there be nothing wrong.'
'Amen, Poole,' said the lawyer.

Thereupon the servant knocked in a very guarded manner; the door was opened on the chain; and a voice asked from within, 'Is that you, Poole?'

'It's all right,' said Poole. 'Open the door.'

The hall, when they entered it, was brightly lighted up; the fire was built high; and about the hearth the whole of the servants, men and women, stood huddled together like a flock of sheep. At the sight of Mr Utterson, the housemaid broke into hysterical whimpering; and the cook, crying out, 'Bless God! it's Mr Utterson,' ran forward as if to take him in her arms.

'What, what? Are you all here?' said the lawyer, peevishly. 'Very irregular, very unseemly: your master would be far from pleased.'

'They're all afraid,' said Poole.

Blank silence followed, no one protesting; only the maid lifted up her voice and now wept loudly.

'Hold your tongue!' Poole said to her, with a ferocity of accent that testified to his own jangled nerves; and indeed when the girl had so suddenly raised the note of her lamentation, they had all started and turned towards the inner door with faces of dreadful expectation. 'And now,' continued the butler, addressing the knife-boy, 'reach me a candle, and we'll get this through hands at once.' And then he begged Mr Utterson to follow him, and led the way to the back garden.

'Now, sir,' said he, 'you come as gently as you can. I want you to hear, and I don't want you to be heard. And see here, sir, if by any chance he was to ask you in, don't go.'

Mr Utterson's nerves, at this unlooked-for termination, gave a jerk that nearly threw him from his balance; but he recollected his courage, and followed the butler into the laboratory building and through the surgical theatre, with its lumber of crates and bottles, to the foot of the stair. Here Poole motioned him to stand on one side and listen; while he himself, setting down the candle and making a great and obvious call on his resolution, mounted the

guarded: cautious
unseemly: unsuitable
with a ferocity...nerves: with a fierceness in his voice
  that showed how worried he was
lamentation: weeping
knife-boy: the boy whose job it was to clean the
  table knives
unlooked-for termination: unexpected ending (to what
  Poole was saying)
resolution: determination

COMMENTARY
They come to the house and find all the servants gathered in the hall. Poole leads Utterson to the door of Jekyll's study.

steps, and knocked with a somewhat uncertain hand on the red baize of the cabinet door.

'Mr Utterson, sir, asking to see you,' he called; and even as he did so, once more violently signed to the lawyer to give ear.

A voice answered from within: 'Tell him I cannot see any one,' it said, complainingly.

'Thank you, sir,' said Poole, with a note of something like triumph in his voice; and taking up his candle, he led Mr Utterson back across the yard and into the great kitchen, where the fire was out and the beetles were leaping on the floor.

'Sir,' he said, looking Mr Utterson in the eyes, 'was that my master's voice?'

'It seems much changed,' replied the lawyer, very pale, but giving look for look.

'Changed? Well, yes, I think so,' said the butler. 'Have I been twenty years in this man's house, to be deceived about his voice? No, sir; master's made away with; he was made away with eight days ago, when we heard him cry out upon the name of God; and who's in there instead of him, and *why* it stays there, is a thing that cries to Heaven, Mr Utterson!'

'This is a very strange tale, Poole; this is rather a wild tale, my man,' said Mr Utterson, biting his finger. 'Suppose it were as you suppose, supposing Dr Jekyll to have been – well, murdered, what could induce the murderer to stay? That won't hold water; it doesn't commend itself to reason.'

'Well, Mr Utterson, you are a hard man to satisfy, but I'll do it yet,' said Poole. 'All this last week (you must know) him, or it, or whatever it is that lives

REWIND: …cabinet door.
Utterson has received an evening visit from Poole, Dr Jekyll's butler, who seems very upset. Poole has begged him to come immediately to Jekyll's house, because he is afraid that 'there's been foul play'. Utterson has gone with him to the house and Poole has taken him to the door of Jekyll's study.

COMMENTARY
Poole shouts in to the study but the person shut inside says he will not see them. Utterson agrees with Poole that the voice does not sound like Jekyll's. But he finds it hard to understand why, if this is Jekyll's murderer, he is still there. Why has he not run away?

made away with: killed
commend itself to reason: make sense

in that cabinet, has been crying night and day for some sort of medicine and cannot get it to his mind. It was sometimes his way – the master's, that is – to write his orders on a sheet of paper and throw it on the stair. We've had nothing else this week back; nothing but papers, and a closed door, and the very meals left there to be smuggled in when nobody was looking. Well, sir, every day, ay, and twice and thrice in the same day, there have been orders and complaints, and I have been sent flying to all the wholesale chemists in town. Every time I brought the stuff back, there would be another paper telling me to return it, because it was not pure, and another order to a different firm. This drug is wanted bitter bad, sir, whatever for.'

'Have you any of these papers?' asked Mr Utterson.

Poole felt in his pocket and handed out a crumpled note, which the lawyer, bending nearer to the candle, carefully examined. Its contents ran thus: 'Dr Jekyll presents his compliments to Messrs Maw. He assures them that their last sample is impure and quite useless for his present purpose. In the year 18—, Dr J. purchased a somewhat large quantity from Messrs M. He now begs them to search with the most sedulous care, and should any of the same quality be left, to forward it to him at once. Expense is no consideration. The importance of this to Dr J. can hardly be exaggerated.' So far the letter had run composedly enough; but here, with a sudden splutter of the pen, the writer's emotion had broken loose. 'For God's sake,' he had added, 'find me some of the old.'

'This is a strange note,' said Mr Utterson; and then sharply, 'How do you come to have it open?'

'The man at Maw's was main angry, sir, and he threw it back to me like so much dirt,' returned Poole.

'This is unquestionably the doctor's hand, do you know?' resumed the lawyer.

'I thought it looked like it,' said the servant, rather sulkily; and then, with another voice, 'But what matters hand of write?' he said. 'I've seen him!'

'Seen him?' repeated Mr Utterson. 'Well?'

COMMENTARY

Poole tells Utterson that the person in the study has been writing and throwing out orders to wholesale chemists for a particular chemical, but that he has not been able to get what he is looking for. It is clear from the orders that he is desperate for the same product that he had been sold previously. Poole surprises Utterson by telling him that he has seen the person in the study.

with the most sedulous care: extremely
  carefully
Expense is no consideration: it does not
  matter how much it costs

main: very
what matters hand of write? what does the
  handwriting matter?

'That's it!' said Poole. 'It was this way. I came suddenly into the theatre from the garden. It seems he had slipped out to look for his drug, or whatever it is; for the cabinet door was open, and there he was at the far end of the room digging among the crates. He looked up when I came in, gave a kind of cry, and whipped upstairs into the cabinet. It was but for one minute that I saw him, but the hair stood upon my head like quills. Sir, if that was my master, why had he a mask upon his face? If it was my master, why did he cry out like a rat and run from me? I have served him long enough. And then...' the man paused and passed his hand over his face.

'These are all very strange circumstances,' said Mr Utterson, 'but I think I begin to see daylight. Your master, Poole, is plainly seized with one of those maladies that both torture and deform the sufferer; hence, for aught I know, the alteration of his voice; hence the mask and his avoidance of his friends; hence his eagerness to find this drug, by means of which the poor soul retains some hope of ultimate recovery – God grant that he be not deceived! There is my explanation; it is sad enough, Poole, ay, and appalling to consider; but it is plain and natural, hangs well together and delivers us from all exorbitant alarms.'

'Sir,' said the butler, turning to a sort of mottled pallor, 'that thing was not my master, and there's the truth. My master' – here he looked round him, and began to whisper – 'is a tall fine build of a man, and this was more of a dwarf.' Utterson attempted to protest. 'O, sir,' cried Poole, 'do you think I do not know my master after twenty years? do you think I do not know where his head comes to in the cabinet door, where I saw him every morning of my life? No, sir, that thing in the mask was never Dr Jekyll – God knows what it was, but it was never Dr Jekyll; and it is the belief of my heart that there was murder done.'

'Poole,' replied the lawyer, 'if you say that, it will become my duty to make certain. Much as I desire to spare your master's feelings, much as I am puzzled about this note, which seems to prove him to be still alive, I shall consider it my duty to break in that door.'

COMMENTARY
Poole describes how he saw a masked figure in the laboratory. He knows from the person's build and movements that he was not Dr Jekyll. As soon as he saw Poole, the person disappeared into the study.

theatre: the laboratory (which used to be a dissecting theatre)
one of those...sufferer: one of those illnesses which both hurt the person and cause his appearance to change
turning to a sort of mottled pallor: his face going pale and blotchy

'Ah, Mr Utterson, that's talking!' cried the butler.

'And now comes the second question,' resumed Utterson: 'Who is going to do it?'

'Why, you and me, sir,' was the undaunted reply.

'That is very well said,' returned the lawyer; 'and whatever comes of it, I shall make it my business to see you are no loser.'

'There is an axe in the theatre,' continued Poole; 'and you might take the kitchen poker for yourself.'

The lawyer took that *rude* but weighty instrument into his hand, and balanced it. 'Do you know, Poole,' he said, looking up, 'that you and I are about to place ourselves in a position of some peril?'

'You may say so, sir, indeed,' returned the butler.

'It is well, then, that we should be frank,' said the other. 'We both think more than we have said; let us make a clean breast. This masked figure that you saw, did you recognise it?'

'Well, sir, it went so quick, and the creature was so doubled up, that I could hardly swear to that,' was the answer. 'But if you mean, was it Mr Hyde – why, yes, I think it was! You see, it was much of the same bigness; and it had the same quick light way with it; and then who else could have got in by the laboratory door? You have not forgot, sir, that at the time of the murder he had still the key with him? But that's not all. I don't know, Mr Utterson, if ever you met this Mr Hyde?'

FAST FORWARD: to page 58

FAST FORWARD: to page 58

'Yes,' said the lawyer, 'I once spoke with him.'

'Then you must know, as well as the rest of us, that there was something queer about that gentleman – something that gave a man a turn – I don't know rightly how to say it, sir, beyond this: that you *felt in your marrow* – kind of cold and thin.'

---

rude: rough
felt in your marrow: felt in your bones

COMMENTARY

Utterson and Poole agree that they will have to break down the door. Poole admits to Utterson that the figure he saw go into the study was Hyde.

'I own I felt something of what you describe,' said Mr Utterson.

'Quite so, sir,' returned Poole, 'Well, when that masked thing like a monkey jumped up from among the chemicals and whipped into the cabinet, it went down my spine like ice. O, I know it's not evidence, Mr Utterson; I'm book-learned enough for that; but a man has his feelings; and I give you my bible-word it was Mr Hyde!'

'Ay, ay,' said the lawyer. 'My fears incline to the same point. Evil, I fear, founded – evil was sure to come – of that connection. Ay, truly, I believe you; I believe poor Harry is killed; and I believe his murderer (for what purpose, God alone can tell) is still lurking in his victim's room. Well, let our name be vengeance. Call Bradshaw.'

The footman came at the summons, very white and nervous.

'Pull yourself together, Bradshaw,' said the lawyer. 'This suspense, I know, is telling upon all of you' but it is now our intention to make an end of it. Poole, here, and I are going to force our way into the cabinet. If all is well, my shoulders are broad enough to bear the blame. Meanwhile, lest anything should really be amiss, or any malefactor seek to escape by the back, you and the boy must go round the corner with a pair of good sticks, and take your post at the laboratory door. We give you ten minutes, to get to your stations.'

As Bradshaw left, the lawyer looked at his watch. 'And now, Poole, let us get to ours,' he said; and taking the poker under his arm, he led the way into the yard. The scud had banked over the moon, and it was now quite dark. The wind, which only broke in puffs and draughts into that deep well of building, tossed the light of the candle to and fro about their steps, until they came into the shelter of the theatre, where they sat down silently to wait. London hummed solemnly all around; but nearer at hand, the stillness was only broken by the sound of a footfall moving to and fro along the cabinet floor.

'So it will walk all day, sir,' whispered Poole; 'ay, and the better part of the night. Only when a new sample comes from the chemist, there's a bit of a break. Ah, it's an ill conscience that's such an enemy to rest! Ah, sir, there's

COMMENTARY
Utterson agrees that he believes Hyde has killed Jekyll. They prepare to break down the door.

book-learned: educated
give you my bible-word: swear on the bible
telling: having its effect
malefactor: wrong-doer
scud: clouds moving rapidly across the sky
Ah, it's an ill conscience that's such an enemy to rest: he cannot sleep because he has a guilty conscience

blood foully shed in every step of it! But hark again, a little closer – put your heart in your ears Mr Utterson, and tell me, is that the doctor's foot?'

The steps fell lightly and oddly, with a certain swing, for all they went so slowly; it was different indeed from the heavy creaking tread of Henry Jekyll. Utterson sighed. 'Is there never anything else?' he asked.

Poole nodded. 'Once,' he said. 'Once I heard it weeping!'

'Weeping? how that?' said the lawyer, conscious of a sudden chill of horror.

'Weeping like a woman or a lost soul,' said the butler. 'I came away with that upon my heart, that I could have wept too.'

But now the ten minutes drew to an end. Poole disinterred the axe from under a stack of packing straw; the candle was set upon the nearest table to light them to the attack; and they drew near with bated breath to where the patient foot was still going up and down, up and down in the quiet of the night.

'Jekyll,' cried Utterson, with a loud voice, 'I demand to see you.' He paused a moment, but there came no reply. 'I give you fair warning, our suspicions are aroused, and I must and shall see you,' he resumed; 'if not by fair means, then by foul – if not of your consent, then by brute force!'

'Utterson,' said the voice, 'for God's sake, have mercy!'

'Ah, that's not Jekyll's voice – it's Hyde's!' cried Utterson. 'Down with the door, Poole!'

Poole swung the axe over his shoulder; the blow shook the building, and the red baize door leaped against the lock and hinges. A dismal screech, as of mere animal terror, rang from the cabinet. Up went the axe again, and again the panels crashed and the frame bounded; four times the blow fell; but the wood

---

REWIND: …quiet of the night.
Utterson and Poole have agreed that the person in Jekyll's study must be Hyde and that he must have murdered Jekyll. They have decided that if he will not let them in, they will break down the door.

---

disinterred: dug out

COMMENTARY
They get an axe and begin to break down the door.

was tough and the fittings were of excellent workmanship; and it was not until the fifth that the lock burst in sunder, and the wreck of the door fell inwards on the carpet.

The besiegers, appalled by their own riot and the stillness that had succeeded, stood back a little and peered in. There lay the cabinet before their eyes in the quiet lamplight, a good fire glowing and chattering on the hearth, the kettle singing its thin strain, a drawer or two open, papers neatly set forth on the business table, and nearer the fire, the things laid out for tea; the quietest room, you would have said, and, but for the glazed presses full of chemicals, the most commonplace that night in London.

Right in the midst there lay the body of a man sorely contorted and still twitching. They drew near on tiptoe, turned it on its back, and beheld the face of Edward Hyde. He was dressed in clothes far too large for him, clothes of the doctor's bigness; the cords of his face still moved with a semblance of life, but life was quite gone; and by the crushed phial in the hand and the strong smell

COMMENTARY
At last it gives way and they enter the study. They find Hyde's body on the floor; he is dead but in his hand is a small glass container that has had poison in it.

glazed presses: glass-fronted cupboards
sorely contorted: severely twisted
cords: sinews
phial: small glass container

of kernels that hung upon the air, Utterson knew that he was looking on the body of a self-destroyer.

'We have come too late,' he said sternly, 'whether to save or punish. Hyde is gone to his account; and it only remains for us to find the body of your master.'

The far greater proportion of the building was occupied by the theatre, which filled almost the whole ground storey, and was lighted from above, and by the cabinet, which formed an upper storey at one end and looked upon the court. A corridor joined the theatre to the door on the by street; and with this, the cabinet communicated separately by a second flight of stairs. There were besides a few dark closets and a spacious cellar. All these they now thoroughly examined. Each closet needed but a glance, for all they were empty and all, by the dust that fell from their doors, had stood long unopened. The cellar, indeed, was filled with crazy lumber, mostly dating from the times of the surgeon who was Jekyll's predecessor; but even as they opened the door, they were advertised of the uselessness of further search by the fall of a perfect mat of cobweb which had for years sealed up the entrance. Nowhere was there any trace of Henry Jekyll, dead or alive.

Poole stamped on the flags of the corridor. 'He must be buried here,' he said, hearkening to the sound.

'Or he may have fled,' said Utterson, and he turned to examine the door in the by street. It was locked; and lying near by on the flags, they found the key, already stained with rust.

'This does not look like use,' observed the lawyer.

'Use!' echoed Poole. 'Do you not see, sir, it is broken? much as if a man had stamped on it.'

'Ah,' continued Utterson, 'and the fractures, too, are rusty.' The two men looked at each other with a scare. 'This is beyond me, Poole,' said the lawyer. 'Let us go back to the cabinet.'

They mounted the stair in silence, and still, with an occasional awestruck glance at the dead body, proceeded more thoroughly to examine the contents of the cabinet. At one table, there were traces of chemical work, various

---

COMMENTARY
Seeing that Hyde is dead, they search all over for any trace of Jekyll but find none. They begin to look again at the contents of the study.

---

kernels: nuts (he probably has in mind almonds, since the deadly poison cyanide gives off a strong smell of almonds)
closets: cupboards
lumber: junk
flags: stone flooring
like use: as if it has been used recently

measured heaps of some white salt being laid on glass saucers, as though for an experiment in which the unhappy man had been prevented.

'That is the same drug that I was always bringing him,' said Poole; and even as he spoke, the kettle with a startling noise boiled over.

This brought them to the fireside, where the easy chair was drawn cosily up, and the tea things stood ready to the sitter's elbow, the very sugar in the cup. There were several books on a shelf; one lay beside the tea things open, and Utterson was amazed to find it a copy of a pious work for which Jekyll had several times expressed a great esteem, annotated, in his own hand, with startling blasphemies.

Next, in the course of their review of the chamber, the searches came to the cheval-glass, into whose depth they looked with an involuntary horror. But it was so turned as to show them nothing but the rosy glow playing on the roof, the fire sparkling in a hundred repetitions along the glazed front of the presses, and their own pale and fearful countenances stooping to look in.

'This glass has seen some strange things, sir,' whispered Poole.

'And surely none stranger than itself,' echoed the lawyer, in the same tone. 'For what did Jekyll' – he caught himself up at the word with a start, and then conquering the weakness: 'what could Jekyll want with it?' he said.

'You may say that!' said Poole.

Next they turned to the business table. On the desk, among the neat array of papers, a large envelope was uppermost, and bore, in the doctor's hand, the name of Mr Utterson. The lawyer unsealed it, and several enclosures fell to the floor. The first was a will, drawn in the same eccentric terms as the one which he had returned six months before, to serve as a testament in case of death and as a deed of gift in case of disappearance; but in place of the name of Edward Hyde, the lawyer, with indescribable amazement, read the name of Gabriel John Utterson. He looked at Poole, and then back at the papers, and last of all at the dead malefactor stretched upon the carpet.

'My head goes round,' he said. 'He has been all these days in possession; he had no cause to like me; he must have raged to see himself displaced; and he has not destroyed this document.'

COMMENTARY
They examine the study and find nothing unusual until they see a large envelope on the desk. It is addressed to Utterson. It contains Jekyll's will in which he leaves everything to Utterson. The lawyer is amazed that Hyde has not destroyed it.

pious: religious
expressed a great esteem: spoken highly of

He caught the next paper; it was a brief note in the doctor's hand and dated at the top. 'O Poole!' the lawyer cried, 'he was alive and here this day. He cannot have been disposed of in so short a space; he must be still alive, he must have fled! And then, why fled? and how? and in that case can we venture to declare this suicide? O, we must be careful. I foresee that we may yet involve your master in some dire catastrophe.'

'Why don't you read it, sir?' asked Poole.

'Because I fear,' replied the lawyer, solemnly. 'God grant I have no cause for it!' And with that he brought the paper to his eyes, and read as follows:

MY DEAR UTTERSON, – When this shall fall into your hands, I shall have disappeared, under what circumstances I have not the penetration to foresee, but my instinct and all the circumstances of my nameless situation tell me that the end is sure and must be early. Go then, and first read the narrative which Lanyon warned me he was to place in your hands; and if you care to hear more, turn to the confession of
> Your unworthy and unhappy friend,
> HENRY JEKYLL

'There was a third enclosure,' asked Utterson.

'Here, sir,' said Poole, and gave into his hands a considerable packet sealed in several places.

The lawyer put it in his pocket. 'I would say nothing of this paper. If your master has fled or is dead, we may at least save his credit. It is now ten; I must go home and read these documents in quiet; but I shall be back before midnight, when we shall send for the police.'

They went out, locking the door of the theatre behind them; and Utterson, once more leaving the servants gathered about the fire in the hall, trudged back to his office to read the two narratives in which this mystery was now to be explained.

under what circumstances…foresee: although I do not have sufficient understanding to know exactly how it will happen

nameless situation: his situation is nameless because it is unique and so has never been described before

COMMENTARY

There are two other things in the envelope. One is a letter from Jekyll to Utterson. It instructs him to go home and read the letter which Dr Lanyon gave him and then to read the third item in the envelope they found in the desk, which is Jekyll's confession.

9 Dr Lanyon's Narrative

Look out for…
- the elaborate plans contained in Jekyll's letter to Lanyon: how do these affect the way in which you read the rest of this chapter?
- Lanyon's reaction to the letter and his preparations for the visit.
- the appearance and actions of the visitor.
- the revelation at the end of the chapter: what else remains to be explained?

FAST FORWARD: to page 66

On the ninth of January, now four days ago, I received by the evening delivery a registered envelope, addressed in the hand of my colleague and old school-companion, Henry Jekyll. I was a good deal surprised by this; for we were by no means in the habit of correspondence; I had seen the man, dined with him, indeed, the night before; and I could imagine nothing in our intercourse that should justify the formality of registration. The contents increased my wonder; for this is how the letter ran:

10th December 18—

DEAR LANYON, – You are one of my oldest friends; and although we may have differed at times on scientific questions, I cannot remember, at least on my side, any break in our affection. There was never a day when, if you had said to me, "Jekyll, my life, my honour, my reason, depend upon you," I would not have sacrificed my fortune or my left hand to help you. Lanyon, my life,

COMMENTARY
This chapter is the document that was given to Utterson after the death of Dr Lanyon. In it Lanyon tells the story of how he became involved in the life of Dr Jekyll. He begins by describing how he received a letter from Jekyll.

intercourse: relationship
justify the formality of registration: make it necessary to send it by registered post

my honour, my reason, are all at your mercy; if you fail me to-night, I am lost. You might suppose, after this preface, that I am going to ask you for something dishonourable to grant. Judge for yourself.

I want you to postpone all other engagements for to-night – ay, even if you were summoned to the bedside of an emperor; to take a cab, unless your carriage should be actually at the door; and, with this letter in your hand for consultation, to drive straight to my house. Poole, my butler, has his orders; you will find him waiting your arrival with a locksmith. The door of my cabinet is then to be forced; and you are to go in alone; to open the glazed press (letter E) on the left hand, breaking the lock if it be shut; and to draw out, *with all its contents as they stand*, the fourth drawer from the top or (which is the same

thing) the third from the bottom. In my extreme distress of mind, I have a morbid fear of misdirecting you; but even if I am in error, you may know the right drawer by its contents: some powders, a phial, and a paper book. This drawer I beg of you to carry back with you to Cavendish Square exactly as it stands.

That is the first part of the service: now for the second. You should be back, if you set out at once on the receipt of this, long before midnight; but I will leave you that amount of margin, not only in the fear of one of those obstacles that can neither be prevented nor foreseen, but because an hour when your servants are in bed is to be preferred for what will then remain to do. At midnight, then, I have to ask you to be alone in your consulting-room, to admit with your own hand into the house a man who will present himself in my name, and to place in his hands the drawer that you will have brought with you from my cabinet. Then you

---

COMMENTARY

Jekyll's letter goes on to ask Lanyon to help him. He wants him to go to Jekyll's house and, with the servant's help, to break into his study. Then he must remove one of the drawers from one of the cupboards and take it home with him. Then he must wait in his consulting room until he is visited by a stranger. He must give the drawer to this man.

---

for consultation: so that you can refer to it
that amount of margin: that much time to spare

will have played your part and earned my gratitude completely. Five minutes afterwards, if you insist upon an explanation, you will have understood that these arrangements are of capital importance; and that by the neglect of one of them, fantastic as they must appear, you might have charged your conscience with my death or the shipwreck of my reason.

Confident as I am that you will not trifle with this appeal, my heart sinks and my hand trembles at the bare thought of such a possibility. Think of me at this hour, in a strange place, labouring under a blackness of distress that no fancy can exaggerate, and yet well aware that, if you will but punctually serve me, my troubles will roll away like a story that is told. Serve me, my dear Lanyon, and save

Your friend,

H. J.

PS. – I had already sealed this up when a fresh terror struck upon my soul. It is possible that the post office may fail me, and this letter not come into your hands until to-morrow morning. In that case, dear Lanyon, do my errand when it shall be most convenient for you in the course of the day; and once more expect my messenger at midnight. It may then already be too late; and if that night passes without event, you will know that you have seen the last of Henry Jekyll.

Upon the reading of this letter, I made sure my colleague was insane; but till that was proved beyond the possibility of doubt, I felt bound to do as he requested. The less I understood of this farrago, the less I was in a position to judge of its importance; and an appeal so worded could not be set aside without a grave responsibility. I rose accordingly from table, got into a hansom, and drove straight to Jekyll's house. The butler was awaiting my arrival; he had received by the same post as mine a registered letter of instruction, and had sent at once for a locksmith and a carpenter. The tradesmen came while we were yet speaking; and we moved in a body to old Dr Denman's surgical

---

COMMENTARY

Having done that, he will discover what it is all about. After reading the letter Lanyon is convinced that Jekyll is mad, but he does as he has been asked. He goes to Jekyll's house.

capital: the greatest
by the neglect of one of them: if you fail to do any one of them
the shipwreck of my reason: my going mad
made sure: was convinced
farrago: hotchpotch, confused mixture
hansom: a horse-drawn closed carriage for two passengers

theatre, from which (as you are doubtless aware) Jekyll's private cabinet is most conveniently entered. The door was very strong, the lock excellent; the carpenter avowed he would have great trouble, and have to do much damage, if force were to be used; and the locksmith was near despair. But this last was a handy fellow, and after two hours' work, the door stood open. The press marked E was unlocked; and I took out the drawer, had it filled up with straw
▶▶ and tied in a sheet, and returned with it to Cavendish Square.

Here I proceeded to examine its contents. The powders were neatly enough made up, but not with the nicety of the dispensing chemist; so that it was plain they were of Jekyll's private manufacture; and when I opened one of the wrappers, I found what seemed to me a simple crystalline salt of a white colour. The phial, to which I next turned my attention, might have been about half-full of a blood-red liquor, which was highly pungent to the sense of smell, and seemed to me to contain phosphorus and some volatile ether. At the other ingredients I could make no guess. The book was an ordinary version book, and contained little but a series of dates. These covered a period of many years, but I observed that the entries ceased nearly a year ago and quite abruptly. Here and there a brief remark was appended to a date, usually no more than a single word: 'double' occurring perhaps six times in a total of several hundred entries; and once very early in the list and followed by several marks of exclamation, 'total failure!!!' All this, though it whetted my curiosity, told me little that was definite. Here were a phial of some tincture, a paper of some salt, and the record of a series of experiments that had led (like too many

---

REWIND: ...to Cavendish Square.
Dr Lanyon has described how he received a letter from Henry Jekyll. It asked him, as an old friend, to help him. What Jekyll wanted him to do was to break into his study, with the help of Poole and a locksmith, remove a certain drawer, and take it back to his house. Then he was to wait for a man to come in Jekyll's name. This Lanyon has done.

---

nicety: care for detail
volatile ether: diethyl ether, a chemical commonly
    used at that time as an anaesthetic, a solvent,
    and as a constituent of chemical compounds
whetted: sharpened
tincture: a solution of a chemical in alcohol

COMMENTARY
Lanyon goes into Jekyll's study and removes the drawer as requested. When he gets it home he examines it and finds that it contains chemicals and a notebook.

of Jekyll's investigations) to no end of practical usefulness. How could the presence of these articles in my house affect either the honour, the sanity, or the life of my flighty colleague? If his messenger could go to one place, why could he not go to another? And even granting some impediment, why was this gentleman to be received by me in secret? The more I reflected, the more convinced I grew that I was dealing with a case of cerebral disease; and though I dismissed my servants to bed, I loaded an old revolver, that I might be found in some posture of self-defence.

Twelve o'clock had scarce rung out over London, ere the knocker sounded very gently on the door. I went myself at the summons, and found a small man crouching against the pillars of the portico.

'Are you come from Dr Jekyll?' I asked.

He told me 'yes' by a constrained gesture; and when I had bidden him enter, he did not obey me without a searching backward glance into the darkness of the square. There was a policeman not far off, advancing with his bull's eye open; and at the sight, I thought my visitor started and made greater haste.

These particulars struck me, I confess, disagreeably; and as I followed him into the bright light of the consulting-room, I kept my hand ready on my weapon. Here, at last, I had a chance of clearly seeing him. I had never set eyes on him before, so much was certain. He was small, as I have said; I was struck besides with the shocking expression of his face, with his remarkable combination of great muscular activity and great apparent debility of constitution, and – last but not least – with the odd, subjective disturbance caused by his neighbourhood. This bore some resemblance to incipient rigor, and was accompanied by a marked sinking of the pulse. At the time, I set it down to some idiosyncratic, personal distaste, and merely wondered at the acuteness of the symptoms; but I have since had reason to believe the cause to lie much deeper in the nature of man, and to turn on some nobler hinge than the principle of hatred.

This person (who has thus, from the first moment of his entrance, struck in me what I can only describe as a disgustful curiosity) was dressed in a fashion

COMMENTARY
Lanyon is convinced that Jekyll is mad. At midnight he opens the door to Jekyll's messenger, whom he finds disturbing. He lets him in to the consulting room.

flighty: fickle
cerebral: of the brain
found in some posture of self-defence: able to defend myself
portico: porch with columns

bull's eye: lantern with a curved lens
debility: weakness
subjective disturbance caused by his neighbourhood: Lanyon found that being near the man was physically disturbing
incipient rigor: the beginnings of stiffening
a disgustful curiosity: a mixture of disgust (at his appearance) and curiosity (to know what was going on)

that would have made an ordinary person laughable; his clothes, that is to say, although they were of rich and sober fabric, were enormously too large for him in every measurement – the trousers hanging on his legs and rolled up to keep them from the ground, the waist of the coat below his haunches, and the collar sprawling wide upon his shoulders. Strange to relate, this ludicrous accoutrement was far from moving me to laughter. Rather, as there was something abnormal and misbegotten in the very essence of the creature that now faced me – something seizing, surprising and revolting – this fresh disparity seemed but to fit in with and to reinforce it; so that to my interest in the man's nature and character there was added a curiosity as to his origin, his life, his fortune and status in the world.

These observations, though they have taken so great a space to be set down in, were yet the work of a few seconds. My visitor was, indeed, on fire with sombre excitement.

'Have you got it?' he cried. 'Have you got it?' And so lively with his impatience that he even laid his hand upon my arm and sought to shake me.

I put him back conscious at the touch of a certain icy pang about my blood. 'Come, sir,' said I. 'You forget that I have not yet the pleasure of your acquaintance. Be seated, if you please.' And I showed him an example, and sat down myself in my customary seat and with as far an imitation of my ordinary manner to a patient, as the lateness of the hour, the nature of my pre-occupations, and the horror I had of my visitor would suffer me to muster.

'I beg your pardon, Dr Lanyon,' he replied, civilly enough. 'What you say is very well founded; and my impatience has shown its heels to my politeness. I come here at the instance of your colleague, Dr Henry Jekyll, on a piece of business of some moment; and I understood...' he paused and put his hand to his throat, and I could see, in spite of his collected manner, that he was wrestling against the approaches of the hysteria – 'I understood, a drawer...'

But here I took pity on my visitor's suspense, and some perhaps on my own growing curiosity.

ludicrous accoutrement: ridiculous clothing
misbegotten: ill-formed
disparity: mismatch (between clothes and man)
well founded: perfectly sensible
hysteria: attack of uncontrollable excitement and emotion

COMMENTARY
The man is strangely dressed in clothes that are far too big for him and seems very agitated. He demands to know if Lanyon has the drawer. Lanyon tries to calm him down.

'There it is, sir,' said I, pointing to the drawer where it lay on the floor behind a table, and still covered with the sheet.

He sprang to it, and then paused, and laid his hand upon his heart; I could hear his teeth grate with the convulsive action of his jaws; and his face was so ghastly to see that I grew alarmed both for his life and reason.

'Compose yourself,' said I.

He turned a dreadful smile to me, and, as if with the decision of despair, plucked away the sheet. At sight of the contents, he uttered one loud sob of such immense relief that I sat petrified. And the next moment, in a voice that was already fairly well under control, 'Have you a graduated glass?' he asked.

I rose from my place with something of an effort, and gave him what he asked.

He thanked me with a smiling nod, measured out a few minims of the red tincture and added one of the powders. The mixture, which was at first of a reddish hue, began, in proportion as the crystals melted, to brighten in colour, to effervesce audibly, and to throw off small fumes of vapour. Suddenly, and at the same moment, the ebullition ceased, and the compound changed to a dark purple, which faded again more slowly to a watery green. My visitor, who had watched these metamorphoses with a keen eye, smiled, set down the glass upon the table, and then turned and looked upon me with an air of scrutiny.

'And now,' said he, 'to settle what remains. Will you be wise? will you be guided? will you suffer me to take this glass in my hand, and to go forth from your house without further parley? or has the greed of curiosity too much command of you? Think before you answer, for it shall be done as you decide. As you decide, you shall be left as you were before, and neither richer nor wiser, unless the sense of service rendered to a man in mortal distress may be counted as a kind of riches of the soul. Or, if you shall so prefer to choose, a new province of knowledge and new avenues to fame and power shall be laid open to you, here, in this room, upon the instant; and your sight shall be blasted by a prodigy to stagger the unbelief of Satan.'

COMMENTARY

To the man's relief, Lanyon gives him the drawer. He mixes the liquid with the powder, producing a chemical reaction. Then he asks Lanyon if he really wants to watch any more or would he not prefer to let his visitor just depart?

graduated glass: flask with measurements marked down the side
minim: the smallest measurable amount, a drop (0.6 cc)
hue: colour
effervesce: fizz
ebullition: bubbling
metamorphoses: changes
parley: talk
prodigy: remarkable thing

'Sir,' said I, affecting a coolness that I was far from truly possessing, 'you speak enigmas, and you will perhaps not wonder that I hear you with no very strong impression of belief. But I have gone too far in the way of inexplicable services to pause before I see the end.'

'It is well,' replied my visitor. 'Lanyon, you remember your vows: what follows is under the seal of our profession. And now, you who have so long been bound to the most narrow and material views, you who have denied the virtue of transcendental medicine, you who have derided your superiors – behold!'

He put the glass to his lips, and drank at one gulp. A cry followed; he reeled, staggered, clutched at the table and held on, staring with injected eyes, gasping with open mouth; and as I looked, there came, I thought, a change – he seemed to swell – his face became suddenly black, and the features seemed to melt and alter – and the next moment I had sprung to my feet and leaped back against the wall, my arm raised to shield me from that prodigy, my mind submerged in terror.

affecting: pretending to show
enigmas: riddles
the virtue of transcendental medicine: the power of medicine that can take human beings beyond normal experience
derided: mocked

'O God!' I screamed, and 'O God!' again and again; for there before my eyes – pale and shaken, and half fainting, and groping before him with his hands, like a man restored from death – there stood Henry Jekyll.

What he told me in the next hour I cannot bring my mind to set on paper. I saw what I saw, I heard what I heard, and my soul sickened at it; and yet, now when that sight has faded from my eyes, I ask myself if I believe it, and I cannot answer. My life is shaken to its roots; sleep has left me; the deadliest terror sits by me at all hours of the day and night; I feel that my days are numbered, and that I must die; and yet I shall die incredulous. As for the moral turpitude that man unveiled to me, even with tears of penitence, I cannot, even in memory, dwell on it without a start of horror. I will say but one thing, Utterson, and that (if you can bring your mind to credit it) will be more than enough. The creature who crept into my house that night was on Jekyll's own confession, known by the name of Hyde and hunted for in every corner of the land as the murderer of Carew.

HASTIE LANYON

COMMENTARY

Lanyon is horrified to see the man turn into Jekyll before his very eyes. Jekyll then tells him the whole story, which Lanyon is too horrified to write down, for he now realises that Jekyll and the murderer Hyde are one and the same.

moral turpitude: wickedness
penitence: repentance

10 Henry Jekyll's Full Statement of the Case

Look out for...
- Jekyll's assessment of what he was like as a young man.
- his explanation of the duality (two-sidedness) of human beings.
- how he developed the formula to change his appearance.
- his explanation of how things gradually went wrong.

FAST FORWARD: to page 74

I was born in the year 18— to a large fortune, endowed besides with excellent parts, inclined by nature to industry, fond of the respect of the wise and good among my fellow-men, and thus, as might have been supposed, with every guarantee of an honourable and distinguished future. And indeed, the worst of my faults was a certain impatient gaiety of disposition, such as has made the happiness of many, but such as I found it hard to reconcile with my imperious desire to carry my head high, and wear a more than commonly grave countenance before the public. Hence it came about that I concealed my pleasures; and that when I reached years of reflection, and began to look round me and take stock of my progress and position in the world, I stood already committed to a profound duplicity of life. Many a man would have even blazoned such irregularities as I was guilty of; but from the high views that I had set before me, I regarded and hid them with an almost morbid sense of shame. It was thus rather the exacting nature of my aspirations, than any particular

COMMENTARY

The language in this final chapter is difficult. There is not space enough for notes on the meanings of words and phrases so, instead, the commentary has been expanded to provide a fuller explanation of what we are told on each page.

Jekyll's account of his life begins with a description of his character. He was fortunate to be talented and had the opportunity of a successful career. His only weakness was a certain impatient lightheartedness – when he wanted to be seen as serious and 'important'. So he pretended that this lighter side of him did not exist. But he felt guilty about this.

degradation in my faults, that made me what I was and, with even a deeper trench than in the majority of men, severed in me those provinces of good and ill which divide and compound man's dual nature. In this case, I was driven to reflect deeply and inveterately on that hard law in life which lies at the root of religion, and is one of the most plentiful springs of distress. Though so profound a double-dealer, I was in no sense a hypocrite; both sides of me were in dead earnest; I was no more myself when I laid aside restraint and plunged in shame, than when I laboured, in the eye of the day, at the furtherance of knowledge or in the relief of sorrow and suffering. And it chanced that the direction of my scientific studies, which led wholly towards the mystic and the transcendental, reacted and shed a strong light on this consciousness of the perennial war among my members. With every day, and from both sides of my intelligence, the moral and the intellectual, I thus drew steadily nearer to that truth by whose partial discovery I have been doomed to such a dreadful shipwreck: that man is not truly one, but truly two. I say two, because the state of my own knowledge does not pass beyond that point. Others will follow, others will outstrip me on the same lines; and I hazard the guess that man will be ultimately known for a mere polity of multi-farious, incongruous and independent denizens. I, for my part, from the nature of my life, advanced infallibly in one direction and in one direction only. It was on the moral side, and in my own person, that I learned to recognise the thorough and primitive duality of man; I saw that, of the two natures that contended in the field of my consciousness, even if I could rightly be said to be either, it was only because I was radically both; and from an early date, even before the course of my scientific discoveries had begun to suggest the most naked possibility of such a miracle, I had learned to dwell with pleasure, as a beloved day-dream, on the thought of the separation of these elements. If each, I told myself, could but be housed in separate identities, life would be relieved of all that was unbearable; the unjust might go his way, delivered from the aspirations and remorse of his upright twin; and the just could walk steadfastly and securely on his upward path, doing the good things in which he found his pleasure, and no longer

COMMENTARY

So he found that there was a deep division inside him between the civilised, moral part of him and the passionate, physical part. His scientific research led him to think more about experiences beyond those of normal everyday life. He came to the conclusion that each person might be not just two-sided, as he had experienced himself, but actually made up of many different personalities. He began to dream of what it would be like if he could be two separate people, so that each 'half' of him could be complete.

exposed to disgrace and penitence by the hands of this extraneous evil. It was the curse of mankind that these incongruous faggots were thus bound together – that in the agonised womb of consciousness these polar twins should be continuously struggling. How, then, were they dissociated?

I was so far in my reflections when, as I have said, a side light began to shine upon the subject from the laboratory table. I began to perceive more deeply than it has ever yet been stated, the trembling immateriality, the mist-like transience, of this seemingly so solid body in which we walk attired. Certain agents I found to have the power to shake and to pluck back that fleshly vestment, even as a wind might toss the curtains of a pavilion. For two good reasons, I will not enter deeply into this scientific branch of my confession. First, because I have been made to learn that the doom and burthen of our life is bound for ever on man's shoulders; and when the attempt is made to cast it off, it but returns upon us with more unfamiliar and more awful pressure. Second, because, as my narrative will make, alas! too evident, my discoveries were incomplete. Enough, then, that I not only recognised my natural body for the mere aura and effulgence of certain of the powers that made up my spirit, but managed to compound a drug by which these powers should be dethroned from their supremacy, and a second form and countenance substituted, none the less natural to me because they were the expression, and bore the stamp, of lower elements in my soul.

▶▶ I hesitated long before I put this theory to the test of practice. I knew well that I risked death; for any drug that so potently controlled and shook the

---

REWIND: …elements in my soul.
Jekyll's account has begun with a description of his life. As a young man he was aware of a deep divide between the good and evil parts of his personality. This both fascinated and alarmed him. His scientific research made him realise that it might be possible to give a physical form to the other, evil, side of his personality, by the use of certain chemicals.

COMMENTARY

His experiments in the laboratory led him to realise that our physical bodies may not be as solid as we think. In fact they are only a kind of flimsy clothing for our personal qualities: the dominant part of the personality is so strong that it controls what our body is like. He worked out a formula for a drug that would weaken this controlling power so that the other side of the personality could take control and make a new body for itself. At first he was frightened of putting his theory into practice.

very fortress of identity, might by the least scruple of an overdose or at the least inopportunity in the moment of exhibition, utterly blot out that immaterial tabernacle which I looked to it to change. But the temptation of a discovery so singular and profound at last overcame the suggestions of alarm. I had long since prepared my tincture; I purchased at once, from a firm of wholesale chemists, a large quantity of a particular salt, which I knew, from my experiments, to be the last ingredient required; and, late one accursed night, I compounded the elements, watched them boil and smoke together in the glass, and when the ebullition had subsided, with a strong glow of courage, drank off the potion.

The most racking pangs succeeded: a grinding in the bones, deadly nausea, and a horror of the spirit that cannot be exceeded at the hour of birth or death. Then these agonies began swiftly to subside, and I came to myself as if out of a great sickness. There was something strange in my sensations, something indescribably new and, from its very novelty, incredibly sweet. I felt younger, lighter, happier in body; within I was conscious of a heady recklessness, a current of disordered sensual images running like a mill race in my fancy, a solution of the bonds of obligation, an unknown but not an innocent freedom of the soul. I knew myself, at the first breath of this new life, to be more wicked, tenfold more wicked, sold a slave to my original evil; and the thought, in that moment, braced and delighted me like wine. I stretched out my hands, exulting at the freshness of these sensations; and in the act, I was suddenly aware that I had lost in stature.

There was no mirror, at that date, in my room; that which stands beside me as I write was brought there later on, and for the very purpose of those transformations. The night, however, was far gone into the morning – the morning, black as it was, was nearly ripe for the conception of the day – the inmates of my house were locked in the most rigorous hours of slumber; and I was determined, flushed as I was with hope and triumph, to venture in my new shape as far as to my bedroom. I crossed the yard, wherein the constellations looked down upon me, I could have thought, with wonder, the first creature of

COMMENTARY

He knew that if he made the slightest mistake he might kill himself. In the end he decided to try it. He had already produced the liquid part of the formula. Now he bought a particular salt. He combined the two, producing a dramatic chemical reaction. When the liquid stopped bubbling he drank the mixture. He suffered a terrible pain throughout his body and then felt an astonishing change in himself. He felt fresh, lively and...evil, far more evil than he had ever felt before. It was late at night and he was determined to see what he looked like. He crossed the yard towards his bedroom.

that sort that their unsleeping vigilance had yet disclosed to them; I stole through the corridors, a stranger in my own house; and coming to my room, I saw for the first time the appearance of Edward Hyde.

FAST FORWARD: to page 77

I must here speak by theory alone, saying not that which I know, but that which I suppose to be most probable. The evil side of my nature, to which I had now transferred the stamping efficacy, was less robust and less developed than the good which I had just deposed. Again, in the course of my life, which had been, after all, nine-tenths of a life of effort, virtue and control, it had been much less exercised and much less exhausted. And hence, as I think, it came about that Edward Hyde was so much smaller, slighter, and younger than Henry Jekyll. Even as good shone upon the countenance of the one, evil was written broadly and plainly on the face of the other. Evil besides (which I must still believe to be the lethal side of man) had left on that body an imprint of deformity and decay. And yet when I looked upon that ugly idol in the glass, I was conscious of no repugnance, rather a leap of welcome. This, too, was myself.

It seemed natural and human. In my eyes it bore a livelier image of the spirit, it seemed more express and single, than the imperfect and divided countenance, I had been hitherto accustomed to call mine. And in so far I was doubtless right. I have observed that when I wore the semblance of Edward Hyde, none could come near to me at first without a visible misgiving of the flesh. This, as I take it, was because all human beings, as we meet

COMMENTARY
He entered his bedroom, looked in the long mirror and saw Edward Hyde. The passionate, physical side of his personality was less developed than the controlling moral side, which is why, he believes, Hyde's body was smaller, lighter, and rather deformed. He also looked younger.

them, are commingled out of good and evil: and Edward Hyde, alone, in the ranks of mankind, was pure evil.

I lingered but a moment at the mirror: the second and conclusive experiment had yet to be attempted; it yet remained to be seen if I had lost my identity beyond redemption and must flee before daylight from a house that was no longer mine; and hurrying back to my cabinet, I once more prepared and drank the cup, once more suffered the pangs of dissolution, and came to myself once more with the character, the stature, and the face of Henry Jekyll.

That night I had come to the fatal cross roads. Had I approached my discovery in a more noble spirit, had I risked the experiment while under the empire of generous or pious aspirations, all must have been otherwise, and from these agonies of death and birth I had come forth an angel instead of a fiend. The drug had no discriminating action; it was neither diabolical nor divine; but it shook the doors of the prisonhouse of my disposition; and, like the captives of Philippi, that which stood within ran forth. At that time my virtue slumbered; my evil, kept awake by ambition, was alert and swift to seize the occasion; and the thing that was projected was Edward Hyde. Hence, although I had now two characters as well as two appearances, one was wholly evil, and the other was still the old Henry Jekyll, that incongruous compound of whose reformation and improvement I had already learned to despair. The movement was thus wholly toward the worse.

Even at that time, I had not yet conquered my aversion to the dryness of a life of study. I would still be merrily disposed at times; and as my pleasures were (to say the least) undignified, and I was not only well known and highly considered, but growing toward the elderly man, this incoherency of my life

---

REWIND: …was pure evil.
In the mirror Jekyll saw a creature who was smaller than he was normally, and both ugly and lively. He found this creature strangely attractive.

COMMENTARY
The next stage in the experiment was to find out whether he could regain the body of Dr Jekyll. He prepared and drank the mixture again, and found himself as Henry Jekyll once more.

He realised he had reached a turning-point in his life. If he had taken the mixture while he was experiencing thoughts that were purely good, his second body might have been that of an angel. Instead it was that of a devil. So his two persons were: Jekyll – a mixture of good and evil, with good controlling evil – and Hyde, who was pure evil.

The other important fact was that up till then he had always enjoyed taking time off from being respectable to enjoy himself in very unrespectable ways.

was daily growing more unwelcome. It was on this side that the new power tempted me until I fell in slavery. I had but to drink the cup, to doff at once the body of the noted professor, and to assume, like a thick cloak, that of Edward Hyde. I smiled at the notion; it seemed to me at the time to be humorous; and I made my preparations with the most studious care. I took and furnished that house in Soho to which Hyde was tracked by the police; and engaged as housekeeper a creature whom I well knew to be silent and unscrupulous. On the other side, I announced to my servants that a Mr Hyde (whom I described) was to have full liberty and power about my house in the square; and, to parry mishaps, I even called and made myself a familiar object in my second character. I next drew up that will to which you so much objected; so that if anything befell me in the person of Dr Jekyll, I could enter on that of Edward Hyde without pecuniary loss. And thus fortified, as I supposed, on every side, I began to profit by the strange immunities of my position.

Men have before hired bravos to transact their crimes, while their own person and reputation sat under shelter. I was the first that ever did so for his pleasures. I was the first that could thus plod in the public eye with a load of genial respectability, and in a moment, like a schoolboy, strip off these lendings and spring headlong into the sea of liberty. But for me, in my impenetrable mantle, the safety was complete. Think of it – I did not even exist! Let me but escape into my laboratory door, give me but a second or two to mix and swallow the draught that I had always standing ready; and, whatever he had done, Edward Hyde would pass away like the stain of breath upon a mirror; and there in his stead, quietly at home, trimming the midnight lamp in his study, a man who could afford to laugh at suspicion, would be Henry Jekyll.

The pleasures which I made haste to seek in my disguise were, as I have said, undignified: I would scarce use a harder term. But in the hands of Edward Hyde they soon began to turn towards the monstrous. When I would come back from these excursions, I was often plunged into a kind of wonder at my vicarious depravity. This familiar that I called out of my own soul, and set forth alone to do his good pleasure, was a being inherently malign and

COMMENTARY

Now he could do that whenever he wanted to – with no fear of being found out! All he had to do was drink the mixture and, as Edward Hyde, he could do as he liked. He made further preparations. He wrote a will in which he left everything to Hyde, in the event of the death or disappearance of Jekyll.

Now he could begin his double life. He found, however, that the things he wanted to do as Hyde changed from being just 'unrespectable' to something a lot worse. Hyde was evil through and through. (It is important to note that we are never told exactly what 'depravity' he is talking about.)

villainous; his every act and thought centred on self; drinking pleasure with bestial avidity from any degree of torture to another; relentless like a man of stone. Henry Jekyll stood at times aghast before the acts of Edward Hyde; but the situation was apart from ordinary laws, and insidiously relaxed the grasp of conscience. It was Hyde, after all, and Hyde alone, that was guilty. Jekyll was no worse; he woke again to his good qualities seemingly unimpaired; he would even make haste, where it was possible, to undo the evil done by Hyde. And thus his conscience slumbered.

Into the details of the infamy at which I thus connived (for even now I can scarce grant that I committed it) I have no design of entering. I mean but to point out the warnings and the successive steps with which my chastisement approached. I met with one accident which, as it brought on no consequence, I shall no more than mention. An act of cruelty to a child aroused against me the anger of a passerby, whom I recognised the other day in the person of your kinsman; the doctor and the child's family joined him; there were moments when I feared for my life; and at last, in order to pacify their too just resentment, Edward Hyde had to bring them to the door, and pay them in a cheque drawn in the name of Henry Jekyll. But this danger was easily eliminated from the future by opening an account at another bank in the name of Edward Hyde himself; and when, by sloping my own hand backwards, I had supplied my double with a signature, I thought I sat beyond the reach of fate.

Some two months before the murder of Sir Danvers, I had been out for one of my adventures, had returned at a late hour, and woke the next day in bed with somewhat odd sensations. It was in vain I looked about me; in vain I saw the decent furniture and tall proportions of my room in the square; in vain that I recognised the pattern of the bed curtains and the design of the mahogany frame; something still kept insisting that I was not where I was, that I had not wakened where I seemed to be, but in the little room in Soho where I was accustomed to sleep in the body of Edward Hyde. I smiled to myself, and, in my psychological way, began lazily to inquire into the elements of this illusion, occasionally, even as I did so, dropping back into a comfortable morning

COMMENTARY

Jekyll was at first horrified at what Hyde did, but gradually he was able to separate himself from these actions – after all, it was Hyde who committed them, not Jekyll.

He met with occasional problems, such as when he attacked a small girl and was forced by Enfield and the parents to pay compensation – for Hyde had no bank account. However he managed to get round the problem and then opened a bank account for Hyde, also giving him a handwriting style and signature to match.

On one occasion he woke feeling strange. He felt as if instead of being in his usual bed at Jekyll's house he was in the room in Soho where he slept when he was Hyde. This was despite the fact that he knew he had gone to bed in Jekyll's bed. He was only half awake, however.

doze. I was still so engaged when, in one of my more wakeful moments, my eye fell upon my hand. Now, the hand of Henry Jekyll (as you have often remarked) was professional in shape and size; it was large, firm, white and comely. But the hand which I now saw, clearly enough in the yellow light of a mid-London morning, lying half shut on the bed-clothes, was lean, corded, knuckly, of a dusky pallor, and thickly shaded with a swart growth of hair. It was the hand of Edward Hyde.

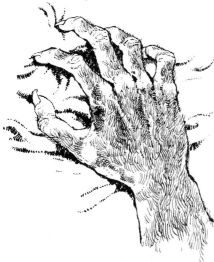

I must have stared upon it for near half a minute, sunk as I was in the mere stupidity of wonder, before terror woke up in my breast as sudden and startling as the crash of cymbals; and bounding from my bed, I rushed to the mirror. At the sight that met my eyes, my blood was changed into something exquisitely thin and icy. Yes, I had gone to bed Henry Jekyll, I had awakened Edward Hyde. How was this to be explained? I asked myself; and then, with another bound of terror – how was it to be remedied? It was well on in the morning; the servants were up; all my drugs were in the cabinet – a long journey, down two pairs of stairs, through the back passage, across the open court and through the anatomical theatre, from where I was then standing horror-struck. It might indeed be possible to cover my face; but of what use was that, when I was unable to conceal the alteration in my stature? And then, with an overpowering sweetness of relief, it came back upon my mind that the servants were already used to the coming and going of my second self. I had soon dressed, as well as I was able, in clothes of my own size; had soon passed through the house, where Bradshaw stared and drew back at seeing Mr Hyde at such an hour and in such a strange array; and ten minutes later, Dr Jekyll

COMMENTARY

Then he looked at his hand and saw that it was Hyde's hand. He had gone to sleep as Jekyll and woken up as Hyde! What was he going to do? He realised that he had to get from the bedroom, across the yard, through the laboratory and into the study. Fortunately the servants had become accustomed to seeing Hyde in the house, so he dressed in Jekyll's bedroom and made his way to the study. Here he took the mixture and became Dr Jekyll once more.

had returned to his own shape and was sitting down, with a darkened brow, to make a feint of breakfasting.

FAST FORWARD: to page 83

Small indeed was my appetite. This inexplicable incident, this reversal of my previous experience, seemed, like the Babylonian finger on the wall, to be spelling out the letters of my judgement; and I began to reflect more seriously than ever before on the issues and possibilities of my double existence. That part of me which I had the power of projecting had lately been much exercised and nourished; it had seemed to me of late as though the body of Edward Hyde had grown in stature, as though (when I wore that form) I were conscious of a more generous tide of blood; and I began to spy a danger that, if this were much prolonged, the balance of my nature might be permanently overthrown, the power of voluntary change be forfeited, and the character of Edward Hyde become irrevocably mine. The power of the drug had not been always equally displayed. Once, very early in my career, it had totally failed me; since then I had been obliged on more than one occasion to double, and once, with infinite risk of death, to treble the amount; and these rare uncertainties had cast hitherto the sole shadow on my contentment. Now, however, and in the light of that morning's accident, I was led to remark that whereas, in the beginning, the difficulty had been to throw off the body of Jekyll, it had of late gradually but decidedly transferred itself to the other side. All things therefore seemed to point to this: that I was slowly losing hold of my original and better self, and becoming slowly incorporated with my second and worse.

Between these two I now felt I had to choose. My two natures had memory in common, but all other faculties were most unequally shared between them. Jekyll (who was a composite) now with the most sensitive apprehensions, now with a greedy gusto, projected and shared in the pleasures and adventures of Hyde; but Hyde was indifferent to Jekyll, or but remembered him as the

COMMENTARY
He felt that this experience was the writing on the wall. He had noticed that Hyde's body seemed to be growing – as the passionate, strong-willed side of his personality developed and grew. There had to be a danger that it would grow so much that it took charge. He might become Hyde and never again be able to return to Jekyll. He felt that he had to make a choice between Jekyll and Hyde.

mountain bandit remembers the cavern in which he conceals himself from pursuit. Jekyll had more than a father's interest; Hyde had more than a son's indifference. To cast in my lot with Jekyll was to die to those appetites which I had long secretly indulged and had of late begun to pamper. To cast it in with Hyde was to die to a thousand interests and aspirations, and to become, at a blow and for ever, despised and friendless. The bargain might appear unequal; but there was still another consideration in the scales; for while Jekyll would suffer smartingly in the fires of abstinence, Hyde would be not even conscious of all that he had lost. Strange as my circumstances were, the terms of this debate are as old and commonplace as man: much the same inducements and alarms cast the die for any tempted and trembling sinner; and it fell out with me, as it falls with so vast a majority of my fellows, that I chose the better part and found wanting in the strength to keep it.

Yes, I preferred the elderly and discontented doctor, surrounded by friends and cherishing honest hopes; and bade a resolute farewell to the liberty, the comparative youth, the light step, leaping pulses and secret pleasures, that I had enjoyed in the disguise of Hyde. I made this choice perhaps with some unconscious reservation, for I neither gave up the house in Soho, nor destroyed the clothes of Edward Hyde, which still lay ready in my cabinet. For two months, however, I was true to my determination; for two months I led a life of such severity as I had never before attained to, and enjoyed the compensations of an approving conscience. But time began at last to obliterate the freshness of my alarm; the praises of conscience began to grow into a thing of course; I began to be tortured with throes and longings, as of Hyde struggling after freedom; and at last, in an hour of moral weakness, I once again compounded and swallowed the transforming draught.

I do not suppose that when a drunkard reasons with himself upon his vice, he is once out of five hundred times affected by the dangers that he runs through his brutish physical insensibility; neither had I, long as I had considered my position, made enough allowance for the complete moral insensibility and insensate readiness to evil which were the leading characters of Edward Hyde.

COMMENTARY

It was a difficult choice. Whichever way he went, he would have to give up things he never wanted to lose: Jekyll's regular life and friends; or Hyde's passions and freedom of action. At last he decided for Jekyll, and for two months he lived purely as the 'elderly and discontented doctor, surrounded by friends…' Unfortunately he was like a reformed drug addict and the further he moved away from that old life, the more he longed to return to it.

Yet it was by these that I was punished. My devil had been long caged, he came out roaring. I was conscious, even when I took the draught, of a more unbridled, a more furious propensity to ill. It must have been this, I suppose, that stirred in my soul that tempest of impatience with which I listened to the civilities of my unhappy victim; I declare at least, before God, no man morally sane could have been guilty of that crime upon so pitiful a provocation; and that I struck in no more reasonable spirit than that in which a sick child may break a plaything. But I had voluntarily stripped myself of all those balancing instincts by which even the worst of us continues to walk with some degree of steadiness among temptations; and in my case, to be tempted, however slightly, was to fall.

Instantly the spirit of hell awoke in me and raged. With a transport of glee, I mauled the unresisting body, tasting delight from every blow; and it was not till weariness had begun to succeed that I was suddenly, in the top fit of my delirium, struck through the heart by a cold thrill of terror. A mist dispersed; I saw my life to be forfeit; and fled from the scene of these excesses, at once glorying and trembling, my lust of evil gratified and stimulated, my love of life screwed to the topmost peg. I ran to the house in Soho, and (to make assurance doubly sure) destroyed my papers; thence I set out through the lamplit streets, in the same divided ecstasy of mind, gloating on my crime, light-headedly devising others in the future, and yet still hastening and still harkening in my wake for the step of the avenger. Hyde had a song upon his lips as he compounded the draught, and as he drank it pledged the dead man. The pangs of

---

REWIND: ...that I was punished.
Jekyll has described how he realised that the Hyde part of his personality was growing stronger and that he was going to have to choose between Jekyll and Hyde. After much thought he chose Jekyll, and for two months lived only as the good doctor. He discovered, however, that it was not so easy to give up Mr Hyde. After a struggle he once again took the potion.

COMMENTARY
Once again he took the mixture and Hyde came back stronger than ever. It was in this state that he attacked and killed Sir Danvers Carew. In a frenzy he attacked the old man and gloried in battering him to death. Then the full horror of what he had done struck him as he realised the danger in which he now stood. He fled to the Soho house and tried to destroy all evidence of Edward Hyde. Then he drank the mixture and became Dr Jekyll.

transformation had not done tearing him, before Henry Jekyll, with streaming tears of gratitude and remorse, had fallen upon his knees and lifted his clasped hand to God. The veil of self-indulgence was rent from head to foot, I saw my life as a whole: I followed it up from the days of childhood, when I had walked with my father's hand, through the self-denying toils of my professional life, to arrive again and again, with the same sense of unreality, at the damned horrors of the evening. I could have screamed aloud; I sought with tears and prayers to smother down the crowd of hideous images and sounds with which my memory swarmed against me; and still, between the petitions, the ugly face of my iniquity stared into my soul. As the acuteness of this remorse began to die away, it was succeeded by a sense of joy. The problem of my conduct was solved. Hyde was henceforth impossible; whether I would or not, I was now confined to the better part of my existence; and, oh, how I rejoiced to think it! with what willing humility I embraced anew the restrictions of natural life! with what sincere renunciation I locked the door by which I had so often gone and come, and ground the key under my heel!

The next day came the news that the murder had been overlooked, that the guilt of Hyde was patent to the world, and that the victim was a man high in public estimation. It was not only a crime, it had been a tragic folly. I think I was glad to know it; I think I was glad to have my better impulses thus buttressed and guarded by the terrors of the scaffold. Jekyll was now my city of refuge; let but Hyde peep out an instant, and the hands of all men would be raised to take and slay him.

I resolved in my future conduct to redeem the past; and I can say with honesty that my resolve was fruitful of some good. You know yourself how earnestly in the last months of last year I laboured to relieve suffering; you know that much was done for others, and that the days passed quietly, almost happily for myself. Nor can I truly say that I wearied of this beneficent and innocent life; I think instead that I daily enjoyed it more completely; but I was still cursed with my duality of purpose; and as the first edge of my penitence wore off, the lower side of me, so long indulged, so recently chained down,

COMMENTARY

At this point he saw everything he had done with complete clarity. The next day he heard that the murder had been discovered and that the dead man was well-known and respected. The hunt was on for Hyde and his only hope was to remain Jekyll for the rest of his life. The problem was that the 'Hyde' side of his personality had become so strong that he could not completely keep it down.

began to growl for licence. Not that I dreamed of resuscitating Hyde; the bare idea of that would startle me to frenzy: no, it was in my own person that I was once more tempted to trifle with my conscience; and it was as an ordinary secret sinner that I at last fell before the assaults of temptation.

There comes an end to all things; the most capacious measure is filled at last; and this brief condescension to my evil finally destroyed the balance of my soul. And yet I was not alarmed; the fall seemed natural, like a return to the old days before I had made my discovery. It was a fine, clear January day, wet under foot where the frost had melted, but cloudless overhead; and the Regent's Park was full of winter chirrupings and sweet with Spring odours. I sat in the sun on a bench; the animal within me licking the chops of memory; the spiritual side a little drowsed, promising subsequent penitence, but not yet moved to begin. After all, I reflected, I was like my neighbours; and then I smiled, comparing myself with other men, comparing my active goodwill with the lazy cruelty of their neglect. And at the very moment of that vainglorious thought, a qualm came over me, a horrid nausea and the most deadly shuddering. These passed away, and left me faint; and then as in its turn the faintness subsided, I began to be aware of a change in the temper of my thoughts, a greater boldness, a contempt of danger, a solution of the bonds of obligation. I looked down; my clothes hung formlessly on my shrunken limbs; the hand that lay on my knee was corded and hairy. I was once more Edward Hyde. A moment before I had been safe of all men's respect, wealthy, beloved – the cloth laying for me in the dining-room at home; and now I was the common quarry of mankind, hunted, houseless, a known murderer, thrall to the gallows.

My reason wavered, but it did not fail me utterly. I have more than once observed that, in my second character, my faculties seemed sharpened to a point and my spirits more tensely elastic; thus it came about that, where Jekyll perhaps might have succumbed, Hyde rose to the importance of the moment. My drugs were in one of the presses of my cabinet: how was I to reach them? That was the problem that (crushing my temples in my hands) I set myself to solve. The laboratory door I had closed. If I sought to enter by the house, my

COMMENTARY

So he remained as Jekyll, but although he was not tempted to take the mixture again, he went back to the kind of behaviour he had indulged in before the existence of Hyde. (Stevenson refers to this as the life of 'an ordinary secret sinner' and leaves it to us to work out what he might mean. We are probably expected to assume that Jekyll had gone back to accosting prostitutes.)

Then suddenly, the following January, as he was walking in Regent's Park, Jekyll felt strange and realised that he was turning into Hyde. He did not panic but plotted swiftly what he would have to do. The main problem was how to get into the house and reach the chemicals unobserved.

own servants would consign me to the gallows. I saw I must employ another hand, and thought of Lanyon. How was he to be reached? how persuaded? Supposing that I escaped capture in the streets, how was I to make my way into his presence? and how should I, an unknown and displeasing visitor, prevail on the famous physician to rifle the study of his colleague, Dr Jekyll? Then I remembered that of my original character, one part remained to me: I could write my own hand; and once I had conceived that kindling spark, the way that I must follow became lighted up from end to end.

Thereupon, I arranged my clothes as best I could, and summoning a passing hansom, drove to an hotel in Portland Street, the name of which I chanced to remember. At my appearance (which was indeed comical enough, however tragic a fate these garments covered) the driver could not conceal his mirth. I gnashed my teeth upon him with a gust of devilish fury; and the smile withered from his face – happily for him – yet more happily for myself, for in another instant I had certainly dragged him from his perch. At the inn, as I entered, I looked about me with so black a countenance as made the attendants tremble; not a look did they exchange in my presence; but obsequiously took my orders, led me to a private room, and brought me wherewithal to write. Hyde in danger of his life was a creature new to me: shaken with inordinate anger, strung to the pitch of murder, lusting to inflict pain. Yet the creature was astute; mastered his fury with a great effort of the will; composed his two important letters, one to Lanyon and one to Poole, and, that he might receive actual evidence of their being posted, sent them out with directions that they should be registered.

Thenceforward, he sat all day over the fire in the private room, gnawing his nails; there he dined, sitting alone with his fears, the waiter visibly quailing before his eye; and thence, when the night was fully come, he set forth in the corner of a closed cab, and was driven to and fro about the streets of the city. He, I say – I cannot say I. That child of Hell had nothing human; nothing lived in him but fear and hatred. And when at last, thinking the driver had begun to grow suspicious, he discharged the cab and ventured on foot, attired

COMMENTARY

If he went there as Hyde he would be arrested. He took a cab to a hotel and rented a room. There he wrote two letters, one to Dr Lanyon, the other to his butler, Poole. After that, he had to sit and wait until it was dark. Then he took a cab and drove about for a while before setting off on foot.

in his misfitting clothes, an object marked out for observation, into the midst of the nocturnal passengers, these two base passions raged within him like a tempest. He walked fast, hunted by his fears, chattering to himself, skulking through the less frequented thoroughfares, counting the minutes that still divided him from midnight. Once a woman spoke to him, offering, I think, a box of lights. He smote her in the face, and she fled.

When I came to myself at Lanyon's, the horror of my old friend perhaps affected me somewhat: I do not know it; it was at least but a drop in the sea to the abhorrence with which I looked back upon these hours. A change had come over me. It was no longer the fear of the gallows, it was the horror of being Hyde that racked me. I received Lanyon's condemnation partly in a dream; it was partly in a dream that I came home to my own house and got into bed. I slept after the prostration of the day, with a stringent and profound slumber which not even the nightmares that wrung me could avail to break. I awoke in the morning shaken, weakened, but refreshed. I still hated and feared the thought of the brute that slept within me, and I had not of course forgotten the appalling dangers of the day before; but I was once more at home, in my own house and close to my drugs; and gratitude for my escape shone so strong in my soul that it almost rivalled the brightness of hope.

I was stepping leisurely across the court after breakfast, drinking the chill of the air with pleasure, when I was seized again with those indescribable sensations that heralded the change; and I had but the time to gain the shelter of my cabinet, before I was once again raging and freezing with the passions of Hyde. It took on this occasion a double dose to recall me to myself; and alas, six hours later, as I sat looking sadly in the fire, the pangs returned, and the drug had to be re-administered. In short, from that day forth it seemed only by a great effort as of gymnastics, and only under the immediate stimulation of the drug, that I was able to wear the countenance of Jekyll. At all hours of the day and night I would be taken with the premonitory shudder; above all, if I slept, or even dozed for a moment in my chair, it was always as Hyde that I awakened. Under the strain of this continually impending doom and by the

COMMENTARY

Still dressed in Jekyll's clothes, which were far too large, he walked to Lanyon's house where he was able to make and drink the mixture.

The next morning, after breakfast, he felt the same warning signs again. This time he was at home and so was able to take a double dose in order to become Jekyll again. After that he could only be Jekyll for short periods and even then only by repeatedly taking the drug and using all his mental concentration.

sleeplessness to which I now condemned myself, ay, even beyond what I had thought possible to man, I became, in my own person, a creature eaten up and emptied by fever, languidly weak both in body and mind, and solely occupied by one thought: the horror of my other self. But when I slept, or when the virtue of the medicine wore off, I would leap almost without transition (for the pangs of transformation grew daily less marked) into the possession of a fancy brimming with images of terror, a soul boiling with causeless hatreds, and a body that seemed not strong enough to contain the raging energies of life. The powers of Hyde seemed to have grown with the sickliness of Jekyll. And certainly the hate that now divided them was equal on each side. With Jekyll, it was a thing of vital instinct. He had now seen the full deformity of that creature that shared with him some of the phenomena of consciousness, and was co-heir with him to death: and beyond these links of community, which in themselves made the most poignant part of his distress, he thought of Hyde, for all his energy of life, as of something not only hellish but inorganic. This was the shocking thing; that the slime of the pit seemed to utter cries and voices; that the amorphous dust gesticulated and sinned; that what was dead, and had no shape, could usurp the offices of life. And this again, that that insurgent horror was knit to him closer than a wife, closer than an eye; lay caged in his flesh, where he heard it mutter and felt it struggle to be born; and at every hour of weakness, and in the confidences of slumber, prevailed against him, and deposed him out of life. The hatred of Hyde for Jekyll was of a different order. His terror of the gallows drove him continually to commit temporary suicide, and return to his subordinate station of a part instead of a person; but he loathed the necessity, he loathed the despondency into which Jekyll was now fallen, and he resented the dislike with which he was himself regarded. Hence the ape-like tricks that he would play me, scrawling in my own hand blasphemies on the pages of my books, burning the letters and destroying the portrait of my father; and indeed, had it not been for his fear of death, he would long ago have ruined himself in order to involve me in the ruin. But his love of life is wonderful; I go further: I, who sicken and freeze at the mere

COMMENTARY

He couldn't sleep, or – if he did – he would automatically wake up as Hyde. Jekyll seemed to become physically weaker, as Hyde's body grew in strength. His whole life became a nightmare as the two halves of his personality fought openly and Jekyll was increasingly unable to win the battle.

thought of him, when I recall the abjection and passion of this attachment, and when I know how he fears my power to cut him off by suicide, I find it in my heart to pity him.

It is useless, and the time awfully fails me, to prolong this description; no one has ever suffered such torments, let that suffice; and yet even to these, habit brought – no, not alleviation – but a certain callousness of soul, a certain acquiescence of despair; and my punishment might have gone on for years, but for the last calamity which has now fallen, and which has finally severed me from my own face and nature. My provision of the salt, which had never been renewed since the date of the first experiment, began to run low. I sent out for a fresh supply, and mixed the draught; the ebullition followed, and the first change of colour, not the second; I drank it, and it was without efficiency. You will learn from Poole how I have had London ransacked; it was in vain; and am now persuaded that my first supply was impure, and that it was that unknown impurity which lent efficacy to the draught.

About a week has passed, and I am now finishing this statement under the influence of the last of the old powders. This, then, is the last time, short of a miracle, that Henry Jekyll can think his own thoughts or see his own face (now how sadly altered!) in the glass. Nor must I delay too long to bring my writing to an end; for if my narrative has hitherto escaped destruction, it has been by a combination of great prudence and great good luck. Should the throes of change take me in the act of writing it, Hyde will tear it in pieces; but if some time shall have elapsed after I have laid it by, his wonderful selfishness and circumscription to the moment will probably save it once again from the action of his ape-like spite. And indeed the doom that is closing on us both has already changed and crushed him. Half an hour from now, when I shall again and for ever reindue that hated personality, I know how I shall sit shuddering and weeping in my chair, or continue, with the most strained and fearstruck ecstasy of listening, to pace up and down this room (my last earthly refuge) and give ear to every sound of menace. Will Hyde die upon the scaffold? or will he find the courage to release himself at the last moment? God knows; I

COMMENTARY

The final calamity arrived when his supplies of the chemical began to run out. He found that new supplies would not have the same effect and realised that it must have been an impurity in the original supply that gave the mixture its special effect. Jekyll has only been able to write this personal statement after taking the last of the old mixture. He expresses the hope that he will have enough time to finish it and put it somewhere where Hyde will not find it and destroy it. In half an hour's time he will become Hyde again, this time for ever. He ends by asking himself how Hyde will end his life – will he be caught and executed or will he take his own life?

am careless; this is my true hour of death, and what is to follow concerns another than myself. Here, then, as I lay down the pen, and proceed to seal up my confession, I bring the life of that unhappy Henry Jekyll to an end.

COMMENTARY
He says that he, Jekyll, does not care what happens to Hyde. So ends the life of Henry Jekyll.

Study guide

HOW TO USE THIS STUDY GUIDE

This study guide is divided into five sections. Each of the first four covers about twenty pages of the story:

1 Chapters 1–3
2 Chapters 4–7
3 Chapters 8–9
4 Chapter 10

The final section looks at the story as a whole. In sections 1–4, there are three types of material:

● **Tracking**

This section takes you through the story chapter by chapter and gives you questions to think about.

● **Character**

This draws your attention to important points about the characters who appear in the section.

● **Key actions**

In each section there is at least one scene which forms a climax or very important point in the action. There are suggestions about how to look at these scenes in more detail.

You can either use this material during your first reading, or you can read the whole story and then turn back to it afterwards. How thoroughly you decide to use it will depend on how much detail you want to study the story in:

● You may just want to use **Tracking** as a check that you are fully understanding the story.
● If you are going to have to write about one or more of the characters, you will find it helpful to go through **Character**.
● **Key actions** will help you if you are going to have to write about the story as a whole and the way in which it is written.
● If you are going to tackle the writing tasks in the final section of this study guide, you will find it helpful to make some notes as you work through the first four sections.

CHAPTERS 1–3

Tracking

When you have reached the end of Chapter 3 think about these points:

1   a   Utterson seems a very dull person. Why do you think Stevenson
       might have chosen such a character to tell this story?
    b   Are there any aspects of his character that make him more
       interesting?
    c   Look again at pages 12 and 13 and the illustration on page 13.
       What are your first feelings and thoughts about this setting where
       so much of the story takes place?
    d   How exactly was the little girl hurt (page 14)?
    e   Who else was there and what did they do?

2   a   How did Utterson's new knowledge about Hyde change his attitude
       towards the will?
    b   Lanyon refers to 'unscientific balderdash' (page 21). What do you
       think he is talking about?
    c   What do Utterson's nightmares tell us about his thoughts and fears?
    d   In what ways do his thoughts and fears change or develop when he
       meets Hyde?
    e   What new information does Utterson get from his conversation
       with Poole?

3   a   How does Jekyll react when Utterson speaks of Hyde? Why do you
       think this is?

Character

1   In this section we meet these characters:
    ● Utterson;
    ● Enfield;
    ● Hyde;
    ● Lanyon;
    ● Jekyll.

    How would you sum up your first impressions of each of them?

2   As you read through the section how do your impressions of Utterson
    develop?

3   By the end of the section, how much do you know about Jekyll? For
    example, what do you know about:
    ● his house?
    ● his work?
    ● his financial position?
    ● what he spends his money on?
    ● his friends?
    ● his family situation?
    ● his relationship with Hyde?

Key actions

Hyde's attack on the little girl
    Make sure that you know:
    ● exactly what happened;
    ● how people reacted to the attack;
    ● what it tells us about Hyde;
    ● what it tells us about people's reactions to Hyde.

Utterson's meeting with Hyde
    Read pages 23–25 again and think about these points:
    ● What does Hyde look like?
    ● How does he speak?
    ● How does he move?

CHAPTERS 4–7

Tracking

1   a   There are very few female characters in this story. What impression
        do you get of the maid servant described on page 31?
    b   Look at the description of the attack on page 32. What are the
        most important features of this? What effect do you think
        Stevenson wanted to have on his readers?
    c   What impression do you get of the police?
    d   Look at the description of Hyde's house on page 35. Does
        anything about it strike you as interesting or unusual?

2   a   Chapter 5 starts with a description of Jekyll's laboratory and
        study (page 36). What clues does this give us about the work the
        Doctor does there?
    b   Jekyll is looking 'deadly sick'. What other indications do we get of
        his state of mind?
    c   Jekyll lies about the letter. How does Utterson find this out? Why
        do you think Jekyll lies? What conclusions does Utterson draw?

3   a   At the beginning of Chapter 6, what makes Utterson happier?
    b   How and why do things change?
    c   What is it about Lanyon's appearance that shocks Utterson most?
    d   What do you think Lanyon is referring to when he talks about a
        'shock' (page 43)?
    e   What do you make of Jekyll's letter? What do you think is really
        going on?

4   a   What do we learn here that adds to our understanding of Jekyll's
        situation?

Character

1   A number of the main characters in this story are quite similar. What
    are the similarities you have noticed between these people:
    ● Jekyll;
    ● Utterson;
    ● Lanyon;
    ● Carew?

2   Compare these two pictures of Jekyll:
    ● that given in Chapter 3;
    ● that given in Chapter 5.
    How has he changed?

3   Compare these two pictures of Lanyon:
    ● that given in Chapter 2;
    ● that given in Chapter 6.
    His appearance and behaviour have changed dramatically. What do
    you think might have caused this?

Key actions

The attack on Carew

The story contains a number of violent actions. Look at this one
carefully and make sure that you have a clear picture of what
happened. Then think about how it is described:
    ● Through whose eyes do we see it?
    ● What is the situation immediately before the attack?
    ● How do the answers to these two questions affect our impressions
      of the attack itself?

Utterson's conversations with Lanyon
> On two occasions (page 21 and page 44) Utterson asks Lanyon about Jekyll. Compare the two:
> - In what ways are they similar?
> - How are they different?
> Remember that in the past Jekyll, Lanyon and Utterson have been close friends. What do you think has been going on to cause these changes in Lanyon's attitude towards Jekyll?

CHAPTERS 8–9

Tracking

1 Chapter 8 builds slowly but inevitably towards the climax of Hyde's death. Look at these important features of the growing tension:
 a Poole's fear: he doesn't explain exactly what he is afraid of. How does this affect us?
 b The time of day and the weather: what kind of picture do these produce in your mind?
 c The behaviour of the servants.
 d The mystery of who is in the room: if it is Jekyll's murderer, why has he not run away?
 e Poole's account of the events of the past week: what does it lead Utterson to fear?
 f The moment they realise that it is definitely not Jekyll in the study: when is this?
 g The breaking down of the door.
 h The discovery of the body: what has happened and how do they react?
 i The mystery of Jekyll's disappearance.
 j The letters: what will be in Jekyll's letters? Why have they been found near Hyde's body?

2 a What frame of mind was Jekyll in when he wrote to Lanyon?
 b What does Lanyon find when he enters Jekyll's study? What conclusions does he draw?
 c Why does Lanyon's visitor offer him the opportunity not to watch him drink the mixture?
 d Why does Lanyon find the transformation so shocking?

Character

1 What fresh light does Chapter 8 throw on:
 - the character of Utterson (for example, his ability to act, and to lead others)?
 - the appearance of Hyde and the effect he has on other people?

2   Shortly after the story recounted in Chapter 9, Dr Lanyon becomes ill
     and dies:
     ● Why did it have such an effect on him?
     ● In what ways does it add to or alter our view of his character?

Key actions

Hyde mixes and takes the poison
     Stevenson builds up to this moment very carefully. It is preceded by:
     ● the letter;
     ● Lanyon's journey to fetch the drawer;
     ● the arrival of the mysterious visitor.
     Look carefully at the description of what happens next (pages 70–71).
     What are the strongest impressions this description of the swallowing
     of the mixture has on you?

CHAPTER 10

This is by far the most demanding chapter in the story, because Stevenson
explores, through Jekyll's confession, the two-sidedness of Dr Jekyll and
men like him. Victorian society claimed to have high moral standards, and
– in public at least – this seemed to be true. There was, however, a vicious
'underside' to this. A respectable professional man like Dr Jekyll would
think nothing of going out for dinner with his professional friends and
colleagues and then stopping at a brothel before rejoining his wife and
family. Child prostitution and other activities which are criminal today
were widespread then.
    Stevenson does not tell us much about the evil acts Jekyll committed
when he was Hyde. He only describes two: the trampling of the little girl
and the murder of Sir Danvers Carew, but the way in which Jekyll writes
makes it clear that Hyde has committed acts which are far more depraved
than these two violent assaults. What these are is left to the reader's
imagination.
    As you read through the chapter again, think about these points:
1   Jekyll's life ends in misery and disgrace. What was there – if anything –
    in his early life to suggest that this might happen?
2   Do you think he is right to say that all people have at least two
    conflicting sides to their personalities?
3   What are the basic ideas behind his experiment with the chemical
    mixture?
4   How and why did Hyde's appearance differ from Jekyll's?
5   What did Dr Jekyll think of the activities of Mr Hyde?
6   How and why did he find it increasingly difficult to remain as Dr
    Jekyll?
7   How would you describe Jekyll's state of mind as he surveys the ruins
    of his life?

8   Do you think he would have acted differently if he had had his time
    over again?

Character

Think back over your earlier judgments of Dr Jekyll. This is the first time
you have heard him speaking frankly about himself. In what ways does his
confession:
- confirm what you already thought?
- add to what you knew?
- lead you to change your mind?

Key actions

Jekyll takes the mixture for the first time (pages 75–77)
> Compare this with the description of what happened when he took it
> in Lanyon's house. That was described by an outsider. Now we get the
> 'inside view'.

LOOKING AT THE STORY AS A WHOLE

Each of the assignments in this section leads to an extended piece of
writing. You may find them easier to tackle if you have worked through at
least some of the material in the earlier sections of this study guide.

Recreating the story

1   The idea behind this story is a very powerful one: that an outwardly
    respectable person can secretly take on a personality and appearance
    that are the opposite of his normal ones. How could such a story be
    told today, in a modern setting? Think of a modern 'Dr Jekyll': what
    kind of person might he or she be? And what would that person's 'Mr
    Hyde' be like? Either
    - make up a short story based on this character, or
    - write a short chapter from a longer story about him or her.

2   The events described in Stevenson's story caused quite a stir in
    London society. Choose one important event from the story and write
    a full newspaper account of it as it might have appeared at the time.

3   Stevenson makes use of three different storytellers: Utterson, Lanyon,
    and Jekyll himself. Choose one section of the story and retell it, using a
    different storyteller. You can choose whatever you wish, but here are
    some suggestions:

- The trampling of the little girl described by her mother.
- The attack on Sir Danvers Carew described by the maid to one of her friends, shortly after she had recovered from the shock.
- The breaking down of the door and the discovery of Hyde's body as told by Poole to a friend.

Character

1 Choose any two of these characters and describe their similarities and differences:
   - Utterson;
   - Lanyon;
   - Jekyll.

   You should include some mention of these points:
   - work and financial position;
   - home life;
   - appearance;
   - personality.

2 Jekyll was born into a wealthy family and was talented and popular. He dies in misery. How could this happen?

Key actions

1 One way of planning a novel, TV play or movie is to begin by listing and describing the key scenes.
   - Make a numbered list of between 8 and 14 key scenes in this story.
   - Describe each one in a short paragraph (not more than 30 words).
   - Write a linking narrative that explains how the story moves from one to the next.

2 Make a list of key scenes as in 1. Choose one of them and write a detailed scenario for a film version. You should include these points:
   - a detailed description of the setting;
   - a list of all the characters who appear in the scene;
   - a point-by-point account of what happens. (This will involve describing the actions of all the characters we can see, not just what Stevenson puts into the story.);
   - important things that people say;
   - a description of the effect you want to achieve in the scene.

Themes and issues

1 It was suggested on page 96 that Stevenson was writing more than a straightforward horror story; he wanted to attack some aspects of Victorian life. He never tells us exactly what these are – and the story would probably never have been published if he had. Nevertheless, he gives us a very vivid picture of Victorian London. Write a description of that London. Here are some suggestions of things you might include:

- the streets and buildings;
- the weather;
- the insides of people's houses;
- people's attitudes towards work and money;
- different social classes.

2 What is a horror story? Do you think this is a 'horror story'? What are the reasons for your answer?

3 In the last chapter, Jekyll spends a lot of time describing the opposing sides of the personality. The effects of these two sides are seen in the rest of the story.

- Go through the story and make a chart listing, side by side, the actions and qualities of Jekyll and Hyde.
- Use the information you have collected to write an explanation of what Jekyll means by his 'profound duplicity [deep-seated two sidedness] of life'.

THE BEACH OF FALESÁ

by
ROBERT LOUIS STEVENSON

Introduction

THE CHARACTERS

Tarleton

Uma

Wiltshire

Father Galuchet

Black Jack

Case

Captain Randall

THE SETTING

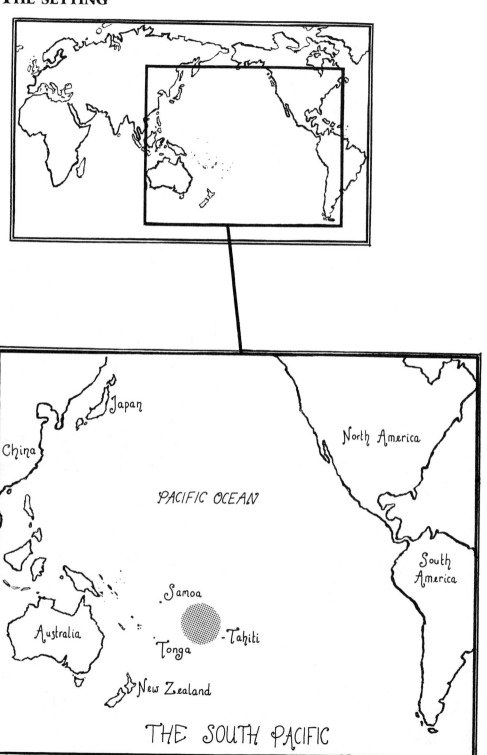

THE SOUTH PACIFIC

FALESÁ

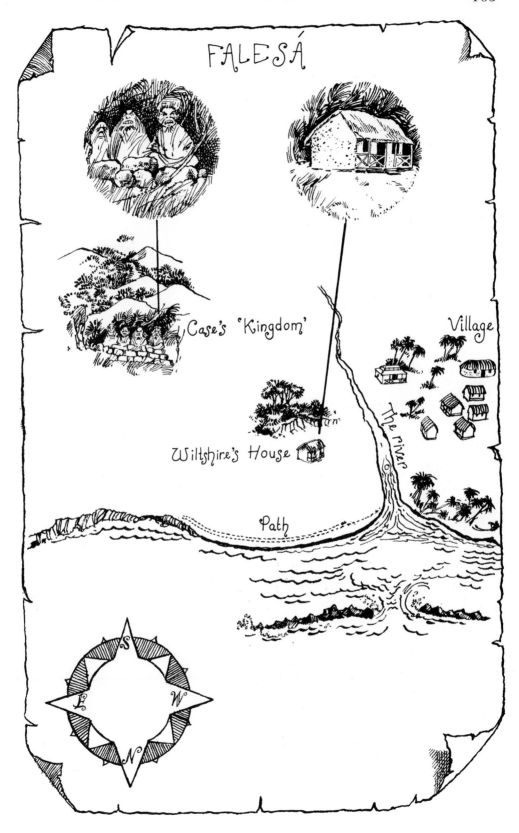

Case's "Kingdom"

Village

Wiltshire's House

The river

Path

1 A South-Sea Bridal

Look out for...
- the character of the storyteller, Wiltshire: what impression do you get of him as a person?
- the attitudes of Wiltshire, Case and Black Jack to the islanders and to women.

I saw that island first when it was neither night nor morning. The moon was to the west, setting, but still broad and bright. To the east, and right amidships of the dawn, which was all pink, the day-star sparkled like a diamond. The land breeze blew in our faces, and smelt strong of wild lime and vanilla; other things besides, but these were the most plain; and the chill of it set me sneezing. I should say I had been for years on a low island near the line, living for the most part solitary among natives. Here was a fresh experience; even the tongue would be quite strange to me; and the look of these woods and mountains, and the rare smell of them, renewed my blood.

The captain blew out the binnacle-lamp.

'There!' said he, 'there goes a bit of smoke, Mr Wiltshire, behind the break of the reef. That's Falesá, where your station is, the last village to the east; nobody lives to windward – I don't know why. Take my glass, and you can make the houses out.'

COMMENTARY
The storyteller is Wiltshire, a white trader in the South Pacific. The company he works for has sent him to Falesá, a village on an island near Samoa (see map on page 104). He arrives there just before dawn and sees the beautiful island at its best. The captain points out to him the village where he will be living.

Bridal: wedding ceremony
amidships: in the middle
day-star: a planet that can be seen just before dawn
the line: the Equator
binnacle-lamp: the lamp used to light the ship's compass
Falesá: the Samoan word for 'holy place' or 'church'

I took the glass; and the shores leaped nearer, and I saw the tangle of the woods and the breach of the surf, and the brown roofs and the black insides of houses peeped among the trees.

'Do you catch a bit of white there to the east'ard?' the captain continued. 'That's your house. Coral built, stands high, veranda you could walk on three abreast; best station in the South Pacific. When old Adams saw it, he took and shook me by the hand. 'I've dropped into a soft thing here,' says he. 'So you have,' says I, 'and time too!' Poor Johnny! I never saw him again but the once, and then he had changed his tune – couldn't get on with the natives, or the whites, or something; and the next time we came around there, he was dead and buried. I took and put up a bit of a stick to him: "John Adams, *obit* eighteen and sixty-eight. Go thou and do likewise." I missed that man. I could never see much harm in Johnny.'

'What did he die of?' I inquired.

'Some kind of sickness,' says the captain. 'It appears it took him sudden. Seems he got up in the night, and filled up on Pain-Killer and Kennedy's Discovery. No go – he was booked beyond Kennedy. Then he had tried to open a case of gin. No go again – not strong enough. Then he must have turned to and run out on the veranda, and capsized over the rail. When they found him, the next day, he was clean crazy – carried on all the time about somebody watering his copra. Poor John!'

'Was it thought to be the island?' I asked.

'Well, it was thought to be the island, or the trouble, or something,' he replied. 'I never could hear but what it was a healthy place. Our last man, Vigours, never turned a hair. He left because of the beach – said he was afraid of Black Jack and Case and Whistling Jimmie, who was still alive at the time, but got drowned soon afterward when drunk. As for old Captain Randall, he's been here any time since eighteen-forty, forty-five. I never could see much harm in Billy, nor much change. Seems as if he might live to be Old Kafoozleum. No, I guess it's healthy.'

'There's a boat coming now,' said I. 'She's right in the pass; looks to be a sixteen-foot whale; two white men in the stern-sheets.'

COMMENTARY

The captain points out to Wiltshire the house and store where he will live and work (his station). He also tells him about the strange things that have happened to previous traders doing his job: John Adams went mad and died, and the last trader left suddenly. He said that he was afraid of some of the other traders on the island, especially Black Jack and Case. Wiltshire sees a boat approaching.

obit: Latin for 'died'
copra: the dried flesh of the coconut, used to make oil. Local people exchanged it for European goods. It was sold by weight, and adding water made it heavier

beach: Europeans who lived off trade and beachcombing on the islands
Old Kafoozleum: Methuselah, who lived for over 900 years (Genesis 5.27)

'That's the boat that drowned Whistling Jimmie!' cried the captain; 'let's see the glass. Yes, that's Case, sure enough, and the darkie. They've got a gallows bad reputation, but you know what a place the beach is for talking. My belief, that Whistling Jimmie was the worst of the trouble; and he's gone to glory, you see. What'll you bet they ain't after gin? Lay you five to two they take six cases.'

When these two traders came aboard I was pleased with the looks of them at once, or, rather, with the looks of both, and the speech of one.

FAST FORWARD: to page 111

I was sick for white neighbours after my four years at the line, which I always counted years of prison; getting tabooed, and going down to the Speak House to see and get it taken off; buying gin and going on a break, and then repenting; sitting in the house at night with the lamp for company; or walking on the beach and wondering what kind of a fool to call myself for being where I was. There were no other whites upon my island, and when I sailed to the next, rough customers made the most of the society. Now to see these two when they came aboard was a pleasure. One was a Negro, to be sure; but they were both rigged out smart in striped pyjamas and straw hats, and Case would have passed muster in a city. He was yellow and smallish, had a hawk's nose to his face, pale eyes, and his beard trimmed with scissors. No man knew his country, beyond he was of English speech; and it was clear he came from a good family and was splendidly educated. He was accomplished too; played the accordion first rate; and give him a piece of string or a cork or a pack of cards, and he could show you tricks equal to any professional. He could speak, when he chose, fit for a drawing-room; and when he chose he could blaspheme worse than a Yankee boatswain, and talk smart to sicken a Kanaka. The way he thought he would pay best at the moment, that was Case's way, and it always seemed to come natural, and like as if he was born to it. He had the

COMMENTARY
Black Jack and Case come aboard and greet Wiltshire warmly. He is delighted to have the company of two 'white men' (i.e. not islanders) after his lonely life for the past four years.

tabooed: put under a religious or magic ban by the local people so that no one would come near him or have anything to do with him – the taboo was the only weapon Polynesians could use against European imperialists

Speak House: the assembly place used by the islanders

going on a break: going off and getting drunk for days on end

Yankee boatswain: American petty officer responsible for calling the ship's crew for duty

Kanaka: South Sea islander

courage of a lion and the cunning of a rat; and if he's not in hell to-day, there's no such place. I know but one good point to the man – that he was fond of his wife, and kind to her. She was a Samoa woman, and dyed her hair red – Samoa style; and when he came to die (as I have to tell of) they found one strange thing – that he had made a will, like a Christian, and the widow got the lot; all this, they said, and all Black Jack's, and the most of Billy Randall's in the bargain, for it was Case that kept the books. So she went off home in the schooner Manu'a, and does the lady to this day in her own place.

But of all this on that first morning I knew no more than a fly. Case used me like a gentleman and like a friend, made me welcome to Falesá, and put his services at my disposal, which was the more helpful from my ignorance of the natives. All the better part of the day we sat drinking better acquaintance in the cabin, and I never heard a man talk more to the point. There was no smarter trader, and none dodgier, in the islands. I thought Falesá seemed to be the right kind of a place; and the more I drank the lighter my heart. Our last trader had fled the place at half an hour's notice, taking a chance passage in a labour ship from up west. The captain, when he came, had found the station

none dodgier: no one more cunning

COMMENTARY
Case and Black Jack tell Wiltshire more about the island.

closed, the keys left with the native pastor, and a letter from the runaway, confessing he was fairly frightened of his life. Since then the firm had not been represented, and of course there was no cargo. The wind, besides, was fair, the captain hoped he could make his next island by dawn, with a good tide, and the business of landing my trade was gone about lively. There was no call for me to fool with it, Case said; nobody would touch my things, everyone was honest in Falesá, only about chickens or an odd knife or an odd stick of tobacco; and the best I could do was to sit quiet till the vessel left, then come straight to his house, see old Captain Randall, the father of the beach, take pot-luck, and go home to sleep when it got dark.

So it was high noon, and the schooner was under way before I set my foot on shore at Falesá.

I had a glass or two on board; I was just off a long cruise, and the ground heaved under me like a ship's deck. The world was like all new painted; my foot went along to music; Falesá might have been Fiddler's Green, if there is such a place, and more's the pity if there isn't! It was good to foot the grass, to look aloft at the green mountains, to see the men with their green wreaths and the women in their bright dresses, red and blue. On we went, in the strong sun and the cool shadow, liking both; and all the children in the town came trotting after with their shaven heads and their brown bodies, and raising a thin kind of a cheer in our wake, like crowing poultry.

'By the bye,' says Case, 'we must get you a wife.'

'That's so,' said I; 'I had forgotten.'

REWIND: …when it got dark.
Wiltshire has met the two traders, Case and the black man 'Black Jack'. They have drunk together and the two traders have made him welcome. He has realised that Case is a clever man and has begun to like him. Case has told him how the last man to do his job left the island very hurriedly. He has then invited Wiltshire to eat with them at Captain Randall's house.

COMMENTARY
The captain does not want to delay, so Wiltshire's goods are unloaded and Case invites him to Captain Randall's house for a meal. They land and walk through the village, where all the people have come to welcome them. Case says that Wiltshire must take a 'wife' from amongst the island girls.

Fiddler's Green: the sailor's haven where they believed they would find wine, women and song

There was a crowd of girls about us, and I pulled myself up and looked among them like a bashaw. They were all dressed out for the sake of the ship being in; and the women of Falesá are a handsome lot to see. If they have a fault, they are a trifle broad in the beam; and I was just thinking so when Case touched me.

'That's pretty,' says he.

I saw one coming on the other side alone. She had been fishing; all she wore was a chemise, and it was wetted through. She was young and very slender for an island maid, with a long face, a high forehead, and a shy, strange, blindish look between a cat's and a baby's.

'Who's she?' said I. 'She'll do.'

'That's Uma,' said Case, and he called her up and spoke to her in the native. I didn't know what he said; but when he was in the midst she looked up at me quick and timid, like a child dodging a blow, then down again, and presently smiled. She had a wide mouth, the lips and the chin cut like any statue's; and the smile came out for a moment and was gone. Then she stood with her head bent, and heard Case to an end, spoke back in the pretty Polynesian voice, looking him full in the face, heard him again in answer, and then with an obeisance started off. I had just a share of the bow, but never another shot of her eye, and there was no more word of smiling.

bashaw: a pasha, a very rich and
   important person
obeisance: low bow

COMMENTARY
Case shows Wiltshire an island girl called Uma.
Wiltshire is immediately attracted to her.

'I guess it's all right,' said Case. 'I guess you can have her. I'll make it square with the old lady. You can have your pick of the lot for a plug of tobacco,' he added, sneering.

I suppose it was the smile stuck in my memory, for I spoke back sharp. 'She doesn't look that sort,' I cried.

'I don't know that she is,' said Case. 'I believe she's as right as the mail. Keeps to herself, don't go round with the gang, and that. Oh, no, don't you misunderstand me – Uma's on the square.' He spoke eager, I thought, and that surprised and pleased me. 'Indeed,' he went on, 'I shouldn't make so sure of getting her, only she cottoned to the cut of your jib. All you have to do is to keep dark and let me work the mother my own way; and I'll bring the girl round to the captain's for the marriage.'

I didn't care for the word marriage, and I said so.

'Oh, there's nothing to hurt in the marriage,' says he. 'Black Jack's the chaplin.'

By this time we had come in view of the house of these three white men; for a Negro is counted a white man, and so is a Chinese! A strange idea, but common in the islands. It was a board house with a strip of rickety veranda. The store was to the front, with a counter, scales, and the finest possible display of trade: a case or two of tinned meats; a barrel of hard bread, a few bolts of cotton stuff, not to be compared with mine; the only thing well represented being the contraband firearms and liquor. 'If these are my only rivals,' thinks I, 'I should do well in Falesá.' Indeed, there was only the one way they could touch me, and that was with the guns and drink.

In the back room was old Captain Randall, squatting on the floor native fashion, fat and pale, naked to the waist, grey as a badger, and his eyes set with drink. His body was covered with grey hair and crawled over by flies; one was in the corner of his eye – he never heeded; and the mosquitoes hummed about the man like bees. Any clean-minded man would have had the creature out at once and buried him; and to see him, and think he was seventy, and remember he had once commanded a ship, and come ashore in his smart togs, and talked big in bars and consulates, and sat in club verandas, turned me sick and sober.

cottoned to the cut of your jib: took a strong liking to you

COMMENTARY
Wiltshire speaks sharply to Case when he mocks Uma. Case says that the two of them must be 'married'; he will arrange it. They arrive at Captain Randall's house and meet the Captain, who is a filthy drunkard.

He tried to get up when I came in, but that was hopeless; so he reached me a hand instead, and stumbled out some salutation.

'Papa's pretty full this morning,' observed Case. 'We've had an epidemic here; and Captain Randall takes gin for a prophylactic – don't you, papa?'

'Never took such a thing in my life!' cried the captain, indignantly. 'Take gin for my health's sake, Mr Wha's-ever-your-name—'s a precautionary measure.'

'That's all right, papa,' said Case. 'But you'll have to brace up. There's going to be a marriage – Mr Wiltshire here is going to get spliced.'

The old man asked to whom.

'To Uma,' said Case.

'Uma!' cried the captain. 'Wha's he want Uma for? 'S he come here for his health, anyway? Wha' 'n hell's he want Uma for?'

'Dry up, papa,' said Case. ''Tain't you that's to marry her. I guess you're not her godfather and godmother. I guess Mr Wiltshire's going to please himself.'

With that he made an excuse to me that he must move about the marriage, and left me alone with the poor wretch that was his partner and (to speak truth) his gull. Trade and station belonged both to Randall; Case and the Negro were parasites; they crawled and fed upon him like the flies, he none the wiser. Indeed, I have no harm to say of Billy Randall beyond the fact that my gorge rose at him, and the time I now passed in his company was like a nightmare.

FAST FORWARD: to page 116

The room was stifling hot and full of flies; for the house was dirty and low and small, and stood in a bad place, behind the village, in the borders of the bush, and sheltered from the trade. The three men's beds were on the floor, and a litter of pans and dishes. There was no standing furniture; Randall, when he was violent, tearing it to laths. There I sat and had a meal which was

salutation: greeting
prophylactic: medicine you take to avoid
   catching a disease
godfather and godmother: Case is confused
   – they play an important part at a
   baptism, not a wedding
his gull: the person he was fooling
Trade and station: house, store and shop
my gorge rose: I felt sick
the trade: south-easterly trade winds
laths: thin strips of wood

COMMENTARY
Wiltshire is introduced to Randall and then left with him, while Case and Black Jack go off.

served us by Case's wife; and there I was entertained all day by that remains of man, his tongue stumbling among low old jokes and long old stories, and his own wheezy laughter always ready, so that he had no sense of my depression. He was nipping gin all the while. Sometimes he fell asleep and awoke again, whimpering and shivering, and every now and again he would ask me why I wanted to marry Uma. 'My friend,' I was telling myself all day, 'you must not come to be an old gentleman like this.'

It might be four in the afternoon, perhaps, when the back door was thrust slowly open, and a strange old native woman crawled into the house almost on her belly. She was swathed in black stuff to her heels; her hair was grey in swatches; her face was tattooed, which was not the practice in that island; her eyes big and bright and crazy. These she fixed upon me with a rapt expression that I saw to be part acting. She said no plain word, but smacked and mumbled with her lips, and hummed aloud, like a child over its Christmas pudding. She came straight across the house, heading for me, and, as soon as she was alongside, caught up my hand and purred and crooned over it like a great cat. From this she slipped into a kind of song.

'Who the devil's this?' cried I, for the thing startled me.

'It's Faavao,' says Randall; and I saw he had hitched along the floor into the farthest corner.

'You ain't afraid of her?' I cried.

'Me 'fraid?' cried the captain. 'My dear friend, I defy her! I don't let her put her foot in here, only I suppose 's different to-day for the marriage. 'S Uma's mother.'

'Well, suppose it is; what's she carrying on about?' I asked, more irritated, perhaps more frightened, than I cared to show; and the captain told me she was making up a quantity of poetry in my praise because I was to marry Uma. 'All right, old lady,' says I, with rather a failure of a laugh, 'anything to oblige. But when you're done with my hand, you might let me know.'

She did as though she understood; the song rose into a cry, and stopped; the woman crouched out of the house, the same way that she came in, and

---

COMMENTARY

Wiltshire is sickened by the filthy Randall. Suddenly they are joined by an elderly island woman, who – Wiltshire learns – is Faavao, Uma's mother. She has come to thank him for marrying her daughter. She blesses the wedding and then leaves.

must have plunged straight into the bush, for when I followed her to the door she had already vanished.

'These are rum manners,' said I.

''S a rum crowd,' said the captain, and, to my surprise, he made the sign of the cross on his bare bosom.

'Hillo!' says I, 'are you a Papist?'

He repudiated the idea with contempt. 'Hard-shell Baptis',' said he. 'But, my dear friend, the Papists got some good ideas too; and th' 's one of 'em. You take my advice, and whenever you come across Uma or Faavao or Vigours, or any of that crowd, you take a leaf out o' the priests, and do what I do. Savvy?' says he, repeated the sign, and winked his dim eye at me. 'No, *sir*!' he broke out again, 'no Papists here!' and for a long time entertained me with his religious opinions.

I must have been taken with Uma from the first, or I should certainly have fled from that house, and got into the clean air, and the clean sea, or some convenient river – though, it's true, I was committed to Case; and, besides, I could never have held my head up in that island if I had run from a girl upon
▶▶ my wedding-night.

The sun was down, the sky all on fire, and the lamp had been some time lighted, when Case came back with Uma and the Negro. She was dressed and scented; her kilt was of fine tapa, looking richer in the folds than any silk; her bust, which was of the colour of dark honey, she wore bare, only for some half

---

REWIND: ...my wedding-night.
Wiltshire has spent several hours with the rambling drunkard Captain Randall. They had been joined by a strange old island woman, Faavao, who it turned out was Uma's mother, who had come to thank Wiltshire for marrying her daughter. When she had gone, Randall has crossed himself, because he has told Wiltshire, although he is not a Catholic, he believes Faavao, like Vigours, is evil.

◀◀

---

tapa: unwoven cloth made from the bark of a tree, the paper mulberry

COMMENTARY
Wiltshire asks Randall why he crossed himself when Faavao came in. Is he a Catholic? Randall tells him that he is a Baptist but believes that the sign of the cross is a protection against evil. Case returns with Black Jack and the girl, Uma.

a dozen necklaces of seeds and flowers; and behind her ears and in her hair she had the scarlet flowers of the hibiscus. She showed the best bearing for a bride conceivable, serious and still; and I thought shame to stand up with her in that mean house and before that grinning Negro. I thought shame, I say; for the mountebank was dressed with a big paper collar, the book he made believe to read from was an odd volume of a novel, and the words of his service not fit to be set down. My conscience smote me when we joined hands; and when she got her certificate I was tempted to throw up the bargain and confess. Here is the document. It was Case that wrote it, signatures and all, in a leaf out of the ledger:

This is to certify that *Uma*, daughter of *Faavao*, of Falesá, island of —, is illegally married to *Mr John Wiltshire* for one night, and Mr John Wiltshire is at liberty to send her to hell next morning.

JOHN BLACKAMOAR,
Chaplain to the Hulks

Extracted from the register
by William T. Randall,
Master Mariner

A nice paper to put in a girl's hand and see her hide away like gold. A man might easily feel cheap for less. But it was the practice in these parts, and (as I told myself) not the least the fault of us white men, but of the missionaries. If they had let the natives be, I had never needed this deception, but taken all the wives I wished, and left them when I pleased, with a clear conscience.

The more ashamed I was, the more hurry I was in to be gone; and our desires thus jumping together, I made the less remark of a change in the traders. Case had been all eagerness to keep me; now, as though he had attained a purpose, he seemed all eagerness to have me go. Uma, he said, could show me to my house, and the three bade us farewell indoors.

COMMENTARY

Black Jack and Case then set up a fake marriage ceremony so that Wiltshire and Uma become 'man and wife' for one night. Then the two of them leave for Wiltshire's house.

When *The Beach of Falesá* was published, Stevenson had problems with censorship. Victorian editors found the fake marriage certificate too shocking and cut it out of the story. It was only published in full in 1979.

mountebank: someone pretending to be something they are not
hibiscus: a shrub with large trumpet-shaped flowers

The night was nearly come; the village smelt of trees and flowers and the sea and bread-fruit-cooking; there came a fine roll of sea from the reef, and from a distance, among the woods and houses, many pretty sounds of men and children. It did me good to breathe free air; it did me good to be done with the captain, and see, instead, the creature at my side. I felt for all the world as though she were some girl at home in the Old Country, and forgetting myself for the minute, took her hand to walk with. He fingers nestled into mine, I heard her breathe deep and quick, and all at once she caught my hand to her face and pressed it there. 'You good!' she cried, and ran ahead of me, and stopped and looked back and smiled, and ran ahead of me again, thus guiding me through the edge of the bush, and by a quiet way to my own house.

FAST FORWARD: to page 119

The truth is, Case had done the courting for me in style – told her I was mad to have her, and cared nothing for the consequences; and the poor soul, knowing that which I was still ignorant of, believed it, every word, and had her head nigh turned with vanity and gratitude. Now, of all this I had no guess; I was one of the most opposed to any nonsense about native women, having seen so many whites eaten up by their wives' relatives, and made fools of into the bargain; and I told myself I must make a stand at once, and bring her to her bearings. But she looked so quaint and pretty as she ran away and then awaited me, and the thing was done so like a child or a kind dog, that the best I could do was just to follow her whenever she went on, to listen for the fall of her bare feet, and to watch in the dusk for the shining of her body. And there was another thought came in my head. She played kitten with me now when we were alone; but in the house she had carried it the way a countess might, so proud and humble. And what with her dress – for all there was so little of it, and that native enough – what with her fine tapa and fine scents, and her red

COMMENTARY
Uma leads Wiltshire back to his house (which he has not yet seen), through the sights, sounds, and smells of this tropical paradise. He is taken with her beauty.

bread-fruit: a large fruit that grows on trees in the South Pacific – it tastes like bread, and is often eaten baked or roasted

flowers and seeds, that were quite as bright as jewels, only larger – it came over me she was a kind of countess really, dressed to hear great singers at a concert, and no even mate for a poor trader like myself.

She was the first in the house; and while I was still without I saw a match flash and the lamplight kindle in the windows. The station was a wonderful fine place, coral built, with quite a wide veranda, and the main room high and wide. My chests and cases had been piled in, and made rather of a mess; and there, in the thick of the confusion, stood Uma by the table, awaiting me. Her shadow went all the way up behind her into the hollow of the iron roof; she stood against it bright, the lamplight shining on her skin. I stopped in the door, and she looked at me, not speaking, with eyes that were eager and yet daunted; then she touched herself on the bosom.

'Me – your wifie,' said she. It had never taken me like that before; but the want of her took and shook all through me, like the wind in the luff of a sail.

I could not speak if I had wanted; and if I could, I would not. I was ashamed to be so much moved about a native, ashamed of the marriage too, and the certificate she had treasured in her kilt; and I turned aside and made believe to rummage among my cases. The first thing I lighted on was a case of gin, the only one that I had brought; and partly for the girl's sake, and partly for horror of the recollections of old Randall, took a sudden resolve. I pried the lid off. One by one I drew the bottles with a pocket corkscrew, and sent Uma out to pour the stuff from the veranda.

She came back after the last, and looked at me puzzled like.

'No good,' said I, for I was now a little better master of my tongue. 'Man he drink, he no good.'

REWIND: …trader like myself.
Wiltshire has spent the time as they walk to his house thinking about Uma's looks and behaviour.

COMMENTARY
Wiltshire is so overwhelmed by Uma's beauty and his feelings for her that on an impulse he pours away the dozen bottles of gin he has brought with him.

Me – your wifie: Europeans and islanders communicated in pidgin, a simplified version of English mixed with bits of other languages – here Uma says, 'I am your wife'

She agreed with this, but kept considering. 'Why you bring him?' she asked, presently. 'Suppose you no want drink, you no bring him, I think.'

'That's all right,' said I. 'One time I want drink too much; now no want. You see, I no savvy, I get one little wifie. Suppose I drink gin, my little wifie be 'fraid.'

To speak to her kindly was about more than I was fit for; I had made my vow I would never let on to weakness with a native, and I had nothing for it but to stop.

She stood looking gravely down at me where I sat by the open case. 'I think you good man,' she said. And suddenly she had fallen before me on the floor. 'I belong you all-e-same pig!' she cried.

savvy: pidgin for 'know' (from the French *savoir*)

COMMENTARY
Uma is impressed by Wiltshire's explanation of what he has done. She tells him she belongs to him now.

2 The Ban

Look out for...
- **the ways in which Wiltshire tries to understand the islanders and what they are thinking: how does he explain them to himself?**
- **Father Galuchet: what part does he play in the story and what are the attitudes of different characters to his religion?**
- **how Case behaves: do you think he is friendly towards Wiltshire?**

I came on the veranda just before the sun rose on the morrow. My house was the last on the east; there was a cape of woods and cliffs behind that hid the sunrise. To the west, a swift, cold river ran down, and beyond was the green of the village, dotted with cocoa-palms and bread-fruits and houses. The shutters were some of them down and some open; I saw the mosquito bars still stretched, with shadows of people new-awakened sitting up inside; and all over the green others were stalking silent, wrapped in their many-coloured sleeping clothes, like Bedouins in Bible pictures. It was mortal still and solemn and chilly, and the light of the dawn on the lagoon was like the shining of a fire.

But the thing that troubled me was nearer hand. Some dozen young men and children made a piece of a half-circle, flanking my house: the river divided them, some were on the near side, some on the far, and one on a boulder in the midst; and they all sat silent, wrapped in their sheets, and stared at me and my house as straight as pointer dogs. I thought it strange as I went out. When I had bathed and come back again, and found them all there, and two or three more along with them, I thought it stranger still. What could they see to gaze at in my house I wondered, and went in.

COMMENTARY
When Wiltshire gets up the next morning he finds a group of islanders standing outside his house staring at him in a strange way. He is puzzled.

pointer dogs: dogs used in hunting – when they see a game bird they stop and point their noses at it, so that the hunter can see where it is

cape: a piece of land jutting out into the sea
cocoa-palms: coconut trees
mosquito bars: nets to protect people from being bitten by mosquitos while they were asleep

But the thought of these starers stuck in my mind, and presently I came out again. The sun was now up, but it was still behind the cape of woods. Say a quarter of an hour had come and gone. The crowd was greatly increased, the far bank of the river was lined for quite a way – perhaps thirty grown folk, and of children twice as many, some standing, some squatted on the ground, and all staring at my house. I have seen a house in a South-Sea village thus surrounded, but then a trader was thrashing his wife inside, and she singing out. Here was nothing – the stove was alight, the smoke coming up in a Christian manner; all was shipshape and Bristol fashion. To be sure, there was a stranger come, but they had a chance to see that stranger yesterday, and took it quiet enough. What ailed them now? I leaned my arms on the rail and stared back. Devil a wink they had in them! Now and then I could see the children chatter, but they spoke so low not even the hum of their speaking came my length. The rest were like graven images: they stared at me, dumb and sorrowful, with their bright eyes; and it came upon me things would look not much different if I were on the platform of the gallows, and these good folk had come to see me hanged.

I felt I was getting daunted, and began to be afraid I looked it, which would never do. Up I stood,

in a Christian manner: just as it should

shipshape and Bristol fashion: exactly as it should be

Devil a wink they had in them!: They did not even blink!

graven images: carved statues, idols – is a reference to the Ten Commandments in the Old Testament, in which the Israelites were told that they must not make statues of gods to worship.

COMMENTARY

The next time Wiltshire goes out onto his verandah, there are far more people standing staring at his house. He is even more puzzled: they are just standing and looking at his house in silence.

made believe to stretch myself, came down the veranda stair, and strolled toward the river. There went a short buzz from one to the other, like what you hear in theatres when the curtain goes up; and some of the nearest gave back the matter of a pace. I saw a girl lay one hand on a young man and make a gesture upward with the other; at the same time she said something in the native with a gasping voice. Three little boys sat beside my path, where I must pass within three feet of them. Wrapped in their sheets, with their shaved heads and bits of topknots, and queer faces, they looked like figures on a chimney-piece. Awhile they sat their ground, solemn as judges. I came up hand over fist, doing my five knots, like a man that meant business; and I thought I saw a sort of a wink and gulp in the three faces. Then one jumped up (he was the farthest off) and ran for his mammy. The other two, trying to follow suit, got foul, came to the ground together bawling, wriggled right out of their sheets, and in a moment there were all three of them scampering for their lives mother-naked and singing out like pigs. The natives, who would never let a joke slip, even at a burial, laughed and let up, as short as a dog's bark.

They say it scares a man to be alone. No such thing. What scares him in the dark or the high bush is that he can't make sure, and there might be an army at his elbow. What scares him worst is to be right in the midst of a crowd, and have no guess of what they're driving at. When that laugh stopped, I stopped too. The boys had not yet made their offing, they were still on the full stretch going the one way, when I had already gone about ship and was sheering off the other. Like a fool I had come out, doing my five knots; like a fool I went back again. It must have been the funniest thing to see, and what knocked me silly, this time no one laughed; only one old woman gave a kind of pious moan, the way you have heard Dissenters in their chapels at the sermon.

'I never saw such dam-fool fools of Kanakas as your people here,' I said once to Uma, glancing out of the window at the starers.

'Savvy nothing,' says Uma, with a kind of disgusted air that she was good at.

And that was all the talk we had upon the matter, for I was put out, and Uma took the thing so much as a matter of course that I was fairly ashamed.

COMMENTARY
Wiltshire approaches the crowd aggressively and makes some of them run away in confusion. The others just stand there and Wiltshire returns to his house, even more confused.

I came up hand over fist: a sailor's term, meaning 'I travelled fast'

five knots: nearly 6 miles per hour

got foul: got tangled up with each other

had not yet...off the other: like sailing boats tacking against the wind they keep going in opposite directions

Dissenters: people who do not belong to the established Church of England and who worship in a chapel, rather than a church

All day, off and on, now fewer and now more, the fools sat at the west end of my house and across the river, waiting for the show, whatever that was – fire to come down from heaven, I suppose, and consume me, bones and baggage. But by evening, like real islanders, they had wearied of the business, and got away, and had a dance instead in the big house of the village, where I heard them singing and clapping hands till, maybe, ten at night, and the next day it seemed they had forgotten I existed. If fire had come down from heaven or the earth opened and swallowed me, there would have been nobody to see the sport or take the lesson, or whatever you like to call it. But I was to find they hadn't forgot either, and kept an eye lifting for phenomena over my way.

I was hard at it both these days getting my trade in order and taking stock of what Vigours had left. This was a job that made me pretty sick, and kept me from thinking on much else, Ben had taken stock the trip before – I knew I could trust Ben – but it was plain somebody had been making free in the meantime. I found I was out by what might easily cover six months' salary and profit, and I could have kicked myself all around the village to have been such a blamed ass, sitting boozing with that Case instead of attending to my own affairs and taking stock.

However, there's no use crying over spilt milk. It was done now, and couldn't be undone. All I could do was to get what was left of it, and my own stuff (my own choice) in order, to go round and get after the rats and cockroaches, and to fix up that store regular Sydney style. A fine show I made of it; and the third morning, when I had lit my pipe and stood in the doorway and looked in, and turned and looked far up the mountain and saw the cocoa-mats waving and posted up the tons of copra, and over the village green and saw the island dandies and reckoned up the yards of print they wanted for their kilts and dresses, I felt as if I was in the right place to make a fortune, and go home again and start a public-house. There was I, sitting in that veranda, in as handsome a piece of scenery as you could find, a splendid sun, and a fine, fresh, healthy trade that stirred up a man's blood like sea-bathing; and the whole thing was clean gone from me, and I was dreaming England, which is,

---

phenomena: strange happenings
taking stock: checking the goods in his
   store
regular Sydney style: Sydney is a large port
   in Australia. Presumably this means the
   same as 'Bristol fashion' – neat, tidy and
   well-organised.
saw the cocoa-mats waving and posted up
   the tons of copra: he saw the tops of the
   coconut trees waving in the breeze and
   counted up in his head the tons of
   copra he would be able to buy

COMMENTARY

The crowd gradually drifts away. Over the next few days Wiltshire organises his store and prepares for trade. He thinks that the prospects should be good.

after all, a nasty, cold, muddy hole, with not enough light to see to read by; and dreaming the looks of my public, by a cant of a broad high-road like an avenue and with the sign on a green tree.

So much for the morning, but the day passed and the devil anyone looked near me, and from all I knew of the natives in other islands I thought this strange. People laughed a little at our firm and their fine stations, and at this station of Falesá in particular; all the copra in the district wouldn't pay for it (I had heard them say) in fifty years, which I supposed was an exaggeration. But when the day went, and no business came at all, I began to get downhearted; and, about three in the afternoon, I went out for a stroll to cheer me up. On the green I saw a white man coming with a cassock on, by which and by the face of him I knew he was a priest. He was a good-natured old soul to look at, gone a little grizzled, and so dirty you could have written with him on a piece of paper.

'Good-day, sir,' said I.

He answered me eagerly in native.

'Don't you speak any English?' said I.

'French,' says he.

'Well,' said I, 'I'm sorry, but I can't do anything there.'

He tried me a while in the French, and then again in native, which he seemed to think was the best chance. I made out he was after more than passing the time of day with me, but had something to communicate, and I listened the harder. I heard the names of Adams and Case and of Randall – Randall the oftenest – and the word 'poison', or something like it, and a native word that he said very often. I went home, repeating it to myself.

'What does fussy-ocky mean?' I asked of Uma, for that was as near as I could come to it.

'Make dead,' said she.

'The devil it does!' says I. 'Did ever you hear that Case had poisoned Johnny Adams?'

'Every man he savvy that,' says Uma, scornful-like. 'Give him white sand – bad sand. He got the bottle still. Suppose he give you gin, you no take him.'

COMMENTARY

Despite Wiltshire's dreams, not one islander comes to his store. Upset, he goes for a walk and meets a French Catholic priest. Wiltshire cannot speak French and the priest cannot speak English, but tries to tell him something in the local language. By talking to Uma later, he discovers that the priest has said that Case poisoned Johnny Adams. Uma tells him that this is common knowledge.

the looks of my public: what my public house would look like
cant: slope
cassock: priest's gown

FAST FORWARD: to page 128

Now I had heard much the same sort of story in other islands, and the same white powder always to the front, which made me think the less of it. For all that, I went over to Randall's place to see what I could pick up, and found Case on the doorstep, cleaning a gun.

'Good shooting here?' says I.

'A-1,' says he. 'The bush is full of all kinds of birds. I wish copra was as plenty,' says he – I thought, slyly – 'but there don't seem anything doing.'

I could see Black Jack in the store, serving a customer.

'That looks like business, though,' said I.

'That's the first sale we've made in three weeks,' said he.

'You don't tell me?' says I. 'Three weeks? Well, well.'

'If you don't believe me,' he cries, a little hot, 'you can go and look at the copra-house. It's half empty to this blessed hour.'

'I shouldn't be much the better for that, you see,' says I. 'For all I can tell, it might have been whole empty yesterday.'

'That's so,' says he, with a bit of a laugh.

'By the by,' I said, 'what sort of a party is that priest? Seems rather a friendly sort.'

At this time Case laughed right out loud. 'Ah!' says he, 'I see what ails you now. Galuchet's been at you.' *Father Galoshes* was the name he went by most, but Case always gave it the French quirk, which was another reason we had for thinking him above the common.

'Yes, I have seen him,' I says. 'I made out he didn't think much of your Captain Randall.'

'That he don't!' says Case. 'It was the trouble about poor Adams. The last day, when he lay dying, there was young Buncombe round. Ever met Buncombe?'

I told him no.

whole empty: completely empty

COMMENTARY
Wiltshire meets Case and asks him about the French priest, whose name he learns is Father Galuchet. Wiltshire says that Father Galuchet has a low opinion of Randall and asks Case why.

'He's a cure, is Buncombe!' laughs Case. 'Well, Buncombe took it in his head that, as there was no other clergyman about, bar Kanaka pastors, we ought to call in Father Galuchet, and have the old man administered and take the sacrament. It was all the same to me, you may suppose; but I said I thought Adams was the fellow to consult. He was jawing away about watered copra and a sight of foolery. 'Look here,' I said, 'you're pretty sick. Would you like to see Galoshes?' He sat right up on his elbow. 'Get the priest,' says he, 'get the priest; don't let me die here like a dog!' He spoke kind of fierce and eager, but sensible enough. There was nothing to say against that, so we went and asked Galuchet if he would come. You bet he would. He jumped in his dirty linen at the thought of it. But we had reckoned without Papa. He's a hard-shelled Baptist, is Papa; no Papists need apply. And he took and locked the door. Buncombe told him he was bigoted, and I thought he would have had a fit. 'Bigoted!' he says. 'Me bigoted? Have I lived to hear it from a jackanapes like you?' And he made for Buncombe, and I had to hold them apart; and there was Adams in the middle, gone luny again, and carrying on about copra like a born fool. It was good as the play, and I was about knocked out of time with laughing, when all of a sudden Adams sat up, clapped his hands to his chest, and went into the horrors. He died hard, did John Adams,' says Case, with a kind of a sudden sternness.

'And what became of the priest?' I asked.

'The priest?' says Case. 'Oh! he was hammering on the door outside, and crying on the natives to come and beat it in, and singing out it was a soul he wished to save, and that. He was in a rare taking, was the priest. But what would you have? Johnny had slipped his cable; no more Johnny in the market; and the administration racket clean played out. Next thing, word gave to Randall that the priest was praying upon Johnny's grave. Papa was pretty full, and got a club, and lit out straight for the place, and there was Galoshes on his knees, and a lot of natives looking on. You wouldn't think Papa cared that much about anything, unless it was liquor; but he and the priest stuck to it two hours, slanging each other in native, and every time Galoshes tried to

COMMENTARY
Case tells Wiltshire that when Johnny Adams was dying, he and another European, Buncombe, sent for the priest, but Captain Randall refused to let him into the house. Later when Adams had been buried, the priest tried to pray at his grave, but Randall prevented him physically.

Kanaka pastors: local people who had been trained to be Protestant ministers
bigoted: so prejudiced against all other beliefs that he would not tolerate them at all
slipped his cable: died
the administration racket clean played out: it is not clear *exactly* what Stevenson means here, but his general meaning must be 'died'

kneel down Papa went for him with the club. There never were such larks in Falesá. The end of it was that Captain Randall knocked over with some kind of a fit or stroke, and the priest got in his goods after all. But he was the angriest priest you ever heard of, and complained to the chiefs about the outrage, as he called it. There was no account, for our chiefs are Protestant here; and, anyway, he had been making trouble about the drum for morning school, and they were glad to give him a wipe. Now he swears old Randall gave Adams poison or something, and when the two meet they grin at each other like baboons.'

He told this story as natural as could be, and like a man that enjoyed the fun; though now I come to think of it after so long, it seems rather a sickening yarn. However, Case never set up to be soft, only to be square and hearty, and a man all round; and, to tell the truth, he puzzled me entirely.

I went home and asked Uma if she were a Popey, which I made out to be the native word for Catholics.

'*E le ai!*' says she. She always used the native when she meant 'no' more than usually strong, and, indeed, there's more of it. 'No good Popey,' she added.

Then I asked her about Adams and the priest, and she told me much the same yarn in her own way. So that I was left not much farther on, but inclined, upon the whole, to think the bottom of the matter was the row about the ►► sacrament, and the poisoning only talk.

> **REWIND:** …the poisoning only talk.
> Wiltshire has gone to see Case to ask him about the priest. Case has told him how Captain Randall and Father Galuchet fell out. When Johnny Adams was dying, he asked for a priest but when Galuchet arrived, Randall refused to let him into the house because he hated the Catholic religion. When Adams had died, Randall found the priest praying at his grave. He attacked him and stopped his prayers by physical force until he himself suffered some kind of attack. After this, the priest continued his prayers. Case has told Wiltshire that this may be why Galuchet is spreading stories about Adams being poisoned.

---

the row about the sacrament: the priest had wanted to perform the sacrament of the last rites, the religious ritual for Catholics at the point of death – since he had been prevented from doing that by Randall, he had said his prayers at the dead man's grave instead

COMMENTARY
The end of Case's story is that Captain Randall got so excited by his attack on the priest that he had a stroke. Wiltshire decides that it is this event that has made the priest tell the story about Case poisoning Johnny Adams.

The next day was a Sunday, when there was no business to be looked for. Uma asked me in the morning if I was going to 'pray'; I told her she bet not, and she stopped home herself, with no more words. I thought this seemed unlike a native, and a native woman, and a woman that had new clothes to show off; however, it suited me to the ground, and I made the less of it. The queer thing was that I came next door to going to church after all, a thing I'm a little likely to forget. I had turned out for a stroll, and heard the hymn tune up. You know how it is. If you hear folk singing, it seems to draw you; and pretty soon I found myself alongside the church. It was a little, long, low place, coral built, rounded off at both ends like a whale-boat, a big native roof on the top of it, windows without sashes and doorways without doors. I stuck my head into one of the windows, and the sight was so new to me – for things went quite different in the islands I was acquainted with – that I stayed and looked on. The congregation sat on the floor mats, the women on one side, the men on the other, all rigged out to kill – the women with dresses and trade hats, the men in white jackets and shirts. The hymn was over; the pastor, a big buck Kanaka, was in the pulpit, preaching for his life; and by the way he wagged his hand, and worked his voice, and made his points, and seemed to argue with the folk, I made out he was a gun at the business. Well, he looked up suddenly and caught my eye, and I give you my word he staggered in the pulpit; his eyes bulged out of his head, his hand rose and pointed at me like as if against his will, and the sermon stopped right there.

COMMENTARY
The next day, Sunday, Wiltshire goes for a walk and finds himself near the local Protestant church, where the islander in charge is preaching. As soon as he sees Wiltshire, he stops in mid-sentence.

whale-boat: a long narrow boat pointed at both ends
without sashes: with no glass in them
trade hats: hats bought from one of the trade shops

a big buck Kanaka: a racially-offensive description of a large male islander. (Remember that Stevenson is putting the words into Wiltshire's mouth, in order to describe a typical European of his time. Stevenson himself was well-known as unprejudiced – indeed, he defended the rights of Polynesians against imperialism.)

It isn't a fine thing to say for yourself, but I ran away; and, if the same kind of a shock was given me, I should run away again to-morrow. To see that palavering Kanaka struck all of a heap at the mere sight of me gave me a feeling as if the bottom had dropped out of the world. I went right home, and stayed there, and said nothing. You might think I would tell Uma, but that was against my system. You might have thought I would have gone over and consulted Case; but the truth was I was ashamed to speak of such a thing, I thought everyone would blurt out laughing in my face. So I held my tongue, and thought all the more; and the more I thought, the less I liked the business.

By Monday night I got it clearly in my head I must be tabooed. A new store to stand open two days in a village and not a man or woman come to see the trade, was past believing.

'Uma,' said I, 'I think I'm tabooed.'

'I think so,' said she.

I thought a while whether I should ask her more, but it's a bad idea to set natives up with any notion of consulting them, so I went to Case. It was dark, and he was sitting alone, as he did mostly, smoking on the stairs.

'Case,' said I, 'here's a queer thing. I'm tabooed.'

'Oh, fudge!' says he; ''tain't the practice in these islands.'

'That may be, or it mayn't,' said I. 'It's the practice where I was before. You can bet I know what it's like; and I tell you for a fact, I'm tabooed.'

'Well,' said he, 'what have you been doing?'

'That's what I want to find out,' said I.

'Oh, you can't be,' said he; 'it ain't possible. However, I'll tell you what I'll do. Just to put your mind at rest, I'll go round and find out for sure. Just you waltz in and talk to Papa.'

'Thank you,' I said, 'I'd rather stay right out here on the veranda. Your house is so close.'

'I'll call Papa out here, then,' says he.

'My dear fellow,' I says, 'I wish you wouldn't. The fact is, I don't take to Mr Randall.'

---

palavering: speaking fast and in a language that Wiltshire could not understand

tabooed: Stevenson had read about a situation just like this and it was one of the things that inspired this story

COMMENTARY

Wiltshire is so frightened by the pastor pointing at him that he runs away. It strengthens his belief that he is under a local taboo. He discusses it with Case, who goes to see what he can find out.

Case laughed, took a lantern from the store, and set out into the village. He was gone perhaps a quarter of an hour, and he looked mighty serious when he came back.

'Well,' said he, clapping down the lantern on the veranda steps, 'I would never have believed it. I don't know where the impudence of these Kanakas 'll go next; they seem to have lost all idea of respect for whites. What we want is a man-of-war – a German, if we could – they know how to manage Kanakas.'

'I *am* tabooed, then?' I cried.

'Something of the sort,' said he. 'It's the worst thing of the kind I've heard yet. But I'll stand by you, Wiltshire, man to man. You come round here to-morrow about nine, and we'll have it out with the chiefs. They're afraid of me, or they used to be; but their heads are so big now, I don't know what to think. Understand me, Wiltshire; I don't count this your quarrel,' he went on, with a great deal of resolution, 'I count it all of our quarrel, I count it the White Man's Quarrel, and I'll stand to it through thick and thin, and there's my hand on it.'

'Have you found out what's the reason?' I asked.

'Not yet,' said Case. 'But we'll fire them down to-morrow.'

Altogether I was pretty well pleased with his attitude, and almost more the next day, when we met to go before the chiefs, to see him so stern and resolved.

FAST FORWARD: to page 134

The chiefs awaited us in one of their big oval houses, which was marked out to us from a long way off by the crowd about the eaves, a hundred strong if there was one – men, women, and children. Many of the men were on their way to work and wore green wreaths, and it put me in thoughts of the first of May at home. This crowd opened and buzzed about the pair of us as we went in, with a sudden angry animation. Five chiefs were there; four mighty, stately

COMMENTARY
Case returns and agrees that there is something strange going on. The next day he takes Wiltshire to meet the chiefs and the local people.

a man-of-war: a warship – he says 'a German, if we could' because Germany was the most powerful foreign power in the South Pacific at this time

the first of May at home: it was traditional in England for country people to assemble on the village green in their best clothes on Mayday and dance around the maypole

men, the fifth old and puckered. They sat on mats in their white kilts and
jackets; they had fans in their hands, like fine ladies; and two of the younger
ones wore Catholic medals, which gave me matter of reflection. Our place was
set, and the mats laid for us over against these grandees, on the near side of
the house; the midst was empty; the crowd, close at our backs, murmured and
craned and jostled to look on, and the shadows of them tossed in front of us
on the clean pebbles of the floor. I was just a hair put out by the excitement of
the commons, but the quiet, civil appearance of the chiefs reassured me, all the
more when their spokesman began and made a long speech in a low tone of
voice, sometimes waving his hand toward Case, sometimes towards me, and
sometimes knocking with his knuckles on the mat. One thing was clear: there
was no sign of anger in the chiefs.

'What's he been saying?' I asked, when he had done.
'Oh, just that they're glad to see you, and they understand by me you wish
to make some kind of complaint, and you're to fire away, and they'll do the
square thing.'

puckered: wrinkled

COMMENTARY
Wiltshire is slightly worried by the
excitement of the crowd, but the
behaviour of the chiefs reassures him.
He cannot, of course, understand what
is said. He asks Case what is going on
and is told that he has been greeted by
the chiefs.

'It took a precious long time to say that,' said I.

'Oh, the rest was sawder and *bonjour* and that,' said Case. 'You know what Kanakas are.'

'Well, they don't get much *bonjour* out of me,' said I. 'You tell them who I am. I'm a white man, and a British subject, and no end of a big chief at home; and I've come here to do them good, and bring them civilization; and no sooner have I got my trade sorted out than they go and taboo me, and no one dare come near my place! Tell them I don't mean to fly in the face of anything legal; and if what they want's a present, I'll do what's fair. I don't blame any man looking out for himself, tell them, for that's human nature; but if they think they're going to come any of their native ideas over me, they'll find themselves mistaken. And tell them plain that I demand the reason of this treatment as a white man and a British subject.'

That was my speech. I knew how to deal with Kanakas: give them plain sense and fair dealing, and – I'll do then that much justice – they knuckle under every time. They haven't any real government or any real law, that's what you've got to knock into their heads; and even if they had, it would be a good joke if it was to apply to a white man. It would be a strange thing if we came all this way and couldn't do what we pleased. The mere idea has always put my monkey up, and I rapped my speech out pretty big. Then Case translated it – or made believe to, rather – and the first chief replied, and then a second, and a third, all in the same style – easy and genteel, but solemn underneath. Once a question was put to Case, and he answered it, and all hands (both chiefs and commons) laughed out aloud, and looked at me. Last of all, the puckered old fellow and the big young chief that spoke first started in to put Case through a kind of catechism. Sometimes I made out that Case was trying to fence, and they stuck to him like hounds, and the sweat ran down his face, which was no very pleasant sight to me, and at some of his answers the crowd moaned and murmured, which was a worse hearing. It's a cruel shame I knew no native, for (as I now believe) they were asking Case about my marriage, and he must have had a tough job of it to clear his feet. But leave Case alone; he had the brains to run a parliament.

COMMENTARY

Wiltshire speaks to the chiefs through Case. He tells them that he will be fair with them if they are fair with them. The chiefs then question Case at length.

sawder: blarney, flattery

put my monkey up: angered me

catechism: a set of questions and answers – he is referring to the questions and answers that people used to learn by heart before they were admitted to full membership of a church

'Well, is that all?' I asked, when a pause came.

'Come along,' says he, mopping his face; 'I'll tell you outside.'

'Do you mean they won't take the taboo off?' I cried.

'It's something queer,' said he. 'I'll tell you outside. Better come away.'

'I won't take it at their hands,' cried I. 'I ain't that kind of a man. You don't find me turn my back on a parcel of Kanakas.'

'You'd better,' said Case.

He looked at me with a signal in his eye; and the five chiefs looked at me civilly enough, but kind of pointed; and the people looked at me and craned and jostled. I remembered the folks that watched my house, and how the pastor had jumped in his pulpit at the bare sight of me; and the whole business seemed so out of the way that I rose and followed Case. The crowd opened again to let us through, but wider than before, the children on the skirts running and singing out, and as we two white men walked away they all stood and watched us.

'And now,' said I, 'what is all this about?'

'The truth is I can't rightly make it out myself. They have a down on you,' says Case.

'Taboo a man because they have a down on him!' I cried. 'I never heard the like.'

'It's worse than that, you see,' said Case. 'You ain't tabooed – I told you that couldn't be. The people won't go near you, Wiltshire, and there's where it is.'

REWIND: …watched us.

Wiltshire and Case have been received by five chiefs and a large number of islanders. Their spokesman has greeted the two men and then Wiltshire has addressed the assembly, telling them that he wants to be treated fairly. Case has acted as interpreter. Then the chiefs have closely questioned Case, before speaking to him at some length and then telling the two men to leave. They are now outside the meeting house.

COMMENTARY

They go outside and Case tells Wiltshire what the chiefs have said. He isn't under a taboo, but the people do not want to have anything to do with him.

'They won't go near me? What do you mean by that? Why won't they go near me?' I cried.

Case hesitated. 'Seems they're frightened,' says he, in a low voice.

I stopped dead short. 'Frightened?' I repeated. 'Are you gone crazy, Case? What are they frightened of?'

'I wish I could make out,' Case answered, shaking his head. 'Appears like one of their tomfool superstitions. That's what I don't cotton to,' he said. 'It's like the business about Vigours.'

'I'd like to know what you mean by that, and I'll trouble you to tell me,' says I.

'Well, you know, Vigours lit out and left all standing,' said he. 'It was some superstition business – I never got the hang of it; but it began to look bad before the end.'

'I've heard a different story about that,' said I, 'and I had better tell you so. I heard he ran away because of you.'

'Oh! well, I suppose he was ashamed to tell the truth,' says Case; 'I guess he thought it silly. And it's a fact that I packed him off. "What would you do, old man?" says he. "Get," says I, "and not think twice about it." I was the gladdest kind of man to see him clear away. It ain't my notion to turn my back on a mate when he's in a tight place, but there was that much trouble in the village that I couldn't see where it might likely end. I was a fool to be so much about with Vigours. They cast it up to me to-day. Didn't you hear Maea – that's the young chief, the big one – ripping out about "Vika"? That was him they were after. They don't seem to forget it, somehow.'

'This is all very well,' said I, 'but don't tell me what's wrong; it don't tell me what they're afraid of – what their idea is.'

'Well, I wish I knew,' said Case. 'I can't say fairer than that.'

'You might have asked, I think,' says I.

'And so I did,' says he. 'But you must have seen for yourself, unless you're blind, that the asking got the other way. I'll go as far as I dare for another white man; but when I find I'm in the scrape myself, I think first of my own

COMMENTARY
Wiltshire demands an explanation but all Case will tell him is that the islanders are afraid of him. Case says that it is the same as what happened to Vigours.

bacon. The loss of me is I'm too good-natured. And I'll take the freedom of telling you you show a queer kind of gratitude to a man who's got into all this mess along of your affairs.'

'There's a thing I'm thinking of,' said I. 'You were a fool to be so much about with Vigours. One comfort, you haven't been much about with me. I notice you've never been inside my house. Own up now; you had word of this before?'

'It's a fact I haven't been,' said he. 'It was an oversight, and I'm sorry for it, Wiltshire. But about coming now. I'll be quite plain.

'You mean you won't?' I asked.

'Awfully sorry, old man, but that's the size of it,' says Case.

'In short, you're afraid?' says I.

'In short, I'm afraid,' says he.

'And I'm still to be tabooed for nothing?' I asked.

'I tell you you're not tabooed,' said he. 'The Kanakas won't go near you, that's all. And who's to make 'em? We traders have a lot of gall, I must say; we make these poor Kanakas take back their laws, and take up their taboos, and that, whenever it happens to suit us. But you don't mean to say you expect a law obliging people to deal in your store whether they want to or not? You don't mean to tell me you've got the gall for that? And if you had, it would be a queer thing to propose to me. I would just like to point out to you, Wiltshire, that I'm a trader myself.'

'I don't think I would talk of gall if I was you,' said I. 'Here's about what it comes to, as well as I can make out: None of the people are to trade with me, and they're all to trade with you. You're to have the copra, and I'm to go to the devil and shake myself. And I don't know any native, and you're the only man here worth mention that speaks English, and you have the gall to up and hint to me my life's in danger, and all you've got to tell me is you don't know why!'

'Well, it *is* all I have to tell you,' said he. 'I don't know – I wish I did.'

'And so you turn your back and leave me to myself! Is that the position?' says I.

---

gall: cheek, nerve

COMMENTARY
Wiltshire asks Case why he is avoiding him. He replies that he is afraid to be seen with him because of the islanders' fear of him. This makes Wiltshire angry.

'If you like to put it nasty,' says he. 'I don't put it so. I say merely, "I'm going to keep clear of you; or, if I don't, I'll get in danger for myself."'

'Well,' says I, 'you're a nice kind of a white man!'

'Oh, I understand; you're riled,' said he. 'I would be myself. I can make excuses.'

'All right,' I said, 'go and make excuses somewhere else. Here's my way, there's yours!'

With that we parted, and I went straight home, in a hot temper, and found Uma trying on a lot of trade goods like a baby.

'Here,' I said, 'you quit that foolery! Here's a pretty mess to have made, as if I wasn't bothered enough anyway! And I thought I told you to get dinner!'

And then I believe I gave her the rough side of my tongue, as she deserved. She stood up at once, like a sentry to his officer; for I must say she was always well brought up, and had a great respect for whites.

'And now,' says I, 'you belong round here, you're bound to understand that. What am I tabooed for, anyway? Or, if I ain't tabooed, what makes the folks afraid of me?'

She stood and looked at me with eyes like saucers.

'You no savvy?' she gasps at last.

'No,' said I. 'How would you expect me to? We don't have any such craziness where I come from.'

'Ese no tell you?' she asked again.

(*Ese* was the name the natives had for Case; it may mean foreign, or extraordinary; or it might mean a mummy-apple; but most like it was only his own name misheard and put in a Kanaka spelling.)

'Not much,' said I.

'Damn Ese!' she cried.

You might think it funny to hear this Kanaka girl come out with a big swear. No such thing. There was no swearing in her – no, nor anger; she was beyond anger, and meant the word simple and serious. She stood there straight as she said it. I cannot justly say that I ever saw a woman look like that before

COMMENTARY

They part angrily. Wiltshire returns home and asks Uma why he is being treated in this way. She is amazed that he does not know. Has Case not told him?

mummy-apple: a tropical fruit

or after, and it struck me mum. Then she made a kind of an obeisance, but it was the proudest kind, and threw her hands out open.

'I 'shamed,' she said. 'I think you savvy. Ese he tell me you savvy, he tell me you no mind, tell me you love me too much. Taboo belong me,' she said, touching herself on the bosom, as she had done upon our wedding-night. 'Now I go 'way, taboo he go 'way too. Then you get too much copra. You like more better, I think. Tofá, alii,' says she in the native – 'Farewell, chief!'

'Hold on!' I cried. 'Don't be in such a hurry.'

She looked at me sidelong with a smile. 'You see, you get copra,' she said, the same as you might offer candies to a child.

'Uma,' said I, 'hear reason. I didn't know, and that's a fact; and Case seems to have played it pretty mean upon the pair of us. But I do know now, and I don't mind; I love you too much. You no go 'way, you no leave me, I too much sorry.'

'You no love me,' she cried, 'you talk me bad words!' And she threw herself in a corner of the floor, and began to cry.

Well, I'm no scholar, but I wasn't born yesterday, and I thought the worst of that trouble was over. However, there she lay – her back turned, her face to the wall – and shook with sobbing like a little child, so that her feet jumped with it. It's strange how it hits a man when he's in love; for there's no use mincing things; Kanaka and all, I was in love with her, or just as good. I tried to take her hand, but she would have none of that. 'Uma,' I said, 'there's no sense in carrying on like that. I want you to stop here, I want my little wifie, I tell you true.'

'No tell me true,' she sobbed.

'All right,' says I, 'I'll wait till you're through with this.' And I sat right down beside her on the floor, and set to smooth her hair with my hand. At first she wriggled away when I touched her; then she seemed to notice me no more; then her sobs grew gradually less, and presently stopped; and the next thing I knew, she raised her face to mine.

'You tell me true? You like me stop?' she asked.

mum: speechless
too much: pidgin for 'a lot'
   or 'very'

COMMENTARY
Uma thought Wiltshire knew. She tells him that the taboo is on her. She says that she will leave him and then he will be free and happy. He tells her that he never wants her to leave him.

'Uma,' I said, 'I would rather have you than all the copra in the South Seas,' which was a very big expression, and the strangest thing was that I meant it.

She threw her arms about me, sprang close up, and pressed her face to mine in the island way of kissing, so that I was all wetted with her tears, and my heart went out to her wholly. I never had anything so near me as this little brown bit of a girl. Many things went together, and all helped to turn my head. She was pretty enough to eat; it seemed she was my only friend in that queer place; I was ashamed that I had spoken rough to her: and she was a woman, and my wife, and a kind of a baby besides that I was sorry for; and the salt of her tears was in my mouth. And I forgot Case and the natives; and I forgot that I knew nothing of the story, or only remembered it to banish the remembrance; and I forgot that I was to get no copra, and so could make no livelihood; and I forgot my employers, and the strange kind of service I was doing them, when I preferred my fancy to their business; and I forgot even that Uma was no true wife of mine, but just a maid beguiled, and that in a pretty shabby style. But that is to look too far on. I will come back to that part of it next.

It was late before we thought of getting dinner. The stove was out, and gone stone-cold; but we fired up after a while, and cooked each a dish, helping and hindering each other, and making a play of it like children. I was so greedy of her nearness that I sat down to dinner with my lass upon my knee, made sure of her with one hand, and ate with the other. Ay, and more than that. She was the worst cook I suppose God made; the things she set her hand to, it would have sickened an honest horse to eat of; yet I made my meal that day on Uma's cookery, and can never call to mind to have been better pleased.

I didn't pretend to myself, and I didn't pretend to her. I saw I was clean gone; and if she was to make a fool of me, she must. And I suppose it was this that set her talking, for now she made sure that we were friends. A lot she told me, sitting in my lap and eating my dish, as I ate hers, from foolery – a lot about herself and her mother and Case, all of which would be very tedious,

beguiled: deceived

COMMENTARY
Wiltshire realises that he has spoken the truth: Uma means more to him than anything in the world.

and fill sheets if I set it down in Beach de Mar, but which I must give a hint of in plain English, and one thing about myself, which had a very big effect on my concerns, as you are soon to hear.

It seems she was born in one of the Line Islands; had been only two or three years in these parts, where she had come with a white man, who was married to her mother and then died; and only the one year in Falesá. Before that they had been a good deal on the move, trekking about after the white man, who was one of those rolling stones that keep going round after a soft job. They talk about looking for gold at the end of a rainbow; but if a man wants an employment that'll last him till he dies, let him start out on the soft-job hunt. There's meat and drink in it too, and beer and skittles, for you never hear of them starving, and rarely see them sober; and as for steady sport, cock-fighting isn't in the same county with it. Anyway, this beachcomber carried the woman and her daughter all over the shop, but mostly to out-of-the-way islands, where there were no police, and he thought, perhaps, the soft job hung out. I've my own view of this old party; but I was just as glad he had kept Uma clear of Apia and Papeete and these flash towns. At last he struck Fale-alii on this island, got some trade – the Lord knows how! – muddled it all away in the usual style, and died worth next to nothing, bar a bit of land at Falesá that he had got for a bad debt, which was what put it in the minds of the mother and daughter to come there and live. It seems Case encouraged them all he could, and helped to get their house built. He was very kind those days, and gave Uma trade, and there is no doubt he had his eye on her from the beginning. However, they had scarce settled, when up turned a young man, a native, and wanted to marry her. He was a small chief, and had some fine mats and old songs in his family, and was 'very pretty', Uma said; and, altogether, it was an extraordinary match for a penniless girl and an out-islander.

At the first word of this I got downright sick with jealousy.

'And you mean to say you would have married him?' I cried.

'Ioe, yes,' said she. 'I like too much!'

'Well!' I said. 'And suppose I had come round after?'

COMMENTARY

Uma tells him about her life. Her mother was married to a white man who wandered round the islands looking for an easy life. He died when Uma was young and she and her mother settled on Falesá. They had some land and Case helped them build their house. He was clearly interested in Uma. Then a young island chief began to court Uma.

Beach de Mar: pidgin English
Line Islands: a group of islands near the Equator, north of Tahiti
Apia: capital of Western Samoa

Papeete: capital of Tahiti
Fale-alii: a village on the island
out-islander: person from outside the island, foreigner

'I like you more better now,' said she. 'But suppose I marry Ioane, I one good wife. I no common Kanaka. Good girl!' says she.

Well, I had to be pleased with that; but I promise you I didn't care about the business one little bit. And I liked the end of that yarn no better than the beginning. For it seems this proposal of marriage was the start of all the trouble. It seems, before that, Uma and her mother had been looked down upon, of course, for kinless folk and out-islanders, but nothing to hurt; and, even when Ioane came forward, there was less trouble at first than might have been looked for. And then, all of a sudden, about six months before my coming, Ioane backed out and left that part of the island, and from that day to this Uma and her mother had found themselves alone. None called at their house – none spoke to them on the roads. If they went to church, the other women drew their mats away and left them in a clear place by themselves. It was a regular excommunication, like what you read of in the Middle Ages; and the cause or sense of it beyond guessing. It was some *talo pepelo*, Uma said, some lie, some calumny; and all she knew of it was that the girls who had been jealous of her luck with Ioane used to twit her with his desertion, and cry out, when they met her alone in the woods, that she would never be married. 'They tell me no man he marry me. He too much 'fraid,' said she.

The only soul that came about them after this desertion was Master Case. Even he was chary of showing himself, and turned up mostly by night; and pretty soon he began to table his cards and make up to Uma. I was still sore about Ioane, and when Case turned up in the same line of business I cut up downright rough.

'Well,' I said, sneering, 'and I suppose you thought Case "very pretty" and "liked too much"?'

'Now you talk silly,' said she. 'White man, he come here, I marry him all-e-same Kanaka; very well! then, he marry all-e-same white woman. Suppose he no marry, he go 'way, woman he stop. All-e-same thief, empty hand, Tonga-heart – no can love! Now you come marry me. You big heart – you no 'shamed island-girl. That thing I love you far too much. I proud.'

COMMENTARY

Suddenly the young man, Ioane, left the island and Uma and her mother found themselves tabooed. Only Case visited them, secretly, and made up to Uma, but she wouldn't have anything to do with him.

kinless: with no family

excommunication: in the past those who offended the authorities in the church could be excommunicated. This meant that they were no longer members of the church. Also, no one had to keep any promises to them or repay debts.

I don't know that ever I felt sicker all the days of my life. I laid down my fork, and put away 'the island-girl'; I didn't seem somehow to have any use for either, and I went and walked up and down in the house, and Uma followed me with her eyes, for she was troubled, and small wonder! But troubled was no word for it with me. I so wanted, and so feared, to make a clean breast of the sweep that I had been.

And just then there came a sound of singing out of the sea; it sprang up suddenly clear and near, as the boat turned the headland, and Uma, running to the window, cried out it was 'Misi' come upon his rounds.

I thought it was a strange thing I should be glad to have a missionary; but, if it was strange, it was still true.

'Uma,' said I, 'you stop here in this room, and don't budge a foot out of it till I come back.'

make a clean breast of the sweep that I had been:
own up to what a bad person I had been

COMMENTARY
Suddenly they hear the sound of islanders singing as the mission boat approaches.

3 The Missionary

Look out for…
- **Tarleton, the missionary: what is his job on the island? How does he help Wiltshire? How has he become involved with Case and his friends?**
- **important information about what happened before the story begins – especially the fate of traders before Wiltshire.**

As I came out on the veranda, the mission-boat was shooting for the mouth of the river. She was a long whale-boat painted white; a bit of an awning astern; a native pastor crouched on the wedge of poop, steering; some four-and-twenty paddles flashing and dipping, true to the boat-song; and the missionary under the awning, in his white clothes, reading in a book; and set him up! It was pretty to see and hear; there's no smarter sight in the islands than a missionary-boat with a good crew and a good pipe to them; and I considered it for half a minute, with a bit of envy perhaps, and then strolled down towards the river.

From the opposite side there was another man aiming for the same place, but he ran and got there first. It was Case; doubtless his idea was to keep me apart from the missionary, who might serve me as interpreter; but my mind was upon other things. I was thinking how he had jockeyed us about the marriage, and tried his hand on Uma before; and at the sight of him rage flew into my nostrils.

'Get out of that, you low, swindling thief!' I cried.

COMMENTARY
Wiltshire watches the mission boat approaching. Suddenly he sees that Case is also going towards the landing-place, to speak to the missionary before he does. Wiltshire is furious.

the wedge of poop: the platform at the rear of the boat
true to the boat-song: the men paddling the boat were singing a work-song and they kept time to the rhythm of it

'What's that you say?' says he.

I gave him the word again, and rammed it down with a good oath. 'And if ever I catch you within six fathoms of my house,' I cried, 'I'll clap a bullet in your measly carcass.'

'You must do as you like about your house,' said he, 'where I told you I have no thought of going; but this is a public place.'

'It's a place where I have private business,' said I. 'I have no idea of a hound like you eavesdropping, and I give you notice to clear out.'

'I don't take it, though,' says Case.

'I'll show you, then,' said I.

'We'll have to see about that,' said he.

He was quick with his hands, but he had neither the height nor the weight, being a flimsy creature alongside a man like me, and, besides, I was blazing to that height of wrath that I could have bit into a chisel. I gave him first the one and then the other, so that I could hear his head rattle and crack, and he went down straight.

'Have you had enough?' cries I. But he only looked up white and blank, and the blood spread upon his face like wine upon a napkin. 'Have you had enough?' I cried again. 'Speak up, and don't lie malingering there, or I'll take my feet to you.'

He sat up at that, and held his head – by the look of him you could see it was spinning – and the blood poured on his pyjamas.

'I've had enough for this time,' says he, and he got up staggering, and sent off by the way that he had come.

The boat was close in; I saw the missionary had laid his book to one side, and I smiled to myself. 'He'll know I'm a man, anyway,' thinks I.

This was the first time, in all my years in the Pacific, I had ever exchanged two words with any missionary, let alone asked one for a favour. I didn't like the lot, no trader does; they look down upon us, and make no concealment; and, besides, they're partly Kanakaized, and suck up with natives instead of with other white men like themselves. I had on a rig of clean, striped pyjamas –

six fathoms: about 10 metres
blazing to that height of wrath: so angry
malingering: pretending to be ill
Kanakaized: 'gone native' – having taken
   up the lifestyle of the islanders

COMMENTARY

He tells Case to clear off but he refuses. Wiltshire attacks him and knocks him to the ground. Case turns and staggers off. Wiltshire prepares to meet the missionary.

for, of course, I had dressed decent to go before the chiefs; but when I saw the missionary step out of this boat in the regular uniform, white duck clothes, pith helmet, white shirt and tie, and yellow boots to his feet, I could have bunged stones at him. As he came nearer, queering me pretty curious (because of the fight, I suppose), I saw he looked mortal sick, for the truth was he had a fever on, and had just had a chill in the boat.

'Mr Tarleton, I believe?' says I, for I had got his name.

'And you, I suppose, are the new trader?' says he.

'I want to tell you first that I don't hold with missions,' I went on, 'and that I think you and the likes of you do a sight of harm, filling up the natives with old wives' tales and bumptiousness.'

'You are perfectly entitled to your opinions,' says he, looking a bit ugly, 'but I have no call to hear them.'

'It so happens that you've got to hear them,' I said. 'I'm no missionary, nor missionary lover; I'm no Kanaka, nor favourer of Kanakas – I'm just a trader; I'm just a common, low Goddamned white man and British subject, the sort you would like to wipe your boots on. I hope that's plain!'

COMMENTARY
Wiltshire greets Tarleton, the missionary – but in an aggressive way.

bumptiousness: big-headedness
I have no call: I do not have to

'Yes, my man,' said he. 'It's more plain than creditable. When you are sober, you'll be sorry for this.'

He tried to pass on, but I stopped him with my hand. The Kanakas were beginning to growl. Guess they didn't like my tone, for I spoke to that man as free as I would to you.

'Now, you can't say I've deceived you,' said I, 'and I can go on. I want a service – I want two services, in fact; and, if you care to give me them, I'll perhaps take more stock in what you call your Christianity.'

He was silent for a moment. Then he smiled. 'You are rather a strange sort of man,' says he.

'I'm the sort of man God made me,' says I. 'I don't set up to be a gentleman,' I said.

'I am not quite so sure,' said he. 'And what can I do for you, Mr—?'

'Wiltshire,' I says, 'though I'm mostly called Welsher; but Wiltshire is the way it's spelt, if the people on the beach could only get their tongues about it. And what do I want? Well, I'll tell you the first thing. I'm what you call a sinner – what I call a sweep – and I want you to help me make it up to a person I've deceived.'

He turned and spoke to his crew in the native. 'And now I am at your service,' said he, 'but only for the time my crew are dining. I must be much farther down the coast before night. I was delayed at Papa-malulu till this morning, and I have an engagement in Fale-alii to-morrow night.'

I led the way to my house in silence, and rather pleased with myself for the way I had managed the talk, for I like a man to keep his self-respect.

'I was sorry to see you fighting,' says he.

'Oh, that's part of the yarn I want to tell you,' I said. 'That's service number two. After you've heard it you'll let me know whether you're sorry or not.'

We walked right in through the store, and I was surprised to find Uma had cleared away the dinner things. This was so unlike her ways that I saw she had done it out of gratitude, and liked her the better. She and Mr Tarleton called

COMMENTARY

Tarleton does not want to have anything to do with him, but Wiltshire calms down and tells him that he needs his services. Tarleton agrees to go to his house.

each other by name, and he was very civil to her seemingly. But I thought little of that; they can always find civility for a Kanaka, it's us white men they lord it over. Besides, I didn't want much Tarleton just then. I was going to do my pitch.

'Uma,' said I, 'give us your marriage certificate.' She looked put out. 'Come,' said I, 'you can trust me. Hand it up.'

She had it about her person, as usual; I believe she thought it was a pass to heaven, and if she had died without having it handy she would go to hell. I couldn't see where she put it the first time, I couldn't see now where she took it from; it seemed to jump into her hand like that Blavatsky business in the papers. But it's the same way with all island women, and I guess they're taught it when young.

'Now,' said I, with the certificate in my hand, 'I was married to this girl by Black Jack, the Negro. The certificate was wrote by Case, and it's a dandy piece of literature, I promise you. Since then I've found that there's a kind of cry in the place against this wife of mine, and so long as I keep her I cannot trade. Now, what would any man do in my place, if he was a man?' I said. 'The first thing he would do is this, I guess.' And I took and tore up the certificate and bunged the pieces on the floor.

'Aue!' cried Uma, and began to clap her hands; but I caught one of them in mine.

'And the second thing that he would do,' said I, 'if he was what I would call a man and you would call a man, Mr Tarleton, is to bring the girl right before you or any other missionary, and to up and say: "I was wrong married to this wife of mine, but I think a heap of her, and now I want to be married to her right." Fire away, Mr Tarleton. And I guess you'd better do it in native; it'll please the old lady,' I said, giving her the proper name of a man's wife upon the spot.

So we had in two of the crew for to witness, and were spliced in our own house; and the parson prayed a good bit, I must say – but not so long as some – and shook hands with the pair of us.

COMMENTARY

Wiltshire tells Tarleton of his 'marriage' to Uma and asks him to marry the two of them properly, according to Christian law. This he does.

do my pitch: make my statement
Blavatsky: Madame Blavatsky (1831–91) was a spiritualist and claimed supernatural powers
Aue!: Alas!

'Mr Wiltshire,' he says, when he had made out the lines and packed off the witnesses, 'I have to thank you for a very lively pleasure. I have rarely performed the marriage ceremony with more grateful emotions.'

That was what you would call talking. He was going on, besides, with more of it, and I was ready for as much taffy as he had in stock, for I felt good. But Uma had been taken up with something half through the marriage, and cut straight in.

'How your hand he get hurt?' she asked.

'You ask Case's head, old lady,' says I.

She jumped with joy, and sang out.

'You haven't made much of a Christian of this one,' says I to Mr Tarleton.

'We didn't think her one of our worst,' says he, 'when she was at Fale-alii; and if Uma bears malice I shall be tempted to fancy she has good cause.'

'Well, there we are at service number two,' said I. 'I want to tell you our yarn, and see if you can let a little daylight in.'

'Is it long?' he asked.

'Yes,' I cried; 'it's a goodish bit of a yarn!'

'Well, I'll give you all the time I can spare,' says he, looking at his watch. 'But I must tell you fairly, I haven't eaten since five this morning, and, unless you can let me have something, I am not likely to eat again before seven or eight to-night.'

---

made out the lines: completed the
   marriage certificate
taffy: chat, blarney
bears malice: holds it against
   someone

COMMENTARY

Tarleton is very pleased to do this. Wiltshire says that he wants to ask another favour – to help him understand what is going on on the island. Tarleton says he will, but that he must have something to eat first.

'By God, we'll give you dinner!' I cried.

I was a little caught up at my swearing, just when all was going straight; and so was the missionary, I suppose, but he made believe to look out of the window, and thanked us.

So we ran him up a bit of a meal. I was bound to let the old lady have a hand in it, to show off, so I deputized her to brew the tea. I don't think I ever met such tea as she turned out. But that was not the worst, for she got round with the salt-box, which she considered an extra European touch, and turned my stew into sea-water. Altogether, Mr Tarleton had a devil of a dinner of it; but he had plenty of entertainment by the way, for all the while that we were cooking, and afterward, when he was making believe to eat, I kept posting him up on Master Case and the beach of Falesá, and he putting questions that showed he was following close.

'Well,' said he at last, 'I am afraid you have a dangerous enemy. This man Case is very clever and seems really wicked. I must tell you I have had my eye on him for nearly a year, and have rather had the worst of our encounters.

FAST FORWARD: to page 153

About the time when the last representative of your firm ran so suddenly away, I had a letter from Namu, the native pastor, begging me to come to Falesá at my earliest convenience, as his flock were all "adopting Catholic practices". I had great confidence in Namu; I fear it only shows how easily we are deceived. No one could hear him preach and not be persuaded he was a man of extraordinary parts. All our islanders easily acquire a kind of eloquence, and can roll out and illustrate, with a great deal of vigour and fancy, second-hand sermons; but Namu's sermons are his own, and I cannot deny that I have found them means of grace. Moreover, he has a keen curiosity in secular things, does not fear work, is clever at carpentering, and has made himself so much respected among the neighbouring pastors that we call him, in a jest

COMMENTARY

They give him dinner. While he eats, Wiltshire tells him all he knows about the beach of Falesá. Tarleton reveals that he already knows quite a lot about Case and says that he is a dangerous enemy. He tells the story of Namu, one of the local ministers, himself a talented man.

deputized her: gave her the job (in my place)

a man of extraordinary parts: a very talented man

means of grace: good for my soul

secular: everyday, not connected with religion and church

which is half serious, the Bishop of the East. In short, I was proud of the man; all the more puzzled by his letter, and took an occasion to come this way. The morning before my arrival, Vigours had been sent on board the *Lion*, and Namu was perfectly at his ease, apparently ashamed of his letter, and quite unwilling to explain it. This, of course, I could not allow, and he ended up by confessing that he had been much concerned to find his people using the sign of the cross, but since he had learned the explanation his mind was satisfied. For Vigours had the Evil Eye, a common thing in a country of Europe called Italy, where men were often struck dead by that kind of devil, and it appeared the sign of the cross was a charm against its power.

"'And I explain it, Misi," said Namu, "in this way: the country in Europe is a Popey country, and the devil of the Evil Eye may be a Catholic devil, or, at least, used to Catholic ways. So then I reasoned thus: if this sign of the cross were used in a Popey manner it would be sinful, but when it is used only to protect men from a devil, which is a thing harmless in itself, the sign too must be harmless. For the sign is neither good nor bad, even as a bottle is neither good nor bad. But if the bottle be full of gin, the gin is bad; and if the sign made in idolatry be bad, so is the idolatry." And, very like a native pastor, he had a text apposite about the casting out of devils.

"'And who has been telling you about the Evil Eye?" I asked.

'He admitted it was Case. Now, I am afraid you will think me very narrow, Mr Wiltshire, but I must tell you I was displeased, and cannot think a trader at all a good man to advise or have an influence upon my pastors. And, besides, there had been some flying talk in the country of old Adams and his being poisoned, to which I had paid no great heed; but it came back to me at this moment.

"'And is this Case a man of sanctified life?" I asked.

'He admitted he was not; for, though he did not drink, he was profligate with women, and had no religion.

"'Then," said I, "I think the less you have to do with him the better."

---

the *Evil Eye:* it was believed that certain people only had to look at someone or something to cast an evil spell on that person or thing

idolatry: worshipping idols or false gods

apposite: suitable

a man of sanctified life: a good (Christian) man

profligate: immoral

COMMENTARY
Tarleton discovered that Namu had fallen under the influences of Case.

'But it is not easy to have the last word with a man like Namu. He was ready in a moment with an illustration. "Misi," said he, "you have told me there were wise men, not pastors, not even holy, who knew many things useful to be taught – about trees, for instance, and beasts, and to print books, and about the stones that are burned to make knives of. Such men teach you in your college, and you learn from them, but take care not to learn to be unholy. Misi, Case is my college."

'I knew not what to say. Mr Vigours had evidently been driven out of Falesá by the machinations of Case and with something not very unlike the collusion of my pastor. I called to mind it was Namu who had reassured me about Adams and traced the rumour to the ill-will of the priest. And I saw I must inform myself more thoroughly from an impartial source. There is an old rascal of a chief here, Faiaso, whom I dare say you saw to-day at the council; he has been all his life turbulent and sly, a great fomenter of rebellions, and a thorn in the side of the mission and the island. For all that he is very shrewd, and, except in politics or about his own misdemeanours, a teller of the truth. I went to his house, told him what I had heard, and besought him to be frank. I do not think I had ever a more painful interview. Perhaps you will understand me, Mr Wiltshire, if I tell you that I am perfectly serious in these old wives' tales with which you reproached me, and as anxious to do well for these islands as you can be to please and to protect your pretty wife. And you are to remember that I thought Namu a paragon, and was proud of the man as one of the first ripe fruits of the mission. And now I was informed that he had fallen in a sort of dependence upon Case. The beginning of it was not corrupt; it began, doubtless, in fear and respect, produced by trickery and pretence; but I was shocked to find that another element had been lately added, that Namu helped himself in the store, and was believed to be deep in Case's debt. Whatever the trader said, that Namu believed with trembling. He was not alone in this; many in the village lived in a similar subjection; but Namu's case was the most influential, it was through Namu that Case had wrought most evil; and with a certain following among the chiefs, and the pastor in his

COMMENTARY
Namu defended himself against Tarleton's criticisms but Tarleton realised it was Case who had driven Vigours from the island, helped by Namu. From Faiaso, one of the chiefs, Tarleton learned that Namu was completely under Case's control and helped him in his wickedness.

the stones that are burned to make knives of: iron ore (smelted to make iron for knife blades)
machinations: cunning trickery
collusion: close help
fomenter: stirrer-up
misdemeanours: wrongdoings

pocket, the man was as good as master of the village. You know something of Vigours and Adams, but perhaps you have never heard of old Underhill, Adams's predecessor. He was a quiet, mild old fellow, I remember, and we were told he had died suddenly: white men die very suddenly in Falesá. The truth, as I now heard it, made my blood run cold. It seems he was struck with a general palsy, all of him dead but one eye, which he continually winked. Word was started that the helpless old man was now a devil, and this vile fellow Case worked upon the natives' fears, which he professed to share, and pretended he durst not go into the house alone. At last a grave was dug, and the living body buried at the far end of the village. Namu, my pastor, whom I helped to educate, offered up a prayer at the hateful scene.

'I felt myself in a very difficult position. Perhaps it was my duty to have denounced Namu and see him deposed. Perhaps I think so now, but at the time it seemed less clear. He had a great influence, it might prove greater than mine. The natives are prone to superstition; perhaps by stirring them up I might but ingrain and spread these dangerous fancies. And Namu besides, apart from this novel and accursed influence, was a good pastor, an able man, and spiritually minded. Where should I look for a better? How was I to find as good? At that moment, with Namu's failure fresh in my view, the work of my life appeared a mockery; hope was dead in me. I would rather repair such tools as I had than go abroad in quest of others that must certainly prove worse; and a scandal is, at the best, a thing to be avoided when humanly possible. Right or wrong, then, I determined on a quiet course. All that night I denounced and reasoned with the erring pastor, twitting him with his ignorance and want of faith, twitted him with his wretched attitude, making clean the outside of the cup and platter, callously helping at a murder, childishly flying in excitement about a few childish, unnecessary, and inconvenient gestures; and long before day I had him on his knees and bathed in tears of what seemed a genuine repentance. On Sunday I took the pulpit in the morning, and preached from First Kings, nineteenth, on the fire, the earthquake, and the voice, distinguishing the true spiritual power, and referring with such plainness as I dared to recent

---

palsy: paralysis

durst not: did not dare

First Kings, nineteenth: in this book of the Old Testament, the prophet Elijah discovers that God is not to be found in the forces of nature (the wind, the earthquake or the fire) but in 'the still small voice' a person hears when alone

COMMENTARY

Tarleton also learned about the horrible fate suffered by Underhill, the trader before Johnny Adams. He suffered a stroke and was entirely paralysed except for movement in one eye. Case persuaded the islanders that he was a devil and Namu helped them bury him alive. Tarleton was shattered to hear about Namu's behaviour and he spent a whole night making him repent.

events in Falesá. The effect produced was great, and it was much increased when Namu rose in his turn and confessed that he had been wanting in faith and conduct, and was convinced of sin. So far, then, all was well; but there was one unfortunate circumstance. It was nearing the time of our "May" in the island, when the native contributions to the missions are received; it fell in my duty to make a notification on the subject, and this gave my enemy his chance, by which he was not slow to profit.

'News of the whole proceedings must have been carried to Case as soon as church was over, and the same afternoon he made an occasion to meet with me in the midst of the village. He came up with so much intentness and animosity that I felt it would be damaging to avoid him.

'"So," says he, in native, "here is the holy man. He has been preaching against me, but that was not in his heart. He has been preaching upon the love of God; but that was not in his heart, it was between his teeth. Will you know what was in his heart?" cries he. "I will show it to you!" And, making a snatch at my hand, he made believe to pluck out a dollar, and held it in the air.

REWIND: ...not slow to profit.
Mr Tarleton has explained to Wiltshire just how he found out what Case was up to. He had corrupted the local island minister, Namu, with whom Tarleton worked closely. Case got Namu entirely under his influence, making him believe that Vigours was under the 'evil eye' and teaching him to use the catholic sign of the cross as a defence against this evil.

Even worse was what had happened to the trader before Johnny Adams, an old man called Underhill. He suffered a stroke and was entirely paralysed except for movement in one eye. Case persuaded the islanders that he was a devil and Namu helped them bury him alive. Namu later confessed this to Tarleton who then used his next sermon to attack Case as evil.

Unfortunately this was at the same church service as he had invited the islanders to make their annual contribution to mission expenses.

COMMENTARY

The next day, Tarleton preached a powerful sermon against Case. Unfortunately this was the same church service as he had invited the islanders to make their annual contribution to mission expenses. Afterwards Case accuses him of being only interested in money and, by his skill as a conjurer, makes it appear that Tarleton has a fistful of dollars.

May: the time of year when Protestant missions appeal to local congregations for contributions towards their running costs

animosity: hostility

in native: the local language

he made believe to pluck out a dollar: pretended to take a dollar from it

'There went that rumour through the crowd with which Polynesians receive a prodigy. As for myself, I stood amazed. The thing was a common conjuring trick, which I have seen performed at home a score of times; but how was I to convince the villagers of that? I wished I had learned legerdemain instead of Hebrew, that I might have paid the fellow out with his own coin. But there I was; I could not stand there silent, and the best I could find to say was weak.

'"I will trouble you not to lay hands on me again," said I.

'"I have no such thought," said he, "nor will I deprive you of your dollar. Here it is," he said, and flung it at my feet. I am told it lay where it fell three days.'

'I must say it was well played,' said I.

'Oh! he is clever,' said Mr Tarleton, 'and you can now see for yourself how dangerous. He was a party to the horrid death of the paralytic; he is accused of poisoning Adams; he drove Vigours out of the place by lies that might have led to murder; and there is no question but he has now made up his mind to rid himself of you. How he means to try we have no guess; only be sure, it's something new. There is no end to his readiness and invention.'

'He gives himself a sight of trouble,' says I. 'And after all, what for?'

'Why, how many tons of copra may they make in this district?' asked the missionary.

'I dare say as much as sixty tons,' says I.

'And what is the profit to the local trader?' he asked.

'You may call it three pounds,' said I.

'Then you can reckon for yourself how much he does it for,' said Mr Tarleton. 'But the more important thing is to defeat him. It is clear he spread some report against Uma, in order to isolate and have his wicked will of her. Failing of that, and seeing a new rival come upon the scene, he used her in a different way. Now, the first point to find out is about Namu. Uma, when people began to leave you and your mother alone, what did Namu do?'

'Stop away all-e-same,' says Uma.

There went…prodigy: the people made that sound which Polynesians make when they see a 'miracle'
legerdemain: conjuring

COMMENTARY
Wiltshire asks why Case behaves like this and Tarleton suggests that it is for money. He dominates the islanders and so gets all their copra.

'I fear the dog has returned to his vomit,' said Mr Tarleton. 'And now what am I to do for you? I will speak to Namu, I will warn him he is observed; it will be strange if he allow anything to go on amiss when he is put upon his guard. At the same time, this precaution may fail, and then you must turn elsewhere. You have two people at hand to whom you might apply. There is, first of all, the priest, who might protect you by the Catholic interest; they are a wretchedly small body, but they count two chiefs. And then there is old Faiaso. Ah! if it had been some years ago you would have needed no one else; but his influence is much reduced, it has gone into Maea's hands, and Maea, I fear, is one of Case's jackals. In fine, if the worst comes to the worst, you must send up or come yourself to Fale-alii, and, though I am not due at this end of the island for a month, I will just see what can be done.'

So Mr Tarleton said farewell; and half an hour later the crew were singing and the paddles flashing in the missionary-boat.

COMMENTARY
Tarleton realises that Namu is still doing as Case tells him. He says he will speak to him again and will do whatever else he can do to help them.

I fear the dog has returned to his vomit: a popular saying meaning that a person who has done something unpleasant will often return to the scene

4 Devil-work

Look out for...
- what Wiltshire discovers when he explores the island.
- what Case has been doing to gain so much power over the people of Falesá.
- the ways in which the situation begins to change.

Near a month went by without much doing. The same night of our marriage Galoshes called round, and made himself mighty civil, and got into the habit of dropping in about dark and smoking his pipe with the family. He could talk to Uma, of course, and started to teach me native and French at the same time. He was a kind old buffer, though the dirtiest you would wish to see, and he muddled me up with foreign languages worse than the Tower of Babel.

That was one employment we had, and it made me feel less lonesome; but there was no profit in the thing, for though the priest came and sat and yarned, none of his folks could be enticed into my store, and if it hadn't been for the other occupation I struck out, there wouldn't have been a pound of copra in the house. This was the idea: Faavao (Uma's mother) had a score of bearing-trees. Of course we could get no labour, being all as good as tabooed, and the two women and I turned to and made copra with our own hands. It was copra to make your mouth water when it was done – I never understood how much the natives cheated me till I had made that four hundred pounds of

---

one employment we had: one thing we had to do

COMMENTARY
Time passes slowly. Wiltshire and Uma become friendly with Galuchet, the Catholic priest. They pass the time making copra themselves from coconuts belonging to Uma's mother.

my own hand – and it weighed so light I felt inclined to take and water it myself.

When we were at the job a good many Kanakas used to put in the best of the day looking on, and once that nigger turned up. He stood back with the natives and laughed and did the big don and the funny dog, till I began to get riled.

'Here, you nigger!' says I.

'I don't address myself to you, Sah,' says the nigger. 'Only speak to gen'le'um.'

'I know,' says I, 'but it happens I was addressing myself to you Mr Black Jack. And all I want to know is just this: did you see Case's figure-head about a week ago?'

'No, Sah,' says he.

'That's all right, then,' says I; 'for I'll show you the own brother to it, only black, in the inside of about two minutes.'

And I began to walk toward him, quite slow, and my hands down; only there was trouble in my eye, if anybody took the pains to look.

'You're a low, obstropulous fellow, Sah,' says he.

'You bet!' says I.

By that time he thought I was about as near as convenient, and lit out so it would have done your heart good to see him travel. And that was all I saw of that precious gang until what I am about to tell you.

It was one of my chief employments these days to go pot-hunting in the woods, which I found (as Case had told me) very rich in game. I have spoken of the cape which shut up the village and my station from the east. A path went about the end of it, and led into the next bay. A strong wind blew here daily, and as the line of the barrier reef stopped at the end of the cape, a heavy surf ran on the shores of the bay. A little cliffy hill cut the valley in two parts, and stood close on the beach; and at high water the sea broke right on the face of it, so that all passage was stopped. Woody mountains hemmed the place all round; the barrier to the east was particularly steep and leafy, the lower parts of it, along the sea, falling in sheer black cliffs streaked with cinnabar; the upper part lumpy with the tops of the great trees. Some of the trees were

COMMENTARY

Black Jack visits them and Wiltshire sends him off with a flea in his ear. Another way Wiltshire passes the time is to go out hunting, to shoot birds and animals for food.

did the big don and the funny dog: behaved like a great man laughing at a silly little dog

figure-head: face (after Wiltshire had hit him)

obstropulous: obstreperous, causing all sorts of problems

lit out: left quickly

pot-hunting: hunting for food

cinnabar: a bright red mineral

bright green, and some red, and the sand of the beach as black as your shoes. Many birds hovered round the bay, some of them snow-white; and the flying fox (or vampire) flew there in broad daylight, gnashing its teeth.

For a long while I came as far as this shooting, and went no farther. There was no sign of any path beyond, and the cocoa-palms in the front of the foot of the valley were the last this way. For the whole 'eye' of the island, as natives call the windward end, lay desert. From Falesá round about to Papa-malulu, there was neither house, nor man, nor planted fruit-tree; and the reef being mostly absent, and the shores bluff, the sea beat direct among crags, and there was scarce a landing-place.

I should tell you that after I began to go in the woods, although no one appeared to come near my store, I found people willing enough to pass the time of day with me where nobody could see them; and as I had begun to pick up native, and most of them had a word or two of English, I began to hold little odds and ends of conversation, not to much purpose, to be sure, but they took off the worst of the feeling, for it's a miserable thing to be made a leper of.

It chanced one day, toward the end of the month, that I was sitting in this bay in the edge of the bush, looking east, with a Kanaka. I had given him a fill of tobacco, and we were making out to talk as best we could; indeed, he had more English than most.

I asked him if there was a road going eastward.

'One time one road,' said he. 'Now he dead.'

'Nobody he go there?' I asked.

'No good,' said he. 'Too much devil he stop there.'

'Oho!' says I, 'got-um plenty devil, that bush?'

'Man devil, woman devil; too much devil,' said my friend. 'Stop there all-e-time. Man he go there, no come back.'

I thought if this fellow was so well posted on devils and spoke of them so free, which is not common, I had better fish for a little information about myself and Uma.

flying fox

'You think me one devil?' I asked.

'No think devil,' said he, soothingly. 'Thing all-e-same fool.'

'Uma, she devil?' I asked again.

'No, no; no devil. Devil stop bush,' said the young man.

I was looking in front of me across the bay, and I saw the hanging front of the woods pushed suddenly open, and Case, with a gun in his hand, step forth into the sunshine on the black beach. He was got up in light pyjamas, near white, his gun sparkled, he looked mighty conspicuous; and the land-crabs scuttled from all round him to their holes.

'Hullo, my friend!' says I, 'you no talk all-e-same true. Ese he go, he come back.'

'Ese no all-e-same; Ese *Tiapolo*,' says my friend; and, with a 'Good-bye,' slunk off among the trees.

I watched Case all around the beach, where the tide was low; and let him pass me on the homeward way to Falesá. He was in deep thought, and the birds seemed to know it, trotting quite near him on the sand, or wheeling and calling in his ears. When he passed me I could see by the working of his lips that he was talking to himself, and what pleased me mightily, he had still my trade-mark on his brow. I tell you the plain truth: I had a mind to give him a gunful in his ugly mug, but I thought better of it.

All this time, and all the time I was following home, I kept repeating that native word, which I remembered by 'Polly, put the kettle on and make us all some tea,' tea-a-pollo.

'Uma,' says I, when I got back, 'what does *Tiapolo* mean?'

'Devil,' says she.

'I thought *aitu* was the word for that,' I said.

'*Aitu* 'nother kind of devil,' said she; 'stop bush, eat Kanaka. Tiapolo big chief devil, stop home; all-e-same Christian devil.'

'Well, then,' said I, 'I'm no further forward. How can Case be Tiapolo?'

'No all-e-same,' said she. 'Ese belong Tiapolo. Tiapolo too much like; Ese all-e-same his son. Suppose Ese he wish something, Tiapolo he make him.'

COMMENTARY

While they are talking, Case comes out of the bush. Wiltshire asks the islander why Case is not afraid and is told that he is 'Tiapolo'. When he asks Uma what this means, she tells him that it means 'King of the Devils'.

'That's mighty convenient for Ese,' says I. 'And what kind of things does he make for him?'

Well, out came a rigmarole of all sorts of stories, many of which (like the dollar he took from Mr Tarleton's hand) were plain enough to me, but others I could make nothing of; and the thing that most surprised the Kanakas was what surprised me least – namely, that he would go in the desert among all the *aitus*. Some of the boldest, however, had accompanied him, and had heard him speak with the dead and give them orders, and, safe in his protection, had returned unscathed. Some said he had a church there, where he worshipped Tiapolo, and Tiapolo appeared to him; others swore that there was no sorcery at all, that he performed his miracles by the power of prayer, and the church was no church, but a prison, in which he had confined a dangerous *aitu*. Namu had been in the bush with him once, and returned glorifying God for these wonders. Altogether, I began to have a glimmer of the man's position, and the means by which he had acquired it, and though I saw he was a tough nut to crack, I was noways cast down.

'Very well,' said I, 'I'll have a look at Master Case's place of worship myself, and we'll see about the glorifying.'

At this Uma fell in a terrible taking; if I went in the high bush I should never return; none could go there but by the protection of Tiapolo.

'I'll chance it on God's,' said I. 'I'm a good sort of a fellow, Uma, as fellows go, and I guess God'll con me through.'

She was silent for a while. 'I think,' said she, mighty solemn – and then, presently – 'Victoreea, he big chief?'

'You bet!' said I.

'He like you too much?' she asked again.

I told her, with a grin, I believed the old lady was rather partial to me.

'All right,' said she. 'Victoreea he big chief, like you too much. No can help you here in Falesá; no can do – too far off. Maea he be small chief – stop here. Suppose he like you – make you all right. All-e-same God and Tiapolo. God he big chief – got too much work. Tiapolo he small chief – he like too much make-see, work very hard.'

---

unscathed: unhurt
con: guide
Victoreea: Queen Victoria

COMMENTARY
From Uma he learns that in the wild area he has never visited there is a shrine for devil-worshippers. Wiltshire says he will visit this shrine. Uma is very concerned.

'I'll have to hand you over to Mr Tarleton,' said I. 'Your theology's out of its bearings, Uma.'

However, we stuck to this business all the evening, and, with the stories she told me of the desert and its dangers, she came near frightening herself into a fit.

FAST FORWARD: to page 163

I don't remember half a quarter of them, of course, for I paid little heed; but two came back to me kind of clear.

About six miles up the coast there is a sheltered cove they call *Fanga-anaana* – 'the haven full of caves'. I've seen it from the sea myself, as near as I could get my boys to venture in; and it's a little strip of yellow sand, black cliffs overhang it, full of the black mouths of caves; great trees overhang the cliffs, and dangle-down lianas; and in one place, about the middle, a big brook pours over in a cascade. Well, there was a boat going by here, with six young men of Falesá, 'all very pretty,' Uma said, which was the loss of them. It blew strong, there was a heavy head sea, and by the time they opened Fanga-anaana, and saw the white cascade and the shady beach, they were all tired and thirsty, and their water had run out. One proposed to land and get a drink, and, being reckless fellows, they were all of the same mind except the youngest. Lotu was his name; he was a very good young gentleman, and very wise; and he held out that they were crazy, telling them the place was given over to spirits and devils and the dead, and there were no living folk nearer than six miles the one way, and maybe twelve the other. But they laughed at his words, and, being five to one, pulled in, beached the boat, and landed. It was a wonderful pleasant place, Lotu said, and the water excellent. They walked round the beach, but could see nowhere any way to mount the cliffs, which made them easier in their mind; and at last they sat down to make a meal on the food they had brought with them. They were scarce set, when there came out of the mouth

lianas: jungle creepers

COMMENTARY
Uma tells Wiltshire stories about the dangers and magic of the jungle. Two stuck in his mind. In the first, Uma tells how a group of young men sailed round the coast to a deserted beach, where they landed and had a meal.

of one of the black caves six of the most beautiful ladies ever seen; they had flowers in their hair, and the most beautiful breasts, and necklaces of scarlet seeds; and began to jest with these young gentlemen, and the young gentlemen to jest back with them, all but Lotu. As for Lotu, he saw there could be no living woman in such a place, and ran, and flung himself in the bottom of the boat, covered his face, and prayed. All the time the business lasted Lotu made one clean break of prayer, and that was all he knew of it, until his friends came back, and made him sit up, and they put to sea again out of the bay, which was now quite desert, and no word of the six ladies. But, what frightened Lotu most, not one of the five remembered anything of what had passed, but they were all like drunken men, and sang and laughed in the boat, and skylarked. The wind freshened and came squally, and the sea rose extraordinary high; it was such weather as any man in the islands would have turned his back to and fled home to Falesá; but these five were like crazy folk, and cracked on all sail and drove their boat into the seas. Lotu went to the bailing; none of the others thought to help him, but sang and skylarked and carried on, and spoke singular things beyond a man's comprehension, and laughed out loud when they said them. So the rest of the day Lotu bailed for his life in the bottom of the boat, and was all drenched with sweat and cold sea-water; and none heeded him. Against all expectation, they came safe in a dreadful tempest to Papa-malulu, where the palms were singing out, and the cocoanuts flying like cannonballs about the village green; and the same night the five young gentlemen sickened, and spoke never a reasonable word until they died.

'And do you mean to tell me you can swallow a yarn like that?' I asked.

She told me the thing was well known, and with handsome young men alone it was even common; but this was the only case where five had been slain the same day and in a company by the love of the woman-devils; and it had made a great stir in the island, and she would be crazy if she doubted.

'Well, anyway,' says I, 'you needn't be frightened about me. I've no use for the women-devils. You're all the women I want, and all the devil too, old lady.'

To this she answered there were other sorts, and she had seen one with her

---

one clean break of prayer: spent all the time praying

COMMENTARY
They had just started eating when they were greeted by some beautiful girls. Lotu, one of the youths, ran back to the boat and spent his time praying. When the others came back they set off to sail home but were overtaken by a violent storm. They survived but when they got back to the village all of them except Lotu went mad and died.

own eyes. She had gone one day alone to the next bay, and, perhaps, got too near the margin of the bad place. The boughs of the high bush overshadowed her from the cant of the hill, but she herself was outside on a flat place, very stony and growing full of young mummy-apples four and five feet high. It was a dark day in the rainy season, and now there came squalls that tore off the leaves and sent them flying, and now it was all still as in a house. It was in one of these still times that a whole gang of birds and flying-foxes came pegging out of the bush like creatures frightened. Presently after she heard a rustle nearer hand, and saw, coming out of the margin of the trees, among the mummy-apples, the appearance of a lean grey old boar. It seemed to think as it came, like a person; and all of a sudden, as she looked at it coming, she was aware it was no boar, but a thing that was a man with a man's thoughts. At that she ran, and the pig after her, and as the pig ran it holla'd aloud, so that the place rang with it.

'I wish I had been there with my gun,' said I. 'I guess that pig would have holla'd so as to surprise himself.'

But she told me a gun was of no use with the like of these, which were the spirits of the dead.

Well, this kind of talk put in the evening, which was the best of it; but of course it didn't change my notion, and the next day, with my gun and a good

---

REWIND: ...spirits of the dead.
Uma has told Wiltshire two stories about the evil part of the island. In the first a group of young men sailed round the coast to a deserted beach. When they landed they were greeted by some beautiful girls. Lotu, one of the youths, ran back to the boat and spent his time praying. When the others came back they set off to sail home but were overtaken by a violent storm. They survived but when they got back to the village all of them except Lotu went mad and died. In the second story Uma has told Wiltshire that she herself went to this area and was terrified by a ghost that resembled both a pig and a grey old man.

COMMENTARY
Uma tells another story about how she had gone to this area and was terrified by a ghost that resembled both a pig and a grey old man.

and now..., and now...: at one moment..., and at the next...

knife, I set off upon a voyage of discovery. I made, as near as I could, for the place where I had seen Case come out; for if it was true he had some kind of establishment in the bush I reckoned I should find a path. The beginning of the desert was marked off by a wall, to call it so, for it was more of a long mound of stones. They say it reaches right across the island, but how they know it is another question, for I doubt if any one has made the journey in a hundred years, the natives sticking chiefly to the sea and their little colonies along the coast, and that part being mortal high and steep and full of cliffs. Up to the west side of the wall the ground has been cleared, and there are cocoa-palms and mummy-apples and guavas, and lots of sensitive. Just across, the bush begins outright; high bush at that, trees going up like the masts of ships, and ropes of liana hanging down like a ship's rigging, and nasty orchids growing in the forks like funguses. The ground where there was no underwood looked to be a heap of boulders. I saw many green pigeons which I might have shot, only I was there with a different idea. A number of butterflies flopped up and down along the ground like dead leaves; sometimes I would hear a bird calling, sometimes the wind overhead, and always the sea along the coast.

But the queerness of the place it's more difficult to tell of, unless to one who has been alone in the high bush himself. The brightest kind of a day it is always dim down there. A man can see to the end of nothing; whichever way he looks the wood shuts up, one bough folding with another like the fingers of your hand;' and whenever he listens he hears always something new – men talking, children laughing, the strokes of an axe a far way ahead of him, and sometimes a sort of a quick, stealthy scurry near at hand that makes him jump and look to his weapons. It's all very well for him to tell himself that he's alone, bar trees and birds; he can't make out to believe it; whichever way he turns the whole place seems to be alive and looking on. Don't think it was Uma's yarns that put me out; I don't value native talk a fourpenny-piece; it's a thing that's natural in the bush, and that's the end of it.

As I got near the top of the hill, for the ground of the wood goes up in this place steep as a ladder, the wind began to sound straight on, and the leaves to

sensitive plant

COMMENTARY
Wiltshire decides to return to the entrance to the jungle where he had seen Case before (see page 159). It is dark and spooky.

guavas: tropical fruit
sensitive: a plant (*mimosa pudica*) which has leaves which close up if you touch them
a fourpenny-piece: nothing at all (there was no such coin)

toss and switch open and let in the sun. This suited me better; it was the same noise all the time, and nothing to startle. Well, I had got to a place where there was an underwood of what they call wild cocoanut – mighty pretty with its scarlet fruit – when there came the sound of singing in the wind that I thought I had never heard the like of. It was all very fine to tell myself it was the branches; I knew better. It was all very fine to tell myself it was a bird; I knew never a bird that sang like that. It rose and swelled, and died away and swelled again; and now I thought it was like someone weeping, only prettier; and now I thought it was like harps; and there was one thing I made sure of, it was a sight too sweet to be wholesome in a place like that. You may laugh if you like; but I declare I called to mind the six young ladies that came, with their scarlet necklaces, out of the cave at Fanga-anaana, and wondered if they sang like that. We laugh at the natives and their superstitions; but see how many traders take them up, splendidly educated white men, that have been book-keepers (some of them) and clerks in the old country. It's my belief a superstition grows up in a place like the different kinds of weeds; and as I stood there and listened to that wailing I twittered in my shoes.

You may call me a coward to be frightened; I thought myself brave enough to go on ahead. But I went mightily carefully, with my gun cocked, spying all about me like a hunter, fully expecting to see a handsome young woman sitting somewhere in the bush, and fully determined (if I did) to try her with a charge of duck-shot. And sure enough, I had not gone far when I met with a queer thing. The wind came on the top of the wood in a strong puff, the leaves in front of me burst open, and I saw for a second something hanging in a tree. It was gone in a wink, the puff blowing by and the leaves closing. I tell you the truth: I had made up my mind to see an *aitu*; and if the thing had looked like a pig or a woman, it wouldn't have given me the same turn. The trouble was that it seemed kind of square, and the idea of a square thing that was alive and sang knocked me sick and silly. I must have stood quite a while; and I made pretty certain it was right out of the same tree that the singing came. Then I began to come to myself a bit.

COMMENTARY

Suddenly he hears a strange singing sound which comes and goes. All Uma's stories come back to him. He approaches the sound and sees that it comes from a strange square object hanging in a tree.

'Well,' says I, 'if this is really so, if this is a place where there are square things that sing, I'm gone up anyway. Let's have my fun for my money.'

But I thought I might as well take the off-chance of a prayer being any good; so I plumped on my knees and prayed out loud; and all the time I was praying the strange sounds came out of the tree, and went up and down, and changed, for all the world like music, only you could see it wasn't human – there was nothing there that you could whistle.

As soon as I had made an end in proper style, I laid down my gun, stuck my knife between my teeth, walked right up to that tree and began to climb. I tell you my heart was like ice. But presently, as I went up, I caught another glimpse of the thing, and that relieved me, for I thought it seemed like a box; and when I got right up to it I near fell out of the tree with laughing.

A box it was, sure enough, and a candle-box at that, with the brand upon the side of it; and it had banjo-strings stretched so as to sound when the wind blew. I believe they call the thing a Tyrolean harp, whatever that may mean.

'Well, Mr Case,' said I, 'you frightened me once, but I defy you to frighten me again,' I says, and slipped down the tree, and set out again to find my enemy's head office, which I guessed would not be far away.

The undergrowth was thick in this part; I couldn't see before my nose, and must burst my way through by main force and ply the knife as I went, slicing the cords of the lianas and slashing down whole trees at a blow. I call them trees for the bigness, but in truth they were just big weeds, and sappy to cut through like carrot. From all this crowd and kind of vegetation, I was just thinking to myself, the place might have once been cleared, when I came on my nose over a pile of stones, and saw in a moment it was some kind of a work of man. The Lord knows when it was made or when deserted, for this part of the island has lain undisturbed since long before the whites came. A few steps beyond I hit into the path I had been always looking for. It was narrow, but well beaten, and I saw that Case had plenty of disciples. It seems, indeed it was, a piece of fashionable boldness to venture up here with the trader, and a young man scarce reckoned himself grown till he had got his breech tattooed,

Tyrolean harp: he means an Aeolian harp – a kind of harp that has sensitive strings which sound when the wind blows across them, producing eerie and unpredictable music
breech: buttocks

COMMENTARY
He is so frightened that he kneels down and says a prayer. Then, as he gets nearer, he sees that it is an Aeolian harp (see notes). He continues on his way.

for one thing, and seen Case's devils for another. This is mighty like Kanakas: but, if you look at it another way, it's mighty like white folk too.

A bit along the path I was brought up to clear stand, and had to rub my eyes. There was a wall in front of me, the path passing it by a gap; it was tumbledown and plainly very old, but built of big stones very well laid; and there is no native alive to-day upon that island that could dream of such a piece of building! Along all the top of it was a line of queer figures, idols or scarecrows, or what not. They had carved and painted faces ugly to view, their eyes and teeth were of shell, their hair and their bright clothes blew in the wind, and some of them worked with the tugging. There are islands up west where they make these kind of figures till to-day; but if ever they were made in this island, the practice and the very recollection of it are now long forgotten. And the singular thing was that all these bogies were as fresh as toys out of a shop.

Then it came in my mind that Case had let out to me the first day that he was a good forger of island curiosities – a thing by which so many traders turn an honest penny. And with that I saw the whole business, and how this display served the man a double purpose: first of all, to season his curiosities, and then to frighten those that came to visit him.

COMMENTARY
Then he reaches an old tumbledown wall which has been decorated with strange statues, resembling local gods, but clearly made by Case.

But I should tell you (what made the thing more curious) that all the time the Tyrolean harps were hanging round me in the trees, and even while I looked, a green-and-yellow bird (that, I suppose was building) began to tear the hair off the head of one of the figures.

A little farther on I found the best curiosity of the museum. The first I saw of it was a longish mound of earth with a twist to it. Digging off the earth with my hands, I found underneath tarpaulin stretched on boards, so that this was plainly the roof of a cellar. It stood right on the top of the hill, and the entrance as on the far side, between two rocks, like the entrance to a cave. I went as far in as the bend, and, looking round the corner, saw a shining face. It was big and ugly, like a pantomime mask, and the brightness of it waxed and dwindled, and at times smoked.

'Oho!' says I, 'luminous paint!'

And I must say I rather admired the man's ingenuity. With a box of tools and a few mighty simple contrivances he had made out to have a devil of a temple. Any poor Kanaka brought up here in the dark, with the harps whining all round him, and shown that smoking face in the bottom of a hole, would make no kind of doubt but he had seen and heard enough devils for a lifetime. It's easy to find out what Kanakas think. Just go back to yourself anyway round from ten to fifteen years old, and there's an average Kanaka. There are some pious, just as there are pious boys; and most of them, like the boys again, are middling honest and yet think it rather larks to steal, and are easy scared, and rather like to be so. I remember a boy I was at school with at home who played the Case business. He didn't know anything, that boy; he couldn't do anything; he had no luminous paint and no Tyrolean harps; he just boldly said he was a sorcerer, and frightened us out of our boots, and we loved it. And then it came in my mind how the master had once flogged that boy, and the surprise we were all in to see the sorcerer catch it and hum like anybody else. Thinks I to myself: 'I must find some way of fixing it so for Master Case.' And the next moment I had my idea.

building: i.e. a nest

I went back by the path, which, when once you had found it, was quite plain and easy walking; and when I stepped out on the black sands, who should I see but Master Case himself. I cocked my gun and held it handy, and we marked up and passed without a word, each keeping the tail of his eye on the other; and no sooner had we passed than we each wheeled round like fellows drilling, and stood face to face. We had each taken the same notion in his head, you see, that the other fellow might give him the load of his gun in the stern.

'You've shot nothing,' says Case.

'I'm not on the shoot to-day,' said I.

'Well, the devil go with you for me,' says he.

'The same to you,' says I.

But we stuck just the way we were; no fear of either of us moving.

Case laughed. 'We can't stop here all day, though,' said he.

'Don't let me detain you,' says I.

He looked again. 'Look here, Wiltshire, do you think me a fool?' he asked.

'More of a knave, if you want to know,' says I.

'Well, do you think it would better me to shoot you here, on this open beach?' said he. 'Because I don't. Folks come fishing every day. There may be a score of them up the valley now, making copra; there might be half a dozen on the hill behind you, after pigeons; they might be watching us this minute, and I shouldn't wonder. I give you my word I don't want to shoot you. Why should I? You don't hinder me any. You haven't got one pound of copra but what you made with your own hands, like a Negro slave. You're vegetating – that's what I call it – and I don't care where you vegetate, nor yet how long. Give me your word you don't mean to shoot me, and I'll give you a lead and walk away.'

'Well,' said I, 'you're frank and pleasant, ain't you? And I'll be the same. I don't mean to shot you to-day. Why should I? This business is beginning; it ain't done yet, Mr Case. I've given you one turn already. I can see the marks of my knuckles on your head to this blooming hour, and I've more cooking for you. I'm not a paralee, like Underhill. My name ain't Adams, and it ain't Vigours; and I mean to show you that you've met your match.'

COMMENTARY
He returns and just as he leaves the jungle he meets Case. Both men are immediately aware of the hatred between them. Each vows to kill the other but not yet. Wiltshire makes it clear that he knows what happened to the traders before him and will not be frightened off.

each keeping the tail of his eye on the other: watching each other out of the corner of their eyes
paralee: paralysed person

'This is a silly way to talk,' said he. 'This is not the talk to make me move on with.'

'All right,' said I, 'stay where you are. I ain't in any hurry, and you know it. I can put in a day on this beach and never mind. I ain't got any copra to bother with. I ain't got any luminous paint to see to.'

I was sorry I said that last, but it whipped out before I knew. I could see it took the wind out of his sails, and he stood and stared at me with his brow drawn up. Then I suppose he made up his mind he must get to the bottom of this.

'I take you at your word,' says he, and turned his back, and walked right into the devil's bush.

I let him go, of course, for I had passed my word. But I watched him as long as he was in sight, and after he was gone lit out for cover as lively as you would want to see, and went the rest of the way home under the bush, for I didn't trust him sixpence worth. One thing I saw, I had been ass enough to give him warning, and that which I meant to do I must do at once.

You would think I had had about enough excitement for one morning, but there was another turn waiting me. As soon as I got far enough round the cape to see my house I made out there were strangers there; a little farther, and no doubt about it. There was a couple of armed sentinels squatting at my door. I could only suppose the trouble about Uma must have come to a head, and the station been seized. For aught I could think, Uma was taken up already, and these armed men were waiting to do the like with me.

However, as I came nearer, which I did at top speed, I saw there was a third native sitting on the veranda like a guest, and Uma was talking with him like a hostess. Nearer still I made out it was the big young chief, Maea, and that he was smiling away and smoking. And what was he smoking? None of your European cigarettes fit for a cat, not even the genuine big, knock-me-down native article that a fellow can really put in the time with if his pipe is broke – but a cigar, and one of my Mexicans at that, that I could swear to. At sight of this my heart started beating, and I took a wild hope in my head that the trouble was over, and Maea had come round.

lit out for cover: quickly made for the protection of the trees

COMMENTARY

Just as they are parting, Wiltshire lets slip that he knows all about Case's 'shrine'. They both leave. When Wiltshire reaches his house, he finds Maea, a young island chief, waiting to greet him.

Uma pointed me out to him as I came up, and he met me at the head of my own stairs like a thorough gentleman.

'Vilivili,' said he, which was the best they could make of my name, 'I pleased.'

There is no doubt when an island chief wants to be civil he can do it. I saw the way things were from the word go. There was no call for Uma to say to me: 'He no 'fraid Ese now, come bring copra.' I tell you I shook hands with that Kanaka like as if he was the best white man in Europe.

The fact was, Case and he had got after the same girl, or Maea suspected it, and concluded to make hay of the trader on the chance. He had dressed himself up, got a couple of his retainers cleaned and armed to kind of make the thing more public, and, just waiting till Case was clear of the village, came round to put the whole of his business my way. He was rich as well as powerful. I suppose that man was worth fifty thousand nuts per annum. I gave him the price of the beach and quarter cent better, and as for credit, I would have advanced him the inside of the store and the fittings besides, I was so pleased to see him. I must say he bought like a gentleman: rice and tins and biscuits enough for a week's feast, and stuffs by the bolt. He was agreeable besides; he had plenty fun to him; and we cracked jests together, mostly through the interpreter, because he had mighty little English, and my native was still off colour. One thing I made out: he could never really have thought much harm of Uma; he could never have been really frightened, and must just have made believe from dodginess, and because he thought Case had a strong pull in the village and could help him on.

This set me thinking that both he and I were in a tightish place. What he had done was to fly in the face of the whole village, and the thing might cost him his authority. More than that, after my talk with Case on the beach, I thought it might very well cost me my life. Case had as good as said he would pot me if ever I got any copra; he would come home to find the best business in the village had changed hands, and the best thing I thought I could do was to get in first with the potting.

COMMENTARY
Maea has come to tell him that he is going to ignore the taboo and bring Wiltshire copra. Wiltshire is delighted because Maea is wealthy. They do business together. Then Wiltshire realises that he and Maea are both now in danger from Case (because he will not allow his trade to slip away like this).

the price of the beach: the price offered by other white traders

stuffs by the bolt: fabrics by the roll

my native was still off colour: my knowledge of the local language was still poor

'See here, Uma,' says I, 'tell him I'm sorry I made him wait, but I was up looking at Case's Tiapolo store in the bush.'

'He want savvy if you no 'fraid?' translated Uma.

I laughed out. 'Not much!' says I. 'Tell him the place is a blooming toy-shop! Tell him in England we give these things to the kid to play with.'

'He want savvy if you hear devil sing?' she asked next.

'Look here,' I said, 'I can't do it now, because I've got no banjo-strings in stock; but the next time the ship comes round I'll have one of these same contraptions right here in my veranda, and he can see for himself how much devil there is to it. Tell him, as soon as I can get the strings I'll make one for his picaninnies. The name of the concern is a Tyrolean harp; and you can tell him the name means in English that nobody but dam-fools give a cent for it.'

This time he was so pleased he had to try his English again. 'You talk true?' says he.

'Rather!' said I. 'Talk all-e-same Bible. Bring out a Bible here, Uma, if you've such a thing, and I'll kiss it. Or, I'll tell you what's better still,' says I, taking a header, 'ask him if he's afraid to go up there himself by day.'

It appeared he wasn't; he could venture as far as that by day and in company.

'That's the ticket, then!' said I. 'Tell him the man's a fraud and the place foolishness, and if he'll go up there to-morrow he'll see all that's left of it. But tell him this, Uma, and mind he understands it: If he gets talking it's bound to come to Case, and I'm a dead man! I'm playing his game, tell him, and if he says one word my blood will be at his door and be the damnation of him here and after.'

She told him, and he shook hands with me up to the hilt, and, says he: 'No talk. Go up to-mollow. You my friend?'

'No, sir,' says I, 'no such foolishness. I've come here to trade, tell him, and not to make friends. But, as to Case, I'll send that man to glory!'

So off Maea went, pretty well pleased, as I could see.

picaninnies: children

COMMENTARY
Wiltshire talks to Maea about Case's 'shrine' and tells him it is nothing to be afraid of. He says he is going to destroy it that very night.

5 Night in the Bush

Look out for...
- the excitement and danger of Wiltshire's night expedition.
- what he does when he gets to the 'home' of Tiapolo.
- the battle with Case, and the personal qualities each one shows.
- how the conflict ends.

FAST FORWARD: to page 174

W ell, I was committed now; Tiapolo had to be smashed up before next day, and my hands were pretty full, not only with preparations, but with argument. My house was like a mechanics' debating society. Uma was so made up that I shouldn't go into the bush by night, or that, if I did, I was never to come back again. You know her style of arguing: you've had a specimen about Queen Victoria and the devil; and I leave you to fancy if I was tired of it before dark.

At last I had a good idea. 'What was the use of casting my pearls before her?' I thought; some of her own chopped hay would be likelier to do the business.

'I'll tell you what, then,' said I. 'You fish out your Bible, and I'll take that up along with me. That'll make me right.'

She swore a Bible was no use.

'That's just your Kanaka ignorance,' said I. 'Bring the Bible out.'

COMMENTARY
Uma tries to persuade Wiltshire not to go back to the shrine, but he is determined to go. He tells her to fetch the Bible.

a mechanics' debating society: during the nineteenth century, workers who were determined to improve their education formed various self-help societies – some of these were devoted to discussion and debate

made up: determined
casting my pearls: from the proverb 'Do not cast pearls before swine' (which, in turn, comes from the New Testament, Matthew 7.6)

She brought it, and I turned to the title-page, where I thought there would likely be some English, and so there was. 'There!' said I. 'Look at that! *"London: Printed for the British and Foreign Bible Society, Blackfriars,"* and the date, which I can't read owing to its being in these X's. There's no devil in hell can look near the Bible Society, Blackfriars. Why, you silly,' I said, 'how do you suppose we get along with our own *aitus* at home! All Bible Society!'

'I think you no got any,' said she. 'White man, he tell me you no got.'

'Sounds likely, don't it?' I asked. 'Why would these islands all be chock full of them and none in Europe?'

'Well, you no got bread-fruit,' said she.

I could have torn my hair. 'Now, look here, old lady,' said I, 'you dry up, for I'm tired of you. I'll take the Bible, which'll put me as straight as the mail, and ▶▶ that's the last word I've got to say.'

The night fell extraordinary dark, clouds coming up with sundown and overspreading all; not a star showed; there was only an end of a moon, and that not due before the small hours. Round the village, what with the lights and the fires in the open houses, and the torches of many fishers moving on the reef, it kept as gay as an illumination; but the sea and the mountains and woods were all clean gone. I suppose it might be eight o'clock when I took the road, laden like a donkey. First there was that Bible, a book as big as your head, which I had let myself in for by my own tomfoolery. Then there was my gun, and knife, and lantern, and patent matches, all necessary. And then there was the real plant of the affair in hand, a mortal weight of gunpowder, a pair of dynamite fishing-bombs, and two or three pieces of slow match that I had

---

REWIND: ...I've got to say.'
Wiltshire is determined to go back to the shrine, but Uma has tried to persuade him not to. In the end he has tricked her into believing that he has special protection and has promised that he will take a bible with him as additional protection.

lighting a slow match, or fuse

COMMENTARY
Using the Bible, he tricks her into believing everything will be all right, but he has to promise to take it with him. He sets off into the night with various items of equipment, including explosives.

pulled out of the tin cases and spliced together the best way I could; for the match was only trade stuff, and a man would be crazy that trusted it. Altogether, you see, I had the materials of a pretty good blow-up! Expense was nothing to me; I wanted that thing done right.

As long as I was in the open, and had the lamp in my house to steer by, I did well. But when I got to the path, it fell so dark I could make no headway, walking into trees and swearing there, like a man looking for the matches in his bed-room. I knew it was risky to light up, for my lantern would be visible all the way to the point of the cape, and as no one went there after dark, it would be talked about, and come to Case's ears. But what was I to do? I had either to give the business over and lose caste with Maea, or light up, take my chance, and get through the thing the smartest I was able.

As long as I was on the path I walked hard, but when I came to the black beach I had to run. For the tide was now nearly flowed; and to get through with my powder dry between the surf and the steep hill, took all the quickness I possessed. As it was, even the wash caught me to the knees, and I came near falling on a stone. All this time the hurry I was in, and the free air and smell of the sea, kept my spirits lively; but when I was once in the bush and began to climb the path I took it easier.

The fearsomeness of the wood had been a good bit rubbed off for me by Master Case's banjo-strings and graven images, yet I thought it was a dreary walk, and guessed, when the disciples went up there, they must be badly scared. The light of the lantern, striking among all these trunks and forked branches and twisted rope-ends of lianas, made the whole place, or all that you could see of it, a kind of a puzzle of turning shadows. They came to meet you, solid and quick like giants, and then spun off and vanished; they hove up over your head like clubs, and flew away into the night like birds. The floor of the bush glimmered with dead wood, the way the match-box used to shine after you had struck a lucifer. Big, cold drops fell on me from the branches overhead like sweat. There was no wind to mention; only a little icy breath on a land breeze that stirred nothing; and the harps were silent.

COMMENTARY
He makes his way into the forest.

lose caste: lose face
flowed: fully in

The first landfall I made was when I got through the bush of wild cocoanuts, and came in view of the bogies on the wall. Mighty queer they looked by the shining of the lantern, with their painted faces and shell eyes, and their clothes, and their hair hanging. One after another I pulled them all up and piled them in a bundle on the cellar roof, so as they might go to glory with the rest. Then I chose a place behind one of the big stones at the entrance, buried my powder and two shells, and arranged my match along the passage. And then I had a look at the smoking head, just for good-bye. It was doing fine.

'Cheer up,' says I. 'You're booked.'

It was my first idea to light up and be getting homeward; for the darkness and the glimmer of the dead wood and the shadows of the lantern made me lonely. But I knew where one of the harps hung; it seemed a pity it shouldn't go with the rest; and at the same time I couldn't help letting on to myself that I was mortal tired of my employment, and would like best to be at home and have the door shut. I stepped out of the cellar and argued it fore and back. There was a sound of the sea far down below me on the coast; nearer hand not a leaf stirred; I might have been the only living creature this side of Cape Horn. Well, as I stood there thinking, it seemed the bush woke and became full of little noises. Little noises they were, and nothing to hurt; a bit of a crackle, a bit of a rush; but the breath jumped right out of me and my throat went as dry as a biscuit. It wasn't Case I was afraid of, which would have been common-sense; I never thought of Case; what took me as sharp as the colic, was the old wives' tales – the devil-women and the man-pigs. It was the toss of a penny whether I should run; but I got a purchase on myself, and stepped out, and held up the lantern (like a fool) and looked all round.

In the direction of the village and the path there was nothing to be seen; but when I turned inland it's a wonder to me I didn't drop. There, coming right up out of the desert and the bad bush – there, sure enough, was a devil-woman, just as the way I had figured she would look. I saw the light shine on her bare arms and her bright eyes, and there went out of me a yell so big that I thought it was my death.

colic: severe pain in the abdomen

COMMENTARY

He reaches the shrine. He sets his explosives and lays the fuse. He begins to move back towards the village when he is startled by what looks like a 'devil-woman'.

'Ah! No sing out!' says the devil-woman, in a kind of a high whisper. 'Why you talk big voice? Put out light! Ese he come.'

'My God Almighty, Uma, is that you?' says I.

'*Ioe*,' says she. 'I come quick. Ese here soon.'

'You come alone?' I asked. 'You no 'fraid?'

'Ah, too much 'fraid!' she whispered, clutching me. 'I think die.'

'Well,' says I, with a kind of a weak grin. 'I'm not the one to laugh at you, Mrs Wiltshire, for I'm about the worst scared man in the South Pacific myself.'

She told me in two words what brought her. I was scarce gone, it seems, when Faavao came in, and the old woman had met Black Jack running as hard as he was fit from our house to Case's. Uma neither spoke nor stopped, but lit right out to come and warn me. She was so close at my heels that the lantern was her guide across the beach, and afterwards, by the glimmer of it in the trees, she got her line uphill. It was only when I had got to the top or was in the cellar that she wandered – Lord knows where! – and lost a sight of precious time, afraid to call out lest Case was at the heels of her, and falling in the bush, so that she was all knocked and bruised. That must have been when she got too far to the southward, and how she came to take me in the flank at last and frighten me beyond what I've got the words to tell of.

Well, anything was better than a devil-woman, but I thought her yarn serious enough. Black Jack had no call to be about my house, unless he was set there to watch; and it looked to me as if my tomfool word about the paint, and perhaps some chatter of Maea's, had got us all in a clove hitch. One thing was clear: Uma and I were here for the night; we daren't try to go home before day, and even then it would be safer to strike round up the mountain and come in by the back of the village, or we might walk into an ambuscade. It was plain, too, that the mine should be sprung immediately, or Case might be in time to stop it.

I marched into the tunnel, Uma keeping tight hold of me, opened my lantern and lit the match. The first length of it burned like a spill of paper, and I stood stupid, watching it burn, and thinking we were going aloft with

COMMENTARY

To his relief, he discovers it is Uma, who has come to warn him that Case is coming. Clearly Wiltshire has put him on his guard and he is coming to defend the shrine. Uma and Wiltshire hurry to light the fuse.

Ioe: Yes

clove hitch: a knot used to tie a rope tightly round a post or tree

ambuscade: ambush

Tiapolo, which was none of my views. The second took to a better rate, though faster than I cared about; and at that I got my wits again, hauled Uma clear of the passage, blew out and dropped the lantern, and the pair of us groped our way into the bush until I thought it might be safe, and lay down together by a tree.

'Old lady,' I said, 'I won't forget this night. You're a trump, and that's what's wrong with you.'

She bumped herself close up to me. She had run out the way she was, with nothing on her but her kilt; and she was all wet with the dews and the sea on the black beach, and shook straight on with cold and terror of the dark and the devils.

'Too much 'fraid,' was all she said.

The far side of Case's hill goes down near as steep as a precipice into the next valley. We were on the very edge of it, and I could see the dead wood shine and hear the sea sound far below. I didn't care about the position, which left me no retreat, but I was afraid to change. Then I saw I had made a worse mistake about the lantern, which I should have left lighted, so that I could have had a crack at Case when he stepped into the shine of it. And since I hadn't had the wit to do that, it seemed a senseless thing to leave the good lantern to blow up with the graven images. The thing belonged to me, after all, and was worth money, and might come in handy. If I could have trusted the match, I might have run in still and rescued it. But who was going to trust to the match? You know what trade is. The stuff was good enough for Kanakas to go fishing with, where they've got to look lively anyway, and the most they risk is only to have their hand blown off. But for anyone that wanted to fool around a blow-up like mine that match was rubbish.

Altogether the best I could do was to lie still, see my shot-gun handy, and wait for the explosion. But it was a solemn kind of a business. The blackness of the night was like solid; the only thing you could see was the nasty bogy glimmer of the dead wood, and that showed you nothing but itself; and as for sounds, I stretched my ears till I thought I could have heard the match burn in

COMMENTARY

They move away to a safe place. Wiltshire is concerned that they will be rather exposed if Case comes, but it is the best they can do.

the tunnel, and that bush was as silent as a coffin. Now and then there was a bit of a crack; but whether it was near or far, whether it was Case stubbing his toes within a few yards of me, or a tree breaking miles away, I knew no more than the babe unborn.

And then, all of a sudden, Vesuvius went off. It was a long time coming; but when it came (though I say it that shouldn't) no man could ask to see a better. At first it was just a son of a gun of a row, and a spout of fire, and the wood lighted up so that you could see to read. And then the trouble began. Uma and I were half buried under a wagonful of earth, and glad it was no worse, for one of the rocks at the entrance of the tunnel was fired clean into the air, and fell within a couple of fathoms of where we lay, and bounded over the edge of the hill, and went pounding down into the next valley. I saw I had rather under-calculated our distance, or over-done the dynamite and powder, which you please.

And presently I saw I had made another slip. The noise of the thing began to die off, shaking the island; the dazzle was over; and yet the night didn't come back the way I expected. For the whole wood was scattered with red

Vesuvius: a famous volcano in Italy

COMMENTARY
The explosion is shattering.

coals and brands from the explosion; they were all round me on the flat, some
had fallen below in the valley, and some stuck and flared in the tree-tops. I had
no fear of fire, for these forests are too wet to kindle. But the trouble was that
the place was all lit up – not very bright, but good enough to get shot by; and
the way the coals were scattered, it was just as likely Case might have the
advantage as myself. I looked all round for his white face, you may be sure; but
there was not a sign of him. As for Uma, the life seemed to have been knocked
right out of her by the bang and blaze of it.

There was one bad point in my game. One of the blessed graven images had
come down all afire, hair and clothes and body, not four yards away from me. I
cast a mighty noticing glance all round; there was still no Case, and I made up
my mind I must get rid of that burning stick before he came, or I should be
shot there like a dog.

It was my first idea to have crawled, and then I thought speed was the main
thing, and stood half up to make a rush. The same moment, from somewhere
between me and the sea, there came a flash and a report, and a rifle-bullet
screeched in my ear. I swung straight round and up with my gun, but the brute
had a Winchester, and before I could as much as see him his second shot
knocked me over like a ninepin. I seemed to fly in the air, then came down by
the run and lay half a minute, silly; and then I found my hands empty, and my
gun had flown over my head as I fell. It makes a man mighty wide awake to be
in the kind of box that I was in. I scarcely knew where I was hurt, or whether I
was hurt or not, but turned right over on my face to crawl after my weapon.
Unless you have tried to get about with a smashed leg you don't know what
pain is, and I let out a howl like a bullock's.

This was the unluckiest noise that ever I made in my life. Up to then Uma
had stuck to her tree like a sensible woman, knowing she would be only in the
way; but as soon as she heard me sing out she ran forward. The Winchester
cracked again, and down she went.

I had sat up, leg and all, to stop her; but when I saw her tumble I clapped
down again where I was, lay still, and felt the handle of my knife. I had been

---

box: dangerous situation

COMMENTARY
Unfortunately, the burning debris lights up the night.
Just as Wiltshire is getting up, a shot rings out. A
second shot smashes his leg and the third strikes Uma.

scurried and put out before. No more of that for me. He had knocked over my girl, I had to fix him for it; and I lay there and gritted my teeth, and footed up the chances. My leg was broke, my gun was gone. Case had still ten shots in his Winchester. It looked a kind of hopeless business. But I never despaired nor thought upon despairing: that man had got to go.

For a goodish bit not one of us let on. Then I heard Case begin to move nearer in the bush, but mighty careful. The image had burned out, there were only a few coals left here and there, and the wood was main dark, but had a kind of low glow in it like a fire on its last legs. It was by this that I made out Case's head looking at me over a big tuft of ferns, and at the same time the brute saw me and shouldered his Winchester. I lay quite still, and as good as looked into the barrel: it was my last chance, but I thought my heart would have come right out of its bearings. Then he fired. Lucky for me it was no shot-gun for the bullet struck within an inch of me and knocked the dirt in my eyes.

Just you try and see if you can lie quiet, and let a man take a sitting shot at you and miss you by the hair. But I did, and lucky, too. A while Case stood with the Winchester at the port-arms; then he gave a little laugh to himself and stepped round the ferns.

'Laugh!' thought I. 'If you had the wit of a louse you would be praying!'

I was all as taut as a ship's hawser or the spring of a watch, and as soon as he came within reach of me I had him by the ankle, plucked the feet right out from under him, laid him out, and was upon the top of him, broken leg and all, before he breathed. His Winchester had gone the same road as my shot-gun; it was nothing to me – I defied him now. I'm a pretty strong man anyway, but I never knew what strength was till I got hold of Case. He was knocked out of time by the rattle he came down with, and threw up his hands together, more like a frightened woman, so that I caught both of them with my left. This wakened him up, and he fastened his teeth in my forearm like a weasel. Much I cared. My leg gave me all the pain I had any use for, and I drew my knife and got it in the place.

scurried: made to scuttle away, to turn tail

COMMENTARY

Although Wiltshire has lost his gun, he still has the knife and is not going to give up. Case approaches and fires again, but misses. He steps closer and, as he does so, Wiltshire grabs his foot and pulls him to the ground.

'Now,' said I, 'I've got up; and you're gone up, and a good job too! Do you feel the point of that? That's for Underhill! And there's for Adams! And now here's one for Uma, and that's going to knock your blooming soul right out of you!'

With that I gave him the cold steel for all I was worth. His body kicked under me like a spring sofa; he gave a dreadful kind of a long moan, and lay still.

'I wonder if you're dead? I hope so!' I thought, for my head was swimming. But I wasn't going to take chances; I had his own example too close before me for that; and I tried to draw the knife out to give it him again. The blood came over my hands, I remember, hot as tea; and with that I fainted clean away, and fell with my head on the man's mouth.

When I came to myself it was pitch dark; the cinders had burned out; there was nothing to be seen but the shine of the dead wood; and I couldn't remember where I was nor why I was in such pain, nor what I was all wetted with. Then it came back, and the first thing I attended to was to give him the

COMMENTARY

Wiltshire attacks him frenziedly with the knife and kills him. At this he passes out.

knife again a half a dozen times up to the handle. I believe he was dead already, but it did him no harm and did me good.

'I bet you're dead now,' I said, and then I called to Uma.

Nothing answered, and I made a move to go and grope for her, fouled my broken leg, and fainted again.

When I came to myself the second time the clouds had all cleared away, except a few that sailed there, white as cotton. The moon was up – a tropic moon. The moon at home turns a wood black, but even this old butt-end of a one showed up that forest as green as by day. The night birds – or, rather, they're a kind of early morning bird – sang out with their long, falling notes like nightingales. And I could see the dead man, that I was still half resting on, looking right up into the sky with his eyes open, no paler than when he was alive; and a little way off Uma tumbled on her side. I got over to her the best way I was able, and when I got there she was broad awake and crying, and sobbing to herself with no more noise than an insect. It appears she was afraid to cry out loud, because of the *aitus*. Altogether she was not much hurt, but scared beyond belief; she had come to her senses a long while ago, cried out to me, heard nothing in reply, made out we were both dead, and had lain there ever since, afraid to budge a finger. The ball had ploughed up her shoulder, and she had lost a main quantity of blood; but I soon had that tied up the way it ought to be with the tail of my shirt and a scarf I had on, got her head on my sound knee and my back against a trunk, and settled down to wait for morning. Uma was for neither use nor ornament, and could only clutch hold of me and shake and cry. I don't suppose there was ever anybody worse scared, and, to do her justice, she had had a lively night of it. As for me, I was in a good bit of pain and fever, but not so bad when I sat still; and every time I looked over to Case I could have sung and whistled. Talk about meat and drink! To see that man lying there dead as a herring filled me full.

The night birds stopped after a while; and then the light began to change, the east came orange, the whole wood began to whirr with singing like a musical box, and there was the broad day.

COMMENTARY

When he comes to, he stabs Case several times more, then goes to look for Uma. Eventually he finds her, more frightened than hurt. Gradually, as they wait, dawn comes.

I didn't expect Maea for a long while yet; and, indeed, I thought there was an off-chance he might go back on the whole idea and not come at all. I was the better pleased when, about an hour after daylight, I heard sticks smashing and a lot of Kanakas laughing and singing out to keep their courage up. Uma sat up quite brisk at the first word of it; and presently we saw a party come stringing out of the path, Maea in front, and behind a white man in a pith helmet. It was Mr Tarleton, who had turned up late last night in Falesá, having left his boat and walked the last stage with a lantern.

They buried Case upon the field of glory, right in the hole where he had kept the smoking head. I waited till the thing was done; and Mr Tarleton prayed, which I thought tomfoolery, but I'm bound to say he gave a pretty sick view of the dear departed's prospects, and seemed to have his own ideas of hell. I had it out with him afterward, told him he had scamped his duty, and what he had ought to have done was to up like a man and tell the Kanakas plainly Case was damned, and a good riddance; but I never could get him to see it my way. Then they made me a litter of poles and carried me down to the station. Mr Tarleton set my leg, and made a regular missionary splice of it, so that I limp to this day. That done, he took down my evidence, and Uma's, and Maea's, wrote it all out fine, and had us sign it; and then he got the chiefs and marched over to Papa Randall's to seize Case's papers.

All they found was a bit of a diary, kept for a good many years, and all about the price of copra, and chickens being stolen, and that; and the books of the business and the will I told you of in the beginning, by both of which the whole thing (stock, lock and barrel) appeared to belong to the Samoa woman. It was I that bought her out at a mighty reasonable figure, for she was in a hurry to get home. As for Randall and the black, they had to tramp; got into some kind of a station on the Papa-malulu side; did very bad business, for the truth is neither of the pair was fit for it, and lived mostly on fish, which was the means of Randall's death. It seems there was a nice shoal in one day, and papa went after them with the dynamite; either the match burned too fast, or papa was full, or both, but the shell went off

a regular missionary splice: presumably he means that Mr Tarleton was no doctor and so set ('spliced') the leg clumsily

full: drunk

COMMENTARY

Eventually, Wiltshire and Uma are rescued by Maea and Tarleton.

(in the usual way) before he threw it, and where was papa's hand? Well, there's nothing to hurt in that; the islands up north are all full of one-handed men, like the parties in the 'Arabian Nights'; but either Randall was too old, or he drank too much, and the short and the long of it was that he died. Pretty soon after, the nigger was turned out of the island for stealing from white men, and went off to the west, where he found men of his own colour, in case he liked that, and the men of his own colour took and ate him at some kind of a corroborree, and I'm sure I hope he was to their fancy!

So there was I, left alone in my glory at Falesá; and when the schooner came round I filled her up, and gave her a deck cargo half as high as the house. I must say Mr Tarleton did the right thing by us; but he took a meanish kind of a revenge.

'Now, Mr Wiltshire,' said he, 'I've put you all square with everybody here. It wasn't difficult to do, Case being gone; but I have done it, and given my pledge besides that you will deal fairly with the natives. I must ask you to keep my word.'

Well, so I did. I used to be bothered about my balances, but I reasoned it out this way. We all have queerish balances, and the natives all know it and water their copra in a proportion so that it's fair all round; but the truth is, it did use to bother me, and, though I did well in Falesá, I was half glad when the firm moved me on to another station, where I was under no kind of a pledge and could look my balances in the face.

As for the old lady, you know her as well as I do. She's only the one fault. If you don't keep your eye lifting she would give away the roof off the station. Well, it seems it's natural in Kanakas. She's turned a powerful big woman now, and could throw a London bobby over her shoulder. But that's natural in Kanakas too, and there's no manner of doubt that she's an A-1 wife.

Mr Tarleton's gone home, his trick being over. He was the best missionary I ever struck and now, it seems, he's parsonising down Somerset way. Well, that's best for him; he'll have no Kanakas there to get luny over.

COMMENTARY
Captain Randall later dies, dynamiting fish. Wiltshire is left alone after Tarleton has made him promise never to cheat the islanders.

corroborree: originally a night-time dance of Australian aboriginals – from this it came to mean any noisy meeting
trick: tour of duty

My public-house? Not a bit of it, nor ever likely. I'm stuck here, I fancy. I don't like to leave the kids, you see: and – there's no use talking – they're better here than what they would be in a white man's country, though Ben took the eldest up to Auckland, where he's being schooled with the best. But what bothers me is the girls. They're only half-castes, of course; I know that as well as you do, and there's nobody thinks less of half-castes than I do; but they're mine, and about all I've got. I can't reconcile my mind to their taking up with Kanakas, and I'd like to know where I'm to find the whites?

COMMENTARY
He and Uma and their children are happy at Falesá, which is where he will spend the rest of his life.

Study guide

HOW TO USE THIS STUDY GUIDE

This study guide is divided into six sections. Each of the first five covers one chapter of the story. The final section looks at the story as a whole.

In sections 1–5, there are three types of material:

- **Tracking**

This section takes you through the chapter and gives you questions to think about.

- **Character**

This draws your attention to important points about the characters who appear in the section.

- **Themes and issues**

This story raises a number of important issues and as they occur they are examined in this section.

You can either use this material during your first reading or you can read the whole story and then turn back to it afterwards. How thoroughly you decide to use it will depend on how much detail you want to study the story in:

- You may just want to use **Tracking** as a check that you are fully understanding the story.
- If you are going to have to write about one or more of the characters, you will find it helpful to go through **Character**.
- **Themes and issues** will help you if you are going to have to write about the story as a whole and the important topics which it raises.
- If you are going to tackle the writing tasks in the final section of this study guide, you will find it helpful to make some notes as you work through the first five sections.

CHAPTER 1

Tracking

1   What are the first impressions you get of Falesá and Wiltshire's house?
2   Who were Johnny Adams and Vigours and what happened to each of them?
3   Why do Case and Black Jack come out to the boat?
4   Where do they all go when they leave the boat?
5   What does Case mean by the words 'wife' (page 111) and 'marriage' (page 113)?
6   Why do you think the sight of Captain Randall turns Wiltshire 'sick and sober' (page 113)?
7   When Case and Black Jack leave Wiltshire with Randall, where do they go?
8   Who is the old woman who comes to the house and how do Randall and Wiltshire react to her?
9   What is Wiltshire's reaction to Uma's appearance and behaviour, and how does he feel about the 'marriage' ceremony after he has seen her?
10 How does Uma behave when she and Wiltshire reach his house?
11 How does he feel about it?
12 Why does he throw away all the gin?

Character

1   We see all the events of this story through the eyes of one person, the trader, Wiltshire. As the story proceeds, his character changes and develops, so it important to ensure that you have a clear picture of what he is like at the beginning. These questions are intended to help you do that:
    a   Where has he come from, what has he been doing, and how did he feel about it?
    b   What are his hopes about this new posting?
    c   What is his attitude to the way of life of Black Jack and Case?
    d   How would you describe his general attitude towards the local people?
    e   How does he react to Captain Randall and what do you think this tells us about him?
    f   How does he feel about the 'marriage' ceremony?
    g   How does he feel about Uma?
    h   Can you see any contradictions in his character?

2   We meet several of the main characters in this first chapter. What are your early impressions of:
    ● Case?
    ● Black Jack?
    ● Captain Randall?
    ● Uma?

Themes and issues

1   Although the whole story is set in the South Pacific, most of the action concerns white Europeans and we meet very few Polynesians. Why are Case, Randall and Wiltshire on Falesá, and what are your first impressions of the way in which they treat the local people?

2   What do you understand by the word 'beach' in the title of the story?

3   What is the attitude of the beach towards women, and especially the island women?

4   What ideas do you get so far – if any – of what Robert Louis Stevenson may think about these matters?

CHAPTER 2

Tracking

1   What does Wiltshire find unusual about the people standing outside his house?
2   What does he discover when he does his stocktaking?
3   Who does he meet that afternoon and what does the man he meets talk to him about?
4   How does Case explain Father Galuchet's dislike of Captain Randall?
5   What happens when Wiltshire goes near the church that Sunday and what do you think it means?
6   Why does Case take Wiltshire to meet the chiefs?
7   What does Wiltshire ask Case to tell them?
8   What does Case say is their reply?
9   What is Case's reaction to this situation and how does Wiltshire feel about that?
10 What does Wiltshire discover when he talks to Uma about it?
11 How does this conversation affect their relationship?
12 What do you think is the real cause of the situation that Uma and her mother found themselves in?

Character

1   We learn a lot more about the character of Wiltshire in this chapter.
    Look again at these sections:
    Pages   Topic
    121–123   The way in which he responds to the islanders' behaviour
    129–130   His reaction to what happens when he goes near the church
    133–134   His speech to the chiefs and his response to what Case says
    134–137   His conversation with Case after the meeting with the chiefs
    137–139   What he says to and feels about Uma

2   The other character we begin to learn more about is Case. Look at
    these sections:
    Pages   Topic
    125   The stories about him
    126–127   His explanation of what 'really' happened and the way in
                  which he gives it
    130–131   His reaction to the idea that Wiltshire might be tabooed
    132–134   His behaviour with the chiefs
    134–137   His treatment of Wiltshire after the meeting with the chiefs
    140–141   How he behaved towards Uma and her mother

    Think also about these facts which we learn at the end of this chapter:
    ● Uma and her mother were put under a ban by the islanders;
    ● Case made secret visits to their house and 'made up to' Uma after
      that;
    ● When Wiltshire arrived, he arranged for him to 'marry' Uma;
    ● He later tells Wiltshire he is 'puzzled' by the way in which the
      islanders are behaving towards him.

    What conclusions do you draw about his character?

Themes and issues

1   Much of the chapter is taken up with Wiltshire's attempts to under-
    stand why the islanders are behaving towards him in the way they are.
    How much can you find out from the chapter about these topics:
    ● The organisation of the village and village life?
    ● The ban or taboo on Uma and Wiltshire?
    ● The attitude of Europeans like Case and Wiltshire towards the local
      community?

CHAPTER 3

Tracking

1 Why does Case want to get to the missionary boat before Wiltshire?
2 Why is Wiltshire so angry with him?
3 What is Wiltshire's attitude towards missionaries?
4 What reason does Wiltshire give the missionary for asking him to his house?
5 Why does Wiltshire tear up the fake 'marriage' certificate and how does Uma react?
6 The first request Wiltshire makes to Tarleton is to perform a proper marriage ceremony. What is the second?
7 Who is Namu and what was Tarleton's original opinion of him?
8 What did Tarleton discover had been happening?
9 What did he do on the night he found out?
10 What did he do the following Sunday?
11 How did Case respond?
12 What explanation does Tarleton give for Case's behaviour?

Character

1 Think about the ways in which we add to or change our opinion of Wiltshire after reading this chapter. In particular consider what each of the following tells us about him:
  - His fight with Case;
  - The way he speaks to Tarleton at first;
  - His insistence on a proper marriage to Uma.

2 What opinion did you form of Tarleton? When thinking about him, you should take into account:
  - His reaction to Wiltshire's behaviour at the beginning of the chapter;
  - His response when Wiltshire asks him to perform the marriage ceremony;
  - How he dealt with the problem of Namu;
  - His final advice to Wiltshire.

3 What can we add to our picture of Case after reading this chapter?

Themes and issues

1 The beginning of *The Beach of Falesá* is like a detective story: the reader gradually works out what has been going on before Wiltshire's arrival. Make sure that you understand this background story clearly, especially the parts played by:

- Case;
- Vigours;
- Johnny Adams;
- Underhill;
- Uma and her mother.

2   When Wiltshire first meets Tarleton he describes himself in words beginning, 'I'm no missionary...' (page 145). Look at this section again. What does it tell us about Wiltshire and people like him?

CHAPTER 4

Tracking

1   How do Wiltshire and Uma pass their days under the taboo?
2   Why do you think Black Jack visits their house?
3   Use the illustration on page 105 to find the places Wiltshire describes on pages 157 and 158.
4   What does he learn about this part of the island?
5   What is the difference between an aitu and Tiapolo?
6   What does he learn about Case and Tiapolo?
7   How do you think Uma's story about Fanga-anaana fits into this?
8   What does Wiltshire decide to do?
9   What is the first frightening thing he encounters?
10 What does he discover further up the path?
11 What exactly has Case been up to?
12 What happens later when Wiltshire meets Case?
13 What does Wiltshire discover when he gets home?
14 What is the importance of this?

Character

1   What do the following add to your view of Wiltshire?
    Pages   *Topic*
    160–164 His decision to explore the part of the island where the devils were believed to be
    165–166 His reaction to the wind harp
    167–168 His reaction to the other things he finds
    169–170 The way he behaves when he meets Case
    171–172 His response to Maea's visit

2   We already know that Case is a villain. What do we actually learn about him in this chapter that is new?

Themes and issues

1   This chapter marks an important turning-point. Think carefully about:
   - what Wiltshire discovers in the bush;
   - what Wiltshire lets slip to Case;
   - Maea's visit;
   - what Wiltshire vows to do.
   How have these changed things at Falesá?

2   Although Case is the villain of the story, Stevenson works hard to make
     him a believable one. Which aspects of the behaviour of white men
     does he want Case to represent?

CHAPTER 5

Tracking

1   What do Uma and Wiltshire argue about and how does Wiltshire get
     his own way?
2   How does Wiltshire feel as he travels through the forest?
3   Who is the 'devil woman' he meets and why has she followed him?
4   What does Wiltshire do when he reaches the 'home' of Tiapolo?
5   Why don't he and Uma return home straight away?
6   What immediate problem does the explosion cause them?
7   What happens when Wiltshire tries to get rid of the burning image
     that lands near them?
8   How does Wiltshire manage to turn the tables on Case?
9   What had happened to Uma?
10   How were Uma and Wiltshire rescued?
11   How did Captain Randall die?
12   How did Wiltshire and Uma end the story?

LOOKING AT THE STORY AS A WHOLE

Each of the assignments in this section leads to an extended piece of
writing. You may find them easier to tackle if you have worked through at
least some of the material in the earlier sections of this study guide.

Recreating the story

1   As you read this story, you realise that a lot has gone on before it
     begins. Part of the enjoyment of reading is trying to find out exactly
     what happened before Wiltshire's arrival at Falesá.
   - Work out the main events. You will need to look particularly at
     Chapter 1 (pages 108–109); Chapter 2 (pages 125–128, 139–142);
     Chapter 3 (pages 149–155); Chapter 4 (pages 159–160, 164–168).

- Decide exactly what must have happened and in what order.
- Write a detailed account of 'the story before the story'.

2   Write two dialogues between Case and Black Jack:
- Just before they set out to greet the boat bringing Wiltshire to Falesá, they discuss Wiltshire and his predecessors.
- Immediately after the end of Chapter 4.

3   Tarleton is responsible to the Missionary Society in England that employed him and sent him out to the islands. The Society hears about strange events at Falesá and writes to him demanding a full account. Write the letter he sends in reply.

4   We learn at the end of the story that Wiltshire's firm later transferred him to another station. Uma went with him and together they raised a family. Years later one of their daughters asks her mother exactly what happened at Falesá. Write the story as Uma tells it to her daughter.

Character

1   Most characters are a mixture of good and bad, positive and negative points. Think carefully about the two main characters in this story, Wiltshire and Case:
- What good or positive qualities does Case possess? (This may seem difficult at first, but ask yourself which of his qualities, and abilities, are not actually bad and might be good if they were part of the make-up of a different person – for example, his skill as a conjurer.)
- What bad qualities does Wiltshire have:
  - at the beginning of the story?
  - and at the end of the story?

2   How does Wiltshire change in the course of the story? Compare what he is like in Chapter 1 (especially pages 109–110 and when he agrees to the fake marriage) with what he is like at the end of Chapter 5 (especially his comments on home and family life on pages 185 and 186).
- Make a list of the main changes.
- Make a list of the most important events that led to them.
Use these notes as the basis of an extended piece of writing about 'Wiltshire – the Changing Hero'.

3   An important feature that makes *The Beach of Falesá* a successful story is the skill with which the characters are depicted. Write short character descriptions of any two of these characters:
- Captain Randall;
- Tarleton;
- Father Galuchet;
- Uma.

Themes and issues

1 When *The Beach of Falesá* was published, the 'marriage' certificate was censored. The publisher removed the entire wording of the document. Stevenson was enraged when he found out and explained that the certificate had been copied almost word for word from documents that were common in the South Pacific at the time. Later publishers changed the wording from 'one night' to 'one week'.

   a Make notes on your responses to these questions:
   - Why do you think Stevenson was so angry? Why was it so important to him?
   - Read page 117 again and work out the effect of such changes on the point of the chapter and of the story as a whole.
   - Why do you think publishers did this? What does it tell us about moral and social attitudes at the time?

   b Use your notes as the basis for a piece of writing about the fake marriage and its importance in the story as a whole.

2 Religion and superstition play an important part in this story. Find out all you can about:
   - Tarleton's work as a missionary;
   - the work of local pastors;
   - Father Galuchet and the Roman Catholic Church;
   - Namu;
   - local beliefs in aitu and Tiapolo;
   - how Case manipulated the islanders' beliefs;
   - Wiltshire's attitudes towards missionaries and local beliefs.

   What do you think Stevenson is telling us about the islander's traditional beliefs, and the activities of white traders and missionaries?